I0745711

The Scent of Metal

Sabrina Chase

Copyright © 2013 Sabrina Chase

All rights reserved. No part of this book may be used or reproduced in any matter without written permission, except in the case of brief quotations for the purpose of review.

Cover art by Les Petersen

ISBN-13: 978-1-940006-18-5

Also by Sabrina Chase

SEQUOYAH TRILOGY
The Long Way Home
Raven's Children
Queen of Chaos

GUARDIAN'S COMPACT SERIES
The Last Mage Guardian
Dragonhunters

Firehearted
Jinxers
The Bureau of Substandards Annual Report

ACKNOWLEDGMENTS

Many thanks to all who have given so generously of their time and advice during the writing of this book: the glorious members of STEW (Nisi Shawl, Michael Ehart, Mike Canfield, Doreen Mitchum, Robert Kruger, Victoria Garcia, Elizabeth Coleman, Kristen King, and Yang–Yang Wang), editor Deb Taber, proofreader Roger Ivie, and my mother, who liked it even with the missing chapter.

I'd also thank a few quiet gentlemen who were kind enough to entertain questions, but I didn't get their names…

S. Chase

CHAPTER 1

Lea Santorin stood in the spartan, sterile structure known as the Waiting Room and tried not to grin like an idiot. She still wasn't sure why she'd been picked for this expedition, but she wasn't complaining. Even though the decorating scheme was pretty much all Early Cargo Container. The Waiting Room did feature some windows with a view of what looked like a regular cave, just like on Earth but without stalagmites and stalactites and things. Boring. Except that the Waiting Room existed so shuttles could dock and people could enter the rest of what they'd come all the way to the edge of the solar system to study.

If she looked closely, she could see the join. On one side it was human-made steel, and on the other a rough, fine-structured material they still had trouble making a dent in. Whoever had made it—and the rest of the huge structure discovered in the core of Pluto—was not human. That much they knew. What Lea wanted to know was how anyone had ever thought to drill down through hundreds of meters of Pluto's ice to find the cave and the rest of the structure the cave connected to.

Vagrant gleams of light reflected off the dark ice of the tunnel. The shuttle was coming, and it was carrying the one object they had successfully removed from the alien base. That fact, and its location in a niche in the big foyer-like area connected to the cave, meant it had to be important. For what, she didn't know—but since the whole mission was focused on figuring out the alien base, Lea

1

had persuaded the mission director that she should be allowed to study the object in its original setting. And so, the Gizmo, her name for the thing, was being taken from *Kepler,* the ship that had brought them from Luna Base to Pluto so she could do so. She wondered how long they would let her keep it.

The expedition leaders had waited until *Kepler* was nearly halfway out from Luna Base to tell them what they were really going to investigate. All Lea had been told on Earth, under heavy security restrictions, was that they had found alien wreckage on Pluto. Which was not exactly true, but not completely false either. Pluto, under a coating of ice and rock, *was* an alien construction. Nobody was sure if it was wrecked or abandoned or what. No alien skeletons or equivalent had been found. At least that's what they'd said.

The shuttle slowly rotated and settled to the floor of the cave, and Lea fidgeted impatiently waiting for the docking collar to connect. Some military types in uniforms were first off the shuttle, but Lea paid no attention to them. Her focus was on Dr. Vasili Adi, who was carrying a bulky metal case.

She reached for the case, but Dr. Adi frowned. "I open when we get there. You want to break only one we have?"

"I'm not going to break it! Come on, let's get it plugged in." Lea sped ahead along the rough-walled corridor, turned, stood a few seconds, and ran back to the slower man. "Are you getting paid by the hour or what?"

Dr. Adi gave a long-suffering sigh. "Young Santorina, it has waited for us many years. You can wait a few minutes for an old man, yes? What do you miss in this time?"

"How would I know? That's what I want to find out!" She bounced up and down. "Come *on!*"

They knew the alien base was huge, and also that parts of it were inaccessible, closed off behind doors they couldn't find or that wouldn't open. Lea suspected the Gizmo was a key of some kind. Of course you would leave the key by the door, where you could find it when you came home after visiting the Andromeda Galaxy, right?

This must have been what it was like for the archaeologists who dug up Tutankhamen's tomb. As soon as it was opened up it would take *years* of unpacking and exploring and figuring out the alien technology. And she got to be a part of it. She could spend the rest of her life here in a happy, geeky haze.

Finally Dr. Adi and the case reached the niche in the wall. All of the corridors and spaces they could reach had the same rough-textured surface, uniformly pale gold in color. Light glowed from the ceiling, but not from a separate fixture. At regular intervals the wall had a recessed section framed in a thicker border, looking like a shallow doorway, but it appeared to be merely decorative. The recessed area wasn't more than a few inches deep. The floor was darker and not as rough—it had a resilient feel. The air was dry and cold, with no scent.

Lea's diagnostic gear was spread out around the niche, ready to go. Dr. Adi propped the case on a wheeled equipment cart and unfastened the latches.

"You should be using gloves," he said with disapproval, but Lea had already grabbed the Gizmo.

It was dark but slightly translucent, asymmetrical, and obviously alien. She'd studied the photographs during the months-long trip out and knew every millimeter of its surface. It felt solid and smooth under her fingers, still a bit warm. Had they been keeping it in a heated environment for some reason? She'd have to ask.

Shifting it so it looked just like it had in the original photos, Lea carefully placed the Gizmo back in the niche. "Just like tha—" She stopped, looking around in puzzlement. "Did you hear that?"

"I hear nothing," Dr. Adi said.

Lea wasn't sure she'd heard anything herself. It was more like an echo of a sound instead of the sound itself. An echo that felt like they were in a huge, open space, and for some reason she had a strong feeling that something other than themselves was listening. She shivered. Better get to work and stop imagining things.

She connected probes, watched scanner screens, made notes, and pondered. Dr. Adi was seated on a large equipment crate, reading and occasionally looking over to see what she was doing. A faint vibration in the floor made her glance up, but it subsided and Lea went back to work.

Someone ran by, heading in the direction of the Waiting Room. One of the soldiers. *I still don't know why those guys are here,* she thought, her tongue sticking out in concentration as she tried to get a large probe in a small space. *This isn't a military project.* Yet another question to ask.

Her attention was diverted by the sound of distant voices. Distant shouting voices. Two more soldiers ran by, and a wave of cold washed over her, seeing weapons in their hands. A third followed, yelling into a radio. "Repeat, what is status of shuttle?"

And then the alarm sounded. In the first moment of panic she forgot what it meant, just knew something was badly wrong. Then she remembered. Evacuation. Assemble at the Waiting Room, instructions will follow. Dr. Adi was trying to pack the Gizmo but it wasn't coming loose from its niche.

"Come on, it's an emergency! Leave it!" She grabbed him by the arm and dragged him behind her.

As they got closer to the Waiting Room she could hear more. "What do you mean, we lost the shuttle? What happened?" someone shouted.

The shuttle was gone? How were they going to get out? Lea wedged her way through the crowd to one of the windows. No visible wreckage. Then she noticed something else missing. The dark ice of the tunnel was gone too. She could see stars at the end of the cave. That was impossible. The ice was several hundreds of meters thick. Even if they'd been hit by an asteroid, wouldn't they have felt something? Wouldn't some of the ice remain?

The stars began to disappear again, and then she saw why. The huge bulk of *Kepler* was floating into the cave, and not gracefully. One edge scraped along the floor, bits of metal breaking off as it went. Clouds of gas escaped from the holes created.

"Move back from the windows!" shouted one of the soldiers. "It's coming in fast!"

Lea stayed where she was, feeling numb. If *Kepler* crashed into them they would die anyway. No way to get back home. Only one sealing door between the Waiting Room and the rest of the alien base. *Is it under attack? What is out there more dangerous than bringing the ship in here?*

Behind the dark shape of *Kepler,* the starfield had vanished again. It had been replaced by a shifting, nacreous silver cloud completely filling—and blocking—the opening of the cave. They couldn't get out anymore.

The emergency survey team moved down the rough–surfaced corridors at a jog–trot, looking for changes. Lea did her best to keep up, holding panic at bay by trying to figure out when things had gone wrong. It couldn't have been their arrival; after all, there had been at least three ships from Earth before *Kepler* with lots of people coming inside, and nothing happened then. Removing the Gizmo hadn't done it.

But she had, just before, put the thing back in the niche where it had been found. The surface ablation of the ice layer had started shortly after. One huge chunk of ice had smashed into the shuttle, and others damaged *Kepler* enough it had sought shelter in the cave—now revealed as a landing area for not an alien space station, but a spaceship. A spaceship that was now going somewhere.

"It's my fault," she mumbled, sure of it.

The lead soldier, Ivars, continued his careful, quick sweep of the corridor like he hadn't heard her, weapon always pointed where he looked. "If you know that, then you know how to fix it." The other soldiers behind her didn't even pretend to pay attention to the conversation, and Dr. Adi was still slack–jawed with horror and shock.

"I mean, it was something I did that started it. I don't know *how* I did it."

"Better figure it out fast then." He gestured, and one of the soldiers moved forward, silent and graceful, past an opening in the wall. The man glanced inside, then shook his head. Just another niche. "Our supplies are not infinite."

No, they wouldn't be. *Kepler* had brought a year's supply for the research station but didn't have a year's supply for their crew on board—just enough for the return trip to Earth.

"They'll know something's wrong, won't they? Back home?"

He looked at her finally, his scarred face hard and pale eyes registering a trace of impatience. "And what can they do about it? Tell the *Voyager* probe to intercept us? We probably passed it seconds after this thing woke up. The only way we're getting home again is by turning it around."

"Faster than light," Dr. Adi whispered. It was the first time he'd spoken since it happened. "Always I wonder if I live to see." He laughed, a brief, hysterical burst. "So, maybe I not live."

Lea fell back a little to walk beside him. "We should at least wait a bit to go back, don't you think, Dr. Adi? Give 'em time to calm down? They are probably pretty mad at us now for stealing an entire planet. Planetoid. Whatever."

He shook his head, trying to smile and failing. "Every time we decide what it is, it changes. Now what is it becoming?"

She could ask the same thing about the mission. She'd noticed earlier, in addition to the scientists and other technical people, the significant military presence on *Kepler*. Now that she was spending more time with the soldiers it was clear they weren't here just to move crates—in action, they all had an air of quiet, watchful competence that didn't match the cheerful bravado of her Army cousins. They didn't seem like rent-a-cops either, which was all she could think the expedition would possibly need. If the alien base/ship really was empty.

Lea quickened her pace to stay closer to Ivars. "Anything?" he asked abruptly.

"No," she whispered, feeling her face heat. She hadn't even been paying attention to the handheld displaying the mapped part of the alien ship. She quickly reviewed and heaved a quiet sigh of relief. The map and her memory matched, so far. She hadn't screwed up. Yet. The pounding headache she'd developed wasn't helping her focus.

The corridor—walls, floor, and ceiling—was made of the same not-quite-metal, not-quite-ceramic the rest of the ship was made of. It reminded her of unglazed brick. *That* material, they now knew, didn't change. The kind that did—well, now that the ship was underway, it had reconfigured itself. Which was why everybody not manning the scanners on *Kepler* was running around in teams, trying to map out what the ship looked like *now*. And, hopefully, find the bridge or control section or whatever the aliens had used for steering.

Lea slowed, frowning. The wall on her left showed as a wall on the handheld, but it wasn't made of the static material. "This is morph," she said, using the term they'd come up with. "But it hasn't changed. The map shows it right here."

Ivars dropped one hand from his weapon, letting it dangle from the harness, and examined the wall more closely. "And we don't know if it was morph before, right?"

She shook her head and stepped away as if to look at a different section of wall but really to get away from Ivars. There was nothing she could point to that made her uncomfortable; he'd been curtly polite to her and the other technical people. She'd never even heard him swear. It was just that close up, the part of her brain that had warned her ancestors about saber-toothed tigers woke up and started yammering.

He's just a soldier, you idiot. Lea took off her glove and touched part of the morph that looked different, even more blocky than the rest. It felt tingly, like it had a slight electric charge. More interestingly, it wasn't cold like the rest of the ship. "Hey, Dr. Adi. Does this feel different to you?"

Adi took off his own glove reluctantly and only rested the tips of his fingers on the surface for a brief moment. "No."

"Not warmer?"

He touched the static wall, then the morph again. "It feels same to me. For you, not?"

"Yeah. Not," Lea said slowly. Her headache twinged, and she winced.

"Mark it and move." Ivars gestured, and the soldiers took up their positions around Lea and Dr. Adi.

They continued on for nearly an hour with nothing else differing from the map. Ivars called a halt and let them rest for far too short a time, mostly because Dr. Adi was having a hard time keeping up.

It wasn't long after they started walking again that Lea noticed a wall coming up on the handheld, a wall that wasn't visible ahead in the corridor. The side corridor was, but not the wall. "That section is new," she said, pointing.

Ivars came up and glanced at the handheld for a moment, then stared down the unexplored section. He gave a small shrug. "Let's check it out."

As an unexplored section of an alien ship went, it was disappointing. The section of corridor stretched ahead as far as Lea could see, with the occasional empty niche, and looked exactly like all the rest. Not even dust or an alien candy wrapper to alleviate the boredom.

Somehow I thought this would be a little more interesting.

The soldier in front raised a hand. The others froze, and Lea and

Dr. Adi had to stop with them. "I'm seeing darkness up ahead."

Now that was definitely different. Lea remembered the initial this–is–what–we–know lecture, and one thing that had intrigued her was the ambient light. It had not been on when the first robot explorer was sent in, and if only a mechanical device was present it would not stay on. If a human was present, the lights were on. Depending on how fast the human was traveling—and they'd brought carts and even bicycles—the lights turned on ahead in anticipation so darkness was never seen.

"Long train," said Ivars. "You two, stay in the back," pointing to Lea and Dr. Adi. They proceeded cautiously, staggered down the corridor. The soldier in front flipped down his adaptive optics.

"Empty. Corridor like the rest, but it looks damaged. Wait, it's blocked."

When Ivars finally let them approach, Lea could see for herself. The corridor came to an abrupt and jarringly asymmetrical halt. The lighting was dead here, and the edges of the wall that blocked their path met corridor surfaces that had cracks and buckling.

"Atmosphere?" Ivars barked.

Human–breathable air had been there from the beginning too, and now would be a bad time for that to change along with the interior architecture. Dr. Adi started, then fumbled at one of the pockets of his vest for the sensor. "All is normal," he said. "Pressure and atmospheric mix."

Lea drifted forward, her curiosity overcoming her fear of getting snapped at by Ivars. The material of the ship was hard to damage, yet here it was cracked and worn. Something had blown up or smashed into the wall—but the wall had been patched up afterward. By whom? When?

Two deep cracks darted jaggedly near the edge of the repair boundary and met. A small chunk of the regular wall surface stood out in the junction just enough for her fingers to get a grip, and she pulled. The chunk came loose in her hand, maybe two inches long. She could hear Ivars draw in breath to yell at her, but it never happened. She was feeling rather speechless herself.

The repair material had flowed into the hole as if it had always been there.

Ivars wove his way through the supplies and sleeping bodies, hoping no further emergencies would erupt requiring clear passageways. After the change it had been agreed by the mission command that letting personnel sleep in the alien structure itself was not a good idea until they had a better understanding of what was happening and why. Plus, nobody wanted to. However, adding the three hundred or so surviving people already in place to the full ship's complement made *Kepler* more cramped than before and it had never been precisely roomy.

Colonel Gonafrio was in the briefing room as expected. So was the civilian head of the project, Merrilee Macrae. Given how busy both of them were, Ivars started wondering if his exploration had been more meaningful than he realized.

"The wall sample," he said, taking the sealed plastic bag from a vest pocket. Yeah, that was probably unusual enough for both of them to be interested. The little chunk of alien building material didn't look that remarkable, but it was the first sample anyone had gotten.

"Thank you, Sergeant," said Macrae, picking up the sample. It made sense, she was in charge of the scientists as well as the project as a whole. "Any speculation on how that wall got that way?"

"It looks like a pretty big hit of some kind. It would have to be to crack that stuff." He hesitated, wondering if it was even worth mentioning. "Santorin didn't think that bit would be very useful. Too damaged to tell us much about the rest of it in the ship. She seems to think it might all be connected and able to fix itself, and the fact that this couldn't means it's broken." He shrugged. The scientists would be sending in their own reports, so it would get covered—but if Santorin had gone to the effort of talking about it, it might be important.

"That goop moving in to seal the gap would support that theory, don't you think?" Gonafrio asked dryly. "Your group managed to uncover a lot of interesting clues, and support for theories that up till now we've been making up out of whole cloth and guesswork. If the self-repair on this tub is still working after thousands of years—and the drive—we can't make any assumptions about systems not working. I find it hard to believe the original owners didn't have any kind of alarm for intruders."

"Did your scientists say anything that would indicate they

suspect the age of this ship?" interrupted Macrae.

Ivars shook his head. They had more data than they had revealed to the new scientific team, in particular stored images of a glaciated Earth, from over a hundred thousand years ago. No more recent images had been found: another mystery.

"The location of the damaged wall matches—or matched—a dark ice feature on the original surface. A fairly large, symmetrical feature but not a crater, not in the ice. It happened before the ice showed up. We suspect something damaged the alien ship right around the time the last image was stored, and it has been dormant ever since." Gonafrio opened up his comp, held it up to retina-verify, then plugged in a holo-pad. He tapped in some commands, and a model of the alien ship shimmered into view. Ivars had seen it before, with the few decks they could access highlighted in green. The core was apparently completely inaccessible. Now, however, there was a large red valley scooped out of one side. "That's our best guess, based on your location and the size of the crater."

"Is that why it was empty? Too damaged, and the aliens abandoned it?" Ivars asked.

"It wasn't too damaged to take off," Macrae pointed out. "But who knows? Maybe the aliens didn't have dent-and-ding insurance." She grinned at Gonafrio's sigh. "We're thinking we might be able to get at the core that way. See how deep that hole is?"

"Yeah, but how are we going to get to it?" asked Ivars, doubtfully considering a long march in a spacesuit on the exterior of an alien ship that, as Gonafrio had hinted, might just have working defenses.

"We might be able to put an airlock in that repair wall. If the goop moves in where the wall has a gap, maybe it will move *away* if that material or something like it moves *in,*" Macrae said, waving the plastic bag. "Until we stop messing around in hyperdrive or the twelfth dimension or whatever this thing is doing we can't get out to go on the hull anyway, so that's something else to try." She glanced at Gonafrio. "We want you to keep looking for more information. I wish I could tell you what to look for, but that's why Lea Santorin is on your team."

Ivars frowned. "What about Dr. Adi?"

"He will be more useful analyzing the data coming in from the sensors we got rigged up at the landing tunnel mouth. Maybe we can understand the drive that way. His specialty is high-energy physics, and reading atmosphere sensors wasn't giving him nearly enough to do. The trouble with intelligent people is they can't turn their brains off. If you don't keep them fully occupied in a situation like this they will start thinking about how much trouble we're in and panic. That's another reason to keep him on the ship. His stress levels were making him almost catatonic."

"OK, but why Santorin? She seems a bit…flaky."

Macrae grinned ruefully. "Welcome to my world, Sergeant. I try to think of the science types as 'highly focused' myself. We sent her out for a reason. When we were recruiting for this mission we had a few computer science specialists play with some of the widgets we'd already found and tested. Santorin was on the list because she'd worked on nonbinary nanotube computation. She figured out more in three days than the original researchers had in the previous month. She doesn't always think in a straight line, but she gets there, and she doesn't let preconceived notions restrict her approach. Good attitude to have on an alien ship, wouldn't you say? Besides, you have another mission."

Ivars glanced at Gonafrio. He was looking serious, almost grim. "You are not to communicate this to anyone outside your team, or to Santorin: in addition to your continued search, you will protect Lea Santorin. This has equal priority with discovering anything that can help us get back home. Is that clear?"

"Yes sir. Can I ask why?"

"Judging from the way she figured out the alien tech we brought back to Earth, and by finding this," Macrae nudged the chunk of wall, "she's probably our best hope of making the ship work for us. But if she knows that, there's a good chance she'll freeze up. Just when we need her the most."

Lea jerked awake with a gasp, disoriented and thrashing to get away from whatever had grabbed her ankle. Then she saw it was Ramirez, there to wake her up. M.O., the ship's cat, opened a baleful eye to see who had disturbed his slumber.

"Ten minutes. Same gear as last time," he said, and trotted off without waiting for her reply. Just like last time.

She wasn't sure how many days this had gone on. There may have been a shower at one point, but that could have been a dream. Food was eaten on the run, dry and compressed and nasty. There was never enough time to sleep, even if she'd had a real bed to sleep on. There weren't enough bunks now, and there had never been much privacy, so she had found a raised metal housing that wasn't near anything crucial and used that with a pad and a blanket. The housing was right next to some kind of control cabinet. What it controlled wasn't clear but it generated enough heat to require a fan, so it was warm and had its own built-in white noise generator. M.O. liked it too, so she also got some cat time now and then.

Maybe the location wasn't such a good idea. Her headache had gotten worse, feeling like her brain was in a pressure cooker. The progressively higher-octane analgesics the medic had given her hadn't made a dent. The only thing that helped was sleep, and even then she would have strange dreams. This time she had relived replacing the alien device in its niche, and she had felt again the strange, subaural click, knowing something was not right. Ivars had brushed her confession aside, but even then she had known a change had occurred. *It felt like the entire universe was listening...*

Lea rolled up the pad and blanket, which were promptly reclaimed by M.O., grabbed her pack, and made a quick visit to the facilities. Someday she would have time to brush her teeth, which were feeling a bit furry. Then the corridor outside the general mess for some more insta-meals, stacked in boxes for the "outside" teams. She hadn't eaten in the mess since the incident.

Scrambling to put what she privately called "soldier chow" in her pack on the run, she still was late. She could tell by the way they were all standing and looking at her. Nobody said anything as they moved out, or as they passed through the main airlock or the sealed tunnel that now connected *Kepler* to the Waiting Room.

The soldiers weren't just names to her now, not after all this time, but she still didn't feel like she knew them. Ramirez, who usually came to wake her, was dark, stocky and the most obviously muscular of the group. Lea liked him best because he seemed to disapprove of her the least. Olsen had white-blond hair and eyebrows so pale they were almost invisible. Even though he was rangy and thin and didn't look that strong, he carried the largest weapon of the group. North was darker than Ramirez, had an artificial foot, and despite—or because—of that, moved with complete and graceful silence. If there were black ninjas, North was one.

Then there was Ivars. He was in command but didn't seem to need to say much; the soldiers all understood what to do instinctively no matter what happened. Tall, lean, and wiry, Ivars had sandy hair that might have been red if he let it grow out more than buzz-cut length, and pale eyes that seemed to look through and beyond her. There were several large scars on one side of his face, near his temple, and one eyelid didn't seem to want to close completely. A polite description of his looks would be "rugged"; a more truthful one would be "beat up."

Dr. Adi hadn't come out with them after the first time. When she asked, Ivars just shrugged and said, with even less interest than usual, something about him being reassigned. Now she had no one to talk to. They only went back to *Kepler* to sleep, so she hadn't talked to anyone there except to report what they'd found. Lea had never felt so alone.

Now they were in the round foyer, with three corridors radiating out. All the same pale gold color; nothing to distinguish them from any other area in the alien ship. Ivars glanced at her. "Which way?"

As if she knew. The survey of changes was complete, so now they were looking for anything strange. A stabbing pain in her head made her stagger, and she put a hand against the wall for balance.

"I want to check the Tank first," she mumbled. If she didn't talk to an ordinary human being soon, she would die. Besides, they might have new information.

As she'd expected, Ivars and the rest of the team said nothing but headed out in the direction of the Tank, straight ahead. The corridor opened into another round space, this one three "levels" high. The corridor was on the middle level. Below was the only piece of alien technology they had gotten to work, a huge cylindrical display. It went up the full three levels, with a wide black base that looked like a stack of gradually smaller disks that had then been covered in a flood of tar. Symmetrical, but slightly lumpy and worn.

Tables and equipment racks with overhead cable trays surrounded the display, along with a dedicated team of researchers. From what she understood, they'd been working on the Tank since the first Earth ship arrived two years ago.

"Ten bucks says it's just the mall directory," joked Ramirez. North allowed himself a small grin; Olsen just sighed. Ivars had no reaction but kept scanning the area. The alien mall was a running gag among the soldiers.

The aliens must have had some way to get to the lower level, but the humans hadn't found it. They made do by constructing metal stairs that went over the railing and then down.

Lea spotted one of the researchers she knew and felt her mood lighten. "Jenny!" Jen Chai turned and smiled. "Anything new?" Jenny was a friend she'd made on the trip out, where they had whiled away the boredom with Jenny teaching her some Chinese and Lea trying to explain American slang. Lea hadn't seen her since the incident.

"*Ni hao,* Li–anh! Some indicators are changing, yes. New since the ship leaving." She shrugged. "Still no understanding what they are. Also the display is changing by itself. What we set it to, it shows and then a few minutes later it goes back to this." She waved her hand. "It changes faster now."

The Tank display didn't look like much. Clouds of glowing dust, threads of denser areas running through them. One cloud looked more symmetrical than the others, and it was near the center of the tank.

Interesting, but nothing she could use to dig up a control system. Lea checked in with a few other researchers, who had similar odd but unconnected findings to report. She sighed. There was no help for it, she was going to have to go back out to Corridor–Land and keep looking.

She trudged toward the stairs. The soldiers looked relieved to be moving again, or maybe they didn't like the wide–open spaces of the Tank area.

Halfway up the stairs, one of the researchers below shouted in surprise. Lea glanced over her shoulder and felt her eyes widen. The Tank display was *pulsing,* brightly. *Oh, I hope we didn't push the self–destruct button by mistake.*

"Let's go," snapped Ivars.

Lea started running up the stairs, when a sudden crashing wave of pain made her cry out and stumble. Before she could fall strong hands grabbed her arms and swung her upright, carrying her the rest of the way up and over the railing. Lea clutched her head, trying to understand what was going on. Her headache had vanished. She wasn't in pain anymore. And down below, the Tank was tranquilly displaying what looked like a long, white spiny spindle with dark hollows. It was getting larger. *Or we're getting closer.*

"I think we aren't in drive anymore," Lea whispered.

CHAPTER 2

The systems control room was surprisingly quiet when Merrilee Macrae entered. The expressions of the various techs were tense but focused, and Gonafrio circulated by the stations to get updates. He looked up and nodded when she entered, but didn't say anything. Macrae waited until his path brought him to where she was standing.

"Have we moved to a war footing?" she asked, indicating his Marvin the Martian coffee mug. The one he usually carried, a gag gift from a colleague, said "Starfleet Academy."

Gonafrio grimaced. "Just trying to make sure if anybody gets disintegrated, it isn't us."

"What's the situation?"

"Not much change. The BDR appears to be docked to the spindle, and lots of smaller craft are moving around it."

"BDR?"

"Big Dumb Rock. What we're calling the damn thing that brought us here. The teams are out searching the BDR—I'll let you know if anything comes up." He turned away and continued circulating, and Macrae let him go. She could tell he didn't want to chat, and all her interrogation experience told her that while she could get more information if she pressed him, his willingness to cooperate later would be minimal. Gonafrio had a hot situation on his hands and needed to focus. She could respect that—but she had a job to do too.

Macrae headed up the stairs to the flight bridge. Brigadier

16

General Rory Hiller was there, rubbing his head bald while staring at the main status screen. All of the data down on the systems deck was summarized there, but you didn't get the raw picture. Sometimes that could be important, if you were dealing with the unknown.

Just like before, Macrae waited for him to see her and indicate she could come forward. Hiller and Gonafrio were some of the best military officers she had ever interacted with, but in a situation like this even they could revert to bad habits regarding civilians. It was always best to let the subject think the questioning was *their* idea.

"Well? How are your people handling things? Any problems?" Hiller's voice had a raspy note.

"They want to help. I understand our situation is not good and you and Colonel Gonafrio need to focus on our safety. We might be able to assist you, but not if we don't have any current information."

His big hands closed over the arms of his chair, knuckles whitening. "And what the hell can your people do to help with this?" he snarled. "I don't recall seeing any alien communication specialists in your roster."

Macrae tried to let the irritation radiate away before speaking with casual calm, but she was aware her Tennessee twang was stronger than she usually allowed. "Why don't you let me see the section of your briefing book that deals with unexpected galactic side trips and I'll get them up to speed, then."

A muscle twitched in Hiller's face. "I don't have time for any academic diaper changing. No offense."

"None taken. I will merely point out you also do not have time to allow nearly nine hundred people to be captured or killed by unknown entities with unknown intentions. How do you intend to proceed?"

"I'll send you out to arrest them," Hiller said, with a tight grin.

Macrae sighed. "Ignoring the fact that the jurisdiction of the FBI does not extend beyond the atmosphere of Earth, I am no longer with the Bureau. Come on, Hiller. I can be a weapon, if you'll let me." Just a touch of pleading, here. Not too much, that would be weakness. Just enough to sound like an eager back-bencher.

He shook his head. "What can you do? I need someone or

something that can go out there and get me intel. How are you going to do that, Former Section Head Macrae?"

She looked at him, silent, until he met her gaze. "Don't let the strangeness of this overwhelm your good sense. If these aliens are gods, all-knowing and all-powerful, there is nothing we can do and it would probably be better to do nothing anyway. If they are not gods, even though they are aliens I can tell you two things about them."

Now his expression was frankly disbelieving. "What?"

"They will have motives, and they will leave evidence. That I *can* help you with. Think of it as a crime scene, one where we happen to be present for the crime. I was watching the screens down below. Those smaller objects have been moving around former-Pluto for nearly three hours now, and not one has gone to the big hole we're hiding in. It's impossible to miss. They've even flown by and not noticed our presence. What does that tell you?"

Hiller resumed his head rubbing, but it had a more thoughtful tempo now. "They are waiting for instructions. Or they want to lure us out."

"How do you lure someone out with the silent treatment? Besides, we're in one of their ever-lovin' ships, Hiller! They could spit us out like a watermelon seed if they had the mind to! If you saw some enemy gizmo attached to *Kepler,* wouldn't you shoot first and worry about the paint job later?" She lowered her voice and leaned closer. "They aren't gods. There have to be reasons for their actions. If they are behaving like they don't know we're here, *maybe they don't know.*"

Hiller was silent for a moment, then spoke in the same low tone she had used. There was enough white noise on the command deck that it would be very difficult for them to be overheard without the effort being noticed. "We lost a probe. About forty-five minutes ago."

"Lost how? Enemy action?"

"Possibly. First we lost control. It no longer responded to navigation commands, but we were still getting signal from the sensors. Then we saw some of those small craft come near, lots of signal noise, then it went dead."

"I'd like to see that transmission," Macrae said. Not a demand, and it offered him a way to get her to move. Sure enough, he gestured to one of the people standing by and handed her off. Macrae watched the recording twice, stopping it a few times to study the screen more carefully and call up the calibration grid. Then she headed back to Hiller.

He wasn't delighted to see her again, but he merely looked resigned instead of irritated. "Well?"

"The probe drops out of control shortly after it moves away from line—of—sight. We are having problems with the radio inside the ship too. Assuming their equipment has the same problems, I consider that further evidence those outside craft can't detect us. Also, the size of the things. The largest is barely over three meters long. I don't think they are manned."

There was an arrested expression in his eyes. "How do we know how big these aliens are?"

"Unless they are the size of gerbils you aren't getting much of a crew plus propulsion and possibly weapons. The…BDR is clearly designed for beings about our size, judging from the doorways and railings and other features. It's not proof, but you might want to consider that those things out there are just robots. Maybe nobody's home?"

He let out a pent—up breath. "That would certainly be convenient. I was wondering why there are no other large ships like the BDR in evidence."

"The probe was able to see all of the spindle?"

"That display in the BDR is showing the whole thing in 3—D. Assuming it is reliable, we're the only one docked there." He closed his eyes for a moment, taking a deep breath. Then his eyes snapped open again. "I need to be sure of that. The other things could just be probes, like we're using."

Macrae had a sudden memory of her first FBI partner, Cohen. Her second year on the job. He had drawn his gun during a hostage situation. A man held a terrified teenaged girl close, their heads touching, a knife to her throat. She was already bleeding from where the man had stabbed her to prove he was serious. Suddenly the man flung the girl away and jumped through a nearby window. Real life not being like the movies, the hostage taker bled out from multiple lacerations caused by the shattered glass after landing on the ground two stories below. The look of shuddering relief on her partner's face, when he realized he no longer had to take the shot that might just as well kill the hostage he was trying to save, was briefly echoed in Hiller's eyes.

There were other little signs too. One foot shifted just a fraction forward, more for comfort now than in subconscious preparation for a fight. A barely noticeable relaxation in the tendons of his hands. Hiller hadn't suddenly decided the situation was safe, far from it. He had, however, started to believe he might win. He wouldn't have to take the hundred-to-one shot. Hiller had been afraid of what he thought he would have to do.

"What kind of offensive capability does *Kepler* have?" Macrae asked suddenly. Hiller's fingers tightened, then relaxed slowly, as if he had noticed the tell and was covering it up.

"You've seen the outside yourself when it was being constructed on Luna Base," Hiller said. "No guns."

"That's not what I asked," Macrae said softly, so only his ears would hear. Her interrogator's instincts were firing rapidly now. Hiller was concealing something, something big. "The military didn't need to send the people they did just to watch over a bunch of sheltered civilians. And they didn't send you out with no other offensive capabilities than 9mm sidearms and a bad attitude. I'm still in charge of the project, Hiller. I authorized you and Gonafrio to take whatever actions you saw fit to protect us—but I didn't abdicate. You may *not* do whatever the hell you want without informing me."

"You will not give me orders on my own damn ship," Hiller gritted through clenched teeth. "You may be in charge of the eggheads, but *I* am in command here."

"I was given full authority and responsibility for the whole Pluto project, including the military section, and your damn ship is parked inside *my* jurisdiction and stuffed to the gills with *my* people," Macrae snapped, still being careful to keep her voice low. "Let's get this straight. I have no intention of diminishing your authority over your crew, or taking over from you and Gonafrio. We all need to work together to survive. Now, I'm going to leave. I will send two of my people to assist, one for each of you. I will return in four hours, and I expect a briefing, private as you like, on whatever little surprises you've neglected to mention so far. Whatever reasons for secrecy you had, they got tossed out the window the minute we left the solar system. And if you don't tell me what I want to know, we'll have the same discussion, right here, where the whole damn ship can hear."

It was good to move fast, unhampered by slow civilians. Even though the danger had increased, the possibility of getting answers had too, and Ivars was looking forward to some of those.

The cart slowed to drop off another communications specialist, then sped up. The teams were getting dropped off all over the accessible parts of the ship. Ivars had asked for the dead-end corridor with the broken wall, one of the farthest locations, so they got a cart ride with all the rest of the comm guys. The strange problem with the radios was cutting their effective force by 20 percent. They could set up repeaters, but someone had to monitor them and tweak the settings or the signal dropped. And they really, really needed comms now.

Only silence, except for the soft continuity beep every three minutes. Nothing new from the sensors on *Kepler,* then. That was strange. They'd seen moving objects near the spindle heading for the Big Dumb Rock they called home, and nothing had happened since the teams had left?

"Next stop: hardware, software, and ladies' lingerie. Unass the cart, *effendi,*" said Tomson from the driver's seat. "Don't forget to call Mother, you know how she worries."

"You should worry if Gonafrio finds out you call him Mother." Ramirez grinned. North had already jumped from the cart and was unslinging the repeater gear. Ivars and the others followed. Tomson sped off with the last of the teams down the cross-corridor, waving without looking back.

North crouched in front of the gear, focused and intent as he fine-tuned the repeater settings, listening to the feedback on an earpiece. He looked up and nodded. "Daisy chain in place. We're on channel two-seven-three."

Ivars took out his own earpiece and set the team frequency, then put it back in after making sure the flipper button was set to the main frequency to call back to *Kepler.* "Base, this is Top-Twelve. Dropped and moving to position." Once he heard the acknowledgment beep, he toggled the flipper to the team setting again. Nodding to North, Ivars signaled for Ramirez and Olsen to head out.

He'd picked this location because of the crater. If those were alien ships moving out there and this was home base, wouldn't they want to check out the visible damage? And other than the entry that *Kepler* was plugging up, how else would they get in?

The corridor showed no change since the last time they'd been in it, with the scientists. They jogged down toward the damaged end, scanning for anything unusual.

Something caught Ivars's eye. A brief glimmer on the wall. He skidded to a stop. Staring at the wall, he saw nothing obviously different. He glanced aside—there it was again!

"What is it?" said Ramirez.

"I'm not sure," Ivars said slowly. He closed his nonsynthetic eye, and put one hand over his forehead to shade the light. The synthetics tried to mimic normal human retinal sensitivity, but there was always a bit of slop either side. Now he saw more clearly. A human handprint, just below shoulder height. He put his own hand up for comparison. The print was smaller. "Flip your adaptives. Do you see anything?"

Ramirez moved his night optics into position, and started. "OK, that's weird. Someone's hand—but why is it sparkling?"

Ivars squinted. Ramirez was right. Mostly at the fingertips and a little in the palm, there was a glimmering sheen. "There was something about this wall…Santorin got sidetracked. Said it felt warm. She had her glove off when she touched it."

"Didn't the old guy touch it too?"

Ivars nodded, scanning the wall. Santorin's handprint was the only change he could see. He shrugged. "Guess we can leave it. It's been over a week and nothing happened then." It wasn't until they had taken up position a few yards from the damaged wall that he realized he hadn't seen anything when Santorin touched the wall. Had their arrival triggered something? Such as an intruder detection system? But why now, and not when she had touched it?

The place where Lea spent most of her time now was what the crew of *Kepler* called the Briefing Room. The only breaks were when the military wanted to use it, and then the scientists cleared out and took over a corner of the mess room. The mess room didn't have any screens or data ports, but it did have coffee. It kept her awake, but now she was afraid it was making her twitchy as well.

She felt restless, like there was something she needed to do. What she *needed* to do was pay attention and think and help get everyone back to Earth. That was hard when she couldn't even access the ship's network to check on things. For some reason they didn't want wireless going right now, and of course the mess room didn't have data taps.

That left people. And people had never been Lea's strong point. Scott Benning was going over the latest changes observed in the display tank of former–Pluto. He was a fussy, impatient man prone to outbursts of snappish irritability, possibly due to the fact he was supposed to have returned to Earth with *Kepler* after Lea's fellow passengers were offloaded. He seemed to be taking the sudden detour personally.

"Now the so–called spindle is surprisingly accurate in name, since it shows signs of spinning. Why, we don't know. The default display shows the whole structure but what's left of Pluto is visible too, so the signal isn't coming from us. We can change the display much like before, but that is the default view. It doesn't autochange as it did shortly before we arrived here."

Someone asked about a signal spectrum at the time of arrival, mentioning the flash. Benning spent five minutes cursing about not having the screens or the network before shrugging and saying it probably didn't matter. Lea frowned. How did he know what was important and what wasn't? It was all strange, and tossing out data when they had so little wasn't going to help. She was a bit curious about that flash too, and whatever had been displayed before. She doubted very much it was some kind of abstract art.

Then she remembered that she had downloaded some of the display tank notes to her reader. She didn't need the network to read that. Lea blissfully dived in to the reams of data and graphs, Benning's querulous voice mere background noise now. Maybe there would be something in the early files that would clear up the flash, and how Benning was so sure it wasn't important. A search didn't bring up much except the same report Benning was discussing right now.

So how *had* they figured out the display tank? Lea went all the way back to the very first report, about two years ago. There was a lot of basic physical description of the tank and the room, a section on the first observations made by the discovery team, a table of test parameters, some signal plots….

Lea narrowed her eyes. Test parameters. Unlike the signal plots, which were rudimentary compared to what they had now, the test parameters looked remarkably similar to the current settings. The alien architecture was multivariant, not binary. It should have taken them a lot longer to figure that out—certainly not to the point where they would have a nice tidy table for the first report.

She looked up. Benning was still holding forth. He'd been one of the first to research the display tank; he was one of the coauthors on the first report. She raised her hand. "Excuse me."

Benning stopped in midcomplaint, looking slightly shocked that she had spoken. "Yes?"

"Do we have all the reports for the view tank in the onboard library? I'm looking at the oldest one I could find but it has data that must have been researched earlier."

Benning glowered at her. "I'm not responsible for your inability to do a simple search. Try it again, whenever they let us get back on the network."

"It's report PQ-209-34991. The summary says it is the first collated information from the view tank room and data, but it has the test parameters already figured out and they don't say how they did it. Where did that get documented?" Benning's attitude always made her more stubborn. He didn't like her question, that was clear, and he had a very curious expression on his face, as if he were both furious and yet forcing himself to be silent.

"In case you hadn't noticed, *Ms.* Santorin, I was one of the first researchers to produce data on the view—"

"Yeah, that's why I thought you would know."

For a moment she thought he really was going to explode, and then it just…went away. "There are no earlier reports," Benning said quietly. "The test parameters were in the information left from the first contact team. They must have done it. I used them and they worked."

So that was why Benning was so angry about her questions. He couldn't pose as the clever guy who had figured it out anymore.

Lea shifted in her seat. "We need to know how it was done. Maybe they missed something. Maybe they got lucky the first try or maybe they had a bunch of runs that didn't work at all that didn't get included in the table. How are we going to figure out where the command and control lines are if we don't even understand how we got what we *do* have?" The words came tumbling out so fast they were running together. What was wrong with her? Was it the coffee? She hadn't had that much...("And another thing I noticed, what about—"

Merrilee Macrae walked in the room, her face pale and lips compressed. As she walked by, Lea wondered why her hands were clenched tightly, held straight by her sides. "There's been no change in outside activity," she said, her Tennessee twang sharp and distinct. "Let's send out a few teams. Radio silence required, and let's keep it to four hours max for now."

"Why don't you go, Santorin?" Benning snapped. "You can get the answers to your questions out there."

"Back to babysitting again," North sighed. "Gonafrio hates us."

"Beats staring at a wall and waiting for it to move," Ramirez said, shrugging. "Nothing's happening. Least with the brainiacs we get to walk around." North lifted a hand, conceding the point.

Ivars glanced around the corner. Same old empty alien corridor, nothing to report. He crouched down, leaning against a wall, and considered the situation. They were going about this all wrong. Even though the scientists came from their country, spoke the same language—when they had any words in common—and had the same cultural referents, they were like a strange tribe. The teams were *trained* for situations like this, even ones where there was no briefing data. You found out what was important to that tribe and tried to help them get it, while encouraging them to trust the teams and maybe dial back the gratuitous violence. Granted, the scientists didn't seem the violent type. That should just make it easier.

"So let's not be babysitters. Let's learn what they are looking for and why, and chat 'em up a bit to see if they have better intel than we do. We've done stranger setups. Remember that bunch of bandits in Tajik?" he asked Olsen, who had been on the same team with him then.

Olsen had been staring out in the distance with a grim expression on his face, but at this he shook his head and groaned. "They were *insane.* I thought they were going to kill us just to make us feel part of the family."

"They enjoyed their vendettas. From their point of view we were missing out on the fun." Ivars thought for a moment. "Speaking of missing the fun, according to the remote data the space near the BDR is crawling with little ships. They're saying now maybe robots. So why aren't we seeing any in here?"

Ramirez sat down against the wall near him. "Yeah. We're strangers here; our tech should stand out. Even our drones know to check stuff out that doesn't match established parameters, and those things out there make our tech look like tin cans with string. They should at least be curious, right? But they aren't. Hell, even our immune system knows to check out strange stuff. Except..." his voice trailed off. "Some things know how to turn off the immune response. Makes it look like they belong there. Cancer does that, if the flagging treatments aren't done."

North gave him a pained look. "Are you calling us cancerous?"

"It's all relative, man. To *them*, sure we are. We don't belong here and as far as this—" He waved his hand at the corridor. "—*body* knows, we could take over and do damage. Just like cancer."

"But somehow the immune response hasn't been triggered. Maybe it's because we came here inside one of their ships," Ivars mused.

Ramirez nodded. "Yeah, that's what a virus does. Hides inside a cell where the leukocytes can't sniff it out."

"Great. Upgraded from cancer to a virus," North said, rolling his eyes.

"Some cancers are *caused* by viruses. So—"

Someone lanky was coming down the corridor from the Waiting Room, someone with a familiar awkward gait. Ivars got to his feet. "Hey, here comes Space Cadet."

Lea Santorin was carrying her pack. Usually she grabbed the shoulder straps and hunched her shoulders like the pack was her shell and she was going to pull herself inside. Now it was more like she was holding on for balance. Her long black hair still had odd tufts that stuck out in different directions, which combined with an overall rumpled appearance, always made her look like she'd just woken up. Usually she kept her gaze averted, awkward and shy, but now she was staring at them with an absent expression and a furrowed brow.

"Something wrong?" asked Ramirez. She transferred her absent gaze to him for a moment, then shrugged.

"I don't know." Lea hesitated, then blurted, "Were you guys here before *Kepler?* I mean not *you,* but…military."

"Why? What's on your mind?" Ivars deliberately looked away and adjusted a strap on his gun harness, to appear unconcerned.

As she poured out a torrent of words, which only North, the comm specialist, managed to follow, Ivars watched her face. The possibility they'd guarded against, that the scientists would notice holes in the official Pluto story, was starting to happen. One thing he'd figured out about Santorin and the others—you could bullshit them only so far, and you'd better keep your story straight because they *would* remember. If they found something that didn't fit the pattern they'd bulldog it to death. Now that the whole project had gone haywire Ivars was beginning to doubt the secrets were worth preserving. If Santorin kept digging she'd find out anyway.

"All of us came on *Kepler,*" he said, when she slowed down to take a breath, "but I can ask around for you. You just want to know about this…test parameter table?" Nice and noncommittal. He hadn't said anything untrue, and he was offering to help. That should count for something.

"Yeah. That and—and any stuff that got figured out earlier. I can't believe they didn't write it down…" She trudged on, frowning. "Do we have to go anywhere in particular? I want to try something with the Gizmo."

The Gizmo being the thing Santorin had replaced before the BDR took off. "Sounds good to me," Ivars said. Maybe she was right and that was the key. If it had sent the BDR here, it could take them back. "You lead, we'll follow." Joke, civilian, for the use of.

Santorin glanced at him as they walked, then at his sleeve. "Why do you have all those empty Velcro patches? Isn't that where you put the…thingies? You know, like merit badges?"

Behind him, Ivars heard Olsen choke and turn it into a cough. He hoped his face hadn't shown anything. *Merit badges?*

"I think she means unit patches," North said with care. His voice sounded almost normal. The rigorous team training could prove useful in all kinds of unexpected situations. Like torture, or suddenly encountering massive and hilarious civilian ignorance.

"Whatever," Santorin said, her cheeks going red. She hunched up and clutched the shoulder straps of her pack. "It's just…all you have on your uniforms is your name and the rank marks, and I thought soldiers had to wear other ones, like the one with the eagle head and stuff."

"Hundred and First Airborne," Ivars said before he could stop himself. "Since this is a mostly civilian mission, keeping the military tone dialed back a notch is less confusing."

That got him a suspicious stare, from surprisingly large amber-brown eyes. She'd hardly ever looked at him directly before. People tended to avert their eyes from his damaged face, so it was understandable. Then he recalled she didn't usually look directly at any of the team, even the admittedly handsome Ramirez.

"You're still wearing uniforms."

"Well, we have to do that," he said with a grin. "How else could we remember each other's names? Not to mention rank. Gotta have the rank."

"I don't know why, you all seem to have the same one," she said, pointing. Ivars was conscious of a sinking feeling that he was not doing very well. Yes, they should have probably done something about team members all having similar rank.

"Oh, there are different ranks on board—the four of us just like to work together," he said, striving to be casual. Again, all true. Just not…completely accurate. He braced for more questions, but the niche with the Gizmo had come into view, and Santorin was distracted. She took off her pack and crouched down, rummaging in the contents. Ivars watched as she quickly assembled her test pad and some probes. "You seem to know exactly what you are looking for this time," he commented. *Find out how they think, what they want.*

"Maybe the test parameter table isn't complete. Maybe there are others. We know those work, though. I can almost see a pattern… which would put the next one…*there*." She entered a value in the pad and tapped a button. She looked up, then around, with a puzzled expression. "Did you say something?"

Suddenly Ramirez, North, and Olsen scrambled into a defensive position around Santorin, weapons at the ready. "New doors! Doors in the niches!" North yelled.

Ivars had followed their movements by instinct. On one knee he pulled Santorin down behind him, then aimed his weapon at the nearest opening. Nothing happened. He pointed at Olsen and waved him to the nearest side of the new door now between them and the escape route to *Kepler*. When Olsen gave him the all–clear Ivars sprinted to the far side. He glanced over at Santorin. She was staring at him, her eyes huge, huddled between North and Ramirez. Clutching the test probes to her chest like they would protect her.

The previously empty niche now looked like a regular corridor entrance. He could see the usual floor and walls, and something that looked like a table or counter. That was new. Nothing moved.

"Looks like you found out how to open the rest of the doors," Ivars said finally, unable to find anything that looked like a threat. "Maybe we can find that control room now."

Santorin got shakily to her feet, looking confused. "But the niches don't have morph," she said, her voice trailing off.

"Since it's open, let's take a look." He debated breaking radio silence. This was important, but the orders had been explicit. Nothing the roving robots could pick up—and it made sense. Drawing attention was something they all wanted to avoid. Besides, they'd already gone through the drill with new doors when the BDR went walkabout.

He went through first. There was a brief flicker, as if the lights had dimmed then brightened, and he did a quick scan down both directions of the new corridor. The walls looked different here, a faint pattern visible instead of the bland, uniform surface of the outer corridor. Still no killer robots, but lots and lots of strange new objects. "Let's keep together," he said, looking back. Santorin was rubbing her head with a pained expression.

"So this is where they were keeping everything," North said. Then he frowned. "Hey, wait a minute. That corridor goes a hell of a long way, and it's parallel to the one we were in. Shouldn't it hit the big cave with *Kepler?* Were there any niches in there?"

"No, there weren't, and if there were they'd need airlocks," Ivars said slowly. "You're right, the corridor is rather long."

They walked down past what looked like desks, or worktables, some with a scattering of small devices or components on the surface. Santorin picked up a silvery rod with a curved bladelike end and studied it, entranced.

A cross–corridor was only a few steps ahead. Ivars hugged the wall and peeked around the corner. Another long corridor, at right angles. "This makes no sense. We should see the corridor with the Gizmo by now. What the hell is going on?"

"Oh, *cool!*" exclaimed Santorin. Her eyes were bright and a delighted grin lit up her face. "We're in a completely different part of the ship! *Transporters!* The niches are transporters!"

CHAPTER 3

"What do you mean, it won't work?" Lea griped. "They're designed to operate remotely!" More importantly, what was she going to do if the expedition gadgeteer couldn't come up with a solution?

Fred Wojicz gave her an unperturbed look from under bushy grey eyebrows. "Weren't designed for some crazy woo–woo magic elevator, that's all I know. Ones with tethers don't go through; they hit the back wall or something. Got permission for a radio remote test, that didn't work either once it got through. Big surprise," he said, acidly. "Don't know why I bothered to come."

Fred had not taken kindly to the radio silence rule. Neither did Lea at the moment. If they couldn't send robots or probes to check out the various powered doorways, humans would have to go instead. Specifically, her. It wouldn't be so bad if her headache hadn't come back, with a vengeance. Going through the doorways seemed to make it worse, too. Just as she went through, when there was a flicker of darkness, she'd feel a brief, stabbing pain—like ice on a tooth that had recently gotten a filling.

Perhaps it was the faint whispering noise that had started up. Maybe an old ventilation system? A constant, barely audible background of white sound. Nobody else had mentioned it, but she'd always had sensitive hearing.

Lea left Wojicz with a sigh and reluctantly made her way through the passageways of *Kepler* and up to the more populated areas of the ship. It wasn't fair. All that cool alien tech and she didn't get to play with any of it. Hadn't she found out about the doors in the first place? So why couldn't she check out the gear? For all they knew the ship controls could be there.

31

She knew why, of course. They wanted her to find the door to the important stuff, and she'd shown she could find doors. Other people hadn't, so they got to investigate the equipment. Still not fair.

The so-called mess room was really a mess now. Half the tables were taken up with tech gear and alien gadgets being analyzed. Swags of hazard tape marked the boundary with the section still devoted to food, and someone had put up a large sign that said *Absolutely NO Transmogrification Allowed* and *Death Ray Permits will be Issued by the Captain on the First Tuesday of Each Month*. Beneath the printing scribbled additions to the new rules were already accumulating. Lea walked past, wistfully smiling at the excited conversations she overheard. Standing in the back, watching it all, was Director Macrae.

Lea frowned. Last time she had seen her, Merrilee Macrae had seemed angry about something. Now she was just standing there, her eyes large and dark, her lips compressed so tightly they looked colorless. The director seemed to be watching and waiting for any kind of a breakthrough with a desperate air. Lea scuttled over to the cafeteria line before Macrae saw her.

"Won't be nuttin' hot fo' nother hour," said the guy behind the counter. He was looking out at the horde of techno-geeks with a surly expression. Black slashes of tribal tattoos covered muscular arms, and he was wearing a T-shirt that said *Death from Within*.

"I just wanted something real to eat," said Lea, backing away. "I have to go out again, and I get so tired of that stuff in the plastic pouches…guess I'll try again when I get back."

Before she could leave she heard, "Hey. Waitaminit." She turned back. The counter guy was looking at her now, with hard, angry eyes. "You the one they sendin' out?"

"Well, there's some soldiers that go with me—wait, aren't there others?" That was not a good thing to hear. The counter guy shrugged.

"Maybe, I dunno. Hey, you don' look so good. You gotta eat right, not that MRE shit allatime. That make me look bad. My job, keep you fueled up. You wait right there." He pointed a finger at her, then banged through a swinging door with a round window in it. Lea froze, not daring to leave. *He'd probably hunt me down.* He appeared a moment later with a corn muffin in a paper napkin.

Little drifts of steam rose from the surface. "You take this, eat it. You get back, I have somethin' for ya. Gotta eat right or they run you down." He glared at her, and Lea hastened to eat the corn muffin.

It was heaven. Hot, sweet, and dripping with butter, with little bits of real corn mixed in. It had never been in a plastic pouch, she could tell. "Oh, I'll be back for this," she said with her mouth full. "Don't know when, but I will be back. You're a lifesaver."

The counter guy appeared to be mollified. "M'mamma's recipe," he mumbled. "Glad ya like it. I'm not here when you get back, you just say Ramos had something for you, OK? The guys will know. They'll take care of ya." He gave her a nod, and Lea smiled back. *I think I'm in love. He may be a grouch, but he can cook.*

Still in a blissful, buttery mood, Lea scanned the room. Seeing a knot of uniforms in one corner, she headed over but before she got there she was intercepted.

"It is very good you find all these!" said Jenny. "You go, find some more eh? I thought I go crazy with that no–good Tank, never working like we want."

"How much stuff do you need?" Lea asked. "There's heaps more right there. Don't use it all up—I want to play too."

Lea tried to keep her disappointment from showing but something must have given her away. Jenny suddenly became completely serious.

"We get home and you not having anything to study, I will complain very loudly. Promise!" Jenny grabbed her hand in a firm, hard grip. "Now you go, find the way back." A quick pat on Lea's shoulder and Jenny went back to her project.

That might actually work. When Jenny got her dander up problems got solved in a big hurry. Lea frowned, wondering where the knot in her stomach had come from. It couldn't have been the corn muffin; that would be blasphemy. Besides, it was fading already. She looked up and nearly had another stomach spasm. Ivars was barely an arms length away, watching her.

"T–there's nothing—I mean, Wojicz didn't have any other options," Lea stammered.

"Guess we do it the hard way," Ivars said, calmly. "Let's gear up and head out."

"I'll get my pack—oh." Ivars was pointing to the end of the table. They all had the same kind of gear, which made it imperative to have some unique mark to distinguish one digicam backpack from another. Lea had attached a small purple anodized flashlight to hers, and there it was. "Thanks."

She went to get it with mixed feelings. It was nice not to have to go get it herself, but now they would be going out that much sooner. The pale-haired guy, Olsen, was still focused intently on his reader as she walked behind him, and she sneaked a look over his shoulder. *New excavations of the early nomadic burial ground at Filippovka* was the title.

OK, so what kind of soldier reads stuff like that? Lea wondered as she hefted the pack onto her shoulders. North was reading too, a Bible, which was not so exotic. Now that she really thought about it, none of them acted like she expected. But what had she been expecting? More noise, maybe. Loud banter and teasing. Arguments about favorite movies, sports, music. Complaints about commanding officers or the job. Well, maybe they did complain about her, just not where she could hear.

Quiet, that's what they were. Quiet and watchful.

"What's the plan?" asked Ivars.

Lea sighed. Of course they'd ask her that, since they'd originally wanted to use the remotes to look through doors. Ivars wasn't any more keen on jumping through without checking it out than she was.

"I really wish there was some way we could figure out where the doors go to, I mean, in the ship. Even if we could use radio it wouldn't help, though."

"What if the doors can go different places?" That was North. "If they had a control panel of some kind, with a keypad for a grid address or coordinates, one door could theoretically go anywhere."

Yeah, these were typical dumb grunt soldiers all right.

They were in the heavy transparent plastic tunnel between *Kepler* and the Waiting Room now. Lea glanced at the tunnel and thought. "How would you keep track of where you had been?" she said eventually. "Or prevent two doors trying to get to the same place at the same time?"

North raised an eyebrow. He had such high cheekbones the gesture made him look like a very dark Chinese master. "Whoever built a giant FTL spaceship that can sit around in the Oort cloud for thous—for all those years without needing an oil change to get it to work again probably could figure it out. Who knows, maybe the transporter process wraps us up like a data packet with all the routing info attached."

"Hmm, yeah. And we all have GUIDs to identify us—no, not global, ship. S-UIDs. Squids?"

North laughed. "And what about scope?" He widened his eyes in mock horror. "Oh no, I'm not defined here! Quick, before the garbage collector cycle starts up!"

Lea chuckled, then choked when she saw the rest of the soldiers staring at them both with bemused expressions.

"What language was that?" asked Ramirez.

"Computer geek," Lea mumbled, feeling her face heat.

"Like that blinkenlight thing I showed you," North added, grinning. "You thought that was funny, remember?"

Olsen snorted. "What you were saying was funny?" He shifted the big weapon in his arms, his pale eyebrows and lashes making him look half-asleep. He wasn't acting sleepy, though, more like he wanted to run.

"Yeah. Just maybe not so—accessible." North gave Lea an apologetic shrug.

Maybe if I made jokes about ancient nomadic burial grounds Olsen would find them funny. Ivars didn't say anything, didn't look like he cared, but Lea met his eyes briefly and felt like she stood on the crumbling edge of a giant pit of seething impatience.

"I don't know what to do!" she blurted. "I guess we try the rest of the things that were marked as niches on the map."

"You don't want to try working with the Gizmo again?" Same patient voice. She didn't believe it.

"No. You can't keep poking at something when you don't know what it does; you might not be able to get back to the original state. What if I shut off the doors and people get stuck…wherever they are?"

"You didn't know you would open something, doing that. But you did know it would have an effect."

Lea shrugged. "Not really. I was just following the pattern…and they never did tell me who came up with the original data table."

Patterns. There was a pattern in how the Gizmo responded,

she'd proved that much. If they were lucky, there was a pattern to the niche–transporters and where they ended up. You needed data to find patterns. Data that could only be obtained by going through the stupid doors and this was not going to end well. She patted frantically at her pockets. She hadn't left it back on *Kepler,* had she? Then she felt the lumpy packet of pills and drew a shaky sigh of relief. The label said to take only one every six hours. She took two.

They started systematically going through every available door past the first one they had discovered. Not surprisingly, the first two new doors also connected to the same area. They even startled a researcher packing more alien gadgets in a cardboard box marked *Towels, Paper, Disposable.* When Ivars and North sprinted through, weapons at the ready, the man screamed and lost his grip on the box, spilling some of the devices.

"Sorry about that. We have to clear all of the connectors for your safety…do you have everything? You sure?" Lea listened with half an ear to Ivars soothing the terrified researcher, who could only manage to stammer a few words in response. She was looking at the tables, or work surfaces, or whatever they were. The aliens didn't seem to think much of isolated rooms; everything was along a big corridor, with indentations for the work surfaces leaving the outer edge completely clear. A pathway?

The researcher, with a few colleagues that had come running when he yelled, finally turned to leave, occasionally looking back over his shoulder to make sure they weren't chasing him. Lea watched him go.

Then, to her surprise, she felt a cool, smooth surface pressed into her dangling hand, held in someone else's. Moving with an unknown instinct, she sandwiched the thing by curving her flattened fingers around it and inching it up and inside her jacket sleeve. For a brief moment, there was an image of someone standing in front of her, and then it was gone. Shock held her rooted in place. The person she'd seen had black hair. And a pack. With a purple flashlight. Herself, but seen from the back. How was that even possible? *Maybe I shouldn't have taken two pills at once.* Strangely, feeling the little alien gizmo touch her hand had felt…friendly. Comforting. So, maybe it was just a bit of drug hallucination.

But why had she seen herself from behind? Was it a warning from her subconscious that she really needed to brush her hair?

One of the soldiers had sneakily passed her one of the devices she so desperately wanted to study, and had done it in a way nobody else could have detected. Ivars—Ivars had asked *Do you have everything,* just before. She looked at him from the corner of her eye. Still the same old impassive, hard, battered face. No sign he had done it, but that was not surprising. The others were the same. Why weren't they saying anything, though? All the researchers were gone. *Oh, right. The head cameras.* Since they were going exploring, the soldiers were told to record. The helmets had clips on the side for tiny cameras.

It didn't matter. She had her secret alien device. And if one of the soldiers had given it to her, maybe they didn't despise her that much.

She got a rare chance to rest while Ramirez and North went ahead to see if there were other portal doors along Gadget Alley. Making sure Ivars and Olsen were facing the other way, talking, she hunkered down like she was getting something out of her pack and wiggled the device out of her sleeve.

It was heavy, like metal or ceramic. Dark, but slightly translucent at the surface, much like the Gizmo. One end was thicker, a flattened cylinder, with traces of something that might be writing or just a random design, and then it tapered off to a slender end. The whole thing was maybe six inches long, all rounded and smooth. Lea hefted it, wondering how the aliens had held it. Maybe it was just a fancy toothpick. Or a tentacle-polisher. It didn't seem particularly comforting or friendly now, just an inert device. She tucked it in her pack, wrapped in the knitted cap she wore when she felt especially cold.

"Nothing ahead," North reported. "We should see something new next time."

A stab of pain, leaving through the door. Lea watched carefully, but none of the soldiers showed any reaction when they went through, not even a twinge. Well, they were tough. Tougher than she was, anyway.

The three transporter doors that led to Gadget Alley had all been on the same side of the corridor, the one that paralleled the big cave where *Kepler* resided. To get to new doorways they had to turn a corner, which had doorway niches on both sides. The ones on the left, near the alien ship's surface, were dark. Olsen put up a hand to the darkness and pushed. Lea could see the effort he was making, but his gloved hand never passed the dark surface.

"Maybe that one isn't powered up? Or connected?"

Olsen shook his head. "Or locked. We're not getting through that one, anyway."

Ivars pointed at the first door on the right. It was lit up, not dark. The view was different than the Gadget doors too, more like a real room.

Another stab of pain crossing the threshold. The room felt different too, and it took Lea a moment to figure out why. The whispering breeze noise was more punctuated. More like words, heard from a distance. And louder. Surely the soldiers could hear that? The more it sounded like a voice, the more it creeped her out. She wished they had found an alien body, even one. What if they were energy creatures? *Then they wouldn't need a ship, idiot.*

Lea blinked, trying to shake the echoes of pain from her thoughts. Something else was different here—the presence of dust. A bench ran along one curving wall, and piles of dust and tatters of some kind of material covered the seat and slumped against the back. She went up and hesitantly touched a ragged piece of the stuff. It shattered as soon as her fingertip made contact. There were work surfaces similar to the ones in Gadget Alley, but smaller. They each had a pedestal of dark material that looked like her gizmo, holding an opaque slab.

"That looks like the pictures of the Tank, before they figured out how to turn it on," Lea said.

"Computers?" said North, looking interested.

"Maybe." Lea doubted the aliens would have a need for a desktop equivalent. Maybe it was something else, though, that you wouldn't want to carry around with you like a reader or a laptop. Like ship controls.

Each work place had an L-shaped frame attached to the side. After staring at them for a moment Lea saw one that was positioned so the crossbar was directly in front of the pedestal, but lower. Something to sit on? She looked more closely and saw gritty dust either still clinging to the surface, or in a pile immediately below each crossbar, which had probably been padding at one point. When she tried moving one bar that was still upright, it creaked noisily but didn't move.

"Does anyone know how long this thing was in orbit as Pluto?" Lea asked. Something felt funny, and she looked up. Ivars was shrugging at Olsen and making a face, which instantly disappeared to be replaced by his usual blank expression when he saw her looking at him.

"Well, Pluto was discovered around, what, 1910? So at least that long," Olsen said, with his usual calm.

Lea got a cold feeling in her stomach. Something was wrong, but she didn't know what. *Why do I have the feeling they are hiding something?* But why would they? OK, so what used to be Pluto had been in the solar system for a while. That was pretty obvious. It was also pretty obvious the original owners hadn't been back for a long time too. What she couldn't understand was why that would be a big important secret.

Speculating wouldn't get them home any faster. Lea sighed and turned her attention to the pedestal devices. She might have to get Benning in to get them to work, if they were like the Tank. The reports she had read indicated it took them weeks to get the Tank showing anything. She tugged off one glove and drifted her fingers over the base of one device, trying to feel any hidden buttons or switches or whatever the aliens used. She snatched her hand away, frowning, and moved to another device.

"Something wrong?" Ivars again.

"I think it's broken," Lea murmured, not knowing how to put it better. Like a room with no echoes. Dead. When she got about an arm's–length away from the new device, she could tell right away what had been missing. The whispering sound had been absent near the first, but here it was strong. She swallowed hard, suddenly reluctant to touch it. What else was she going to do? She had to do something. The soldiers wouldn't let themselves be afraid of a chunk of old alien tech.

Lea poked the pedestal quickly, with just one finger. She couldn't help the stifled gasp. Even though the contact had been brief, she had felt the material warm up just as she touched it. Mouth dry, she forced herself to place her palm in contact and hold it there.

There was warmth, but not uncomfortable heat. The whispering was now clear but faint music. At least, she thought it was music. Rhythm and rising and falling tones. Was something showing on the slab–screen? She leaned closer, focusing intently.

The slab flared with light, and Lea stumbled back clasping her bare hand to her chest. A softly three dimensional object, roughly spherical, displayed. It seemed to have a hole dug out of it, like someone had taken an ice cream scoop to it. The hole was flickering, and the edges were a dark orange in contrast to the softer amber of the sphere.

"I'll be damned. That's the BDR!" said Ivars, coming up closer.

"How do you know?"

He pointed to the scoop. "We think something hit it. There's evidence of a crater about that size, on the surface, filled in with ice. At least it was before we left."

"How long ago did this happen?" Lea asked, staring at him. The cold feeling came back, then slowly faded. Ivars didn't look away.

"Can't say."

It could have meant he didn't know. How could he know? Lea was sure, however, he was saying something else. When he put up a hand to his helmet as if to adjust it, almost touching the camera, she knew. He wasn't allowed to tell her, but he wasn't trying to hide that fact any more. OK, she'd just have to ask lots of questions when they got back to *Kepler*. She turned back to the display.

With more fiddling around she discovered the display had the ability to detect things close to it but not actually touching, and you could use that to change what was shown. She used a probe to focus more closely on the crater. Pushing the probe tip closer to the surface popped the view inside the ship. It was disorienting until she figured out how the display was showing levels at different depths, and she got lost a few times.

"What are those bright lines?" asked Ramirez, leaning over her shoulder. There were only a few, short and vertical, and they were scattered almost randomly, mostly on one level. Lea zoomed around in the display, trying to orient herself, and found an area, round, that appeared to be three levels deep. In the center was a square with an alien glyph. It was the first writing she'd seen. How she knew it was writing and not just some abstract symbol, she wasn't sure.

"Look, I found the Tank. I think the bright lines are people. Us." Viewed more closely, the lines were slim cylinders. "Oh, hey! I think we can figure out where the doors go now!"

Ivars grinned. "I get it. Simple but effective. Send some people through and see where they end up. Nice job."

"We can make sure we are really alone on this tub, too," added Olsen.

North was watching the door. Glancing over his shoulder, he said, "That will take a long time. Get someone else to do it."

Ivars nodded. "Should probably report this; it's big enough."

"Just a minute," Lea mumbled. "I'm seeing some other symbols…" More glyphs, tiny ones. She was sure they could be made larger somehow. More important was the pattern. They seemed to be showing up near the niche doors, but not all of them. She brought out her personal display, now looking hopelessly clunky and crude next to the alien one, and tried to match up her map with the 3D one. What was different about those doors, the ones without glyph strings? "They aren't open," she breathed. "Look, this thing is showing which of the doors are working! Huh. That's weird. There's one on the hull side. I thought they were all dark."

"Yeah, you're right. Just past the cross-corridor." Ivars stared at the display, thinking. "Let's take a look and head back."

Lea felt her tiredness turn to excitement. This was much more what she'd been expecting when they first mentioned exploring an alien ship! Going through the transporter door dropped her back down again. The pain washed through her, making her stumble, and darkness crowded at the edges of her vision. She took deep, shaky breaths, willing the headache to go away. *I can't faint. Not here, not in front of them!*

The darkness pulled back. Lea trudged behind North and Ivars, wondering what was wrong with her. Maybe she was going nuts? Stress sometimes did that to people. But did stress make you hear whispers and change moods every five seconds? *Just get back to the ship. The medics will help you.*

They reached the door that Lea had seen in the display. It had been telling the truth: the door was active. She could see corridor floor, a curving black arc against the far wall, and a sloped surface like an angled desk, covered with an ordered array of small, glittering objects and topped by a large display slab. Astonishment held her motionless, then joy set her free—running, heedless of the coming pain, flinging herself through to reach her goal. Lea knew what it was. She could go home, and it wouldn't hurt anymore. They could all go home.

She had found the ship's control panel.

CHAPTER 4

Olsen was waiting outside when Ivars left Gonafrio's office. "What's the fire drill this time?" he asked.

"We just made this ship unsecureable, and what do I plan to do about it?" Ivars sighed. "You know. I gave him a big problem and he wants to share the pain. Never mind it was Space Cadet turning on the doors, not us, and she was doing what they told her to do— find out more about the ship. Trouble with trial and error is you are bound to get some errors in the process."

"So what's he going to do?"

Ivars shrugged. "Guard the points of entry to the dock. Not much else he can do; not enough people. Are we ready to go again? Can't wait to find something else to give Gonafrio a heart attack."

Olsen just smiled in his sleepy way. "Lea Santorin went to talk to one of the guys in the machine shop. Thinks he might be able to figure out a way for us to check out the doorways without going through them."

"Huh. I wouldn't have expected such tactical thinking from her."

Olsen was silent for a moment. "Aren't you being a bit harsh, Mark? She's not one of us; not even military. I'd say she's been doing a pretty good job with no warning or training."

"Maybe." Ivars was not convinced. "I'd feel better if I had some idea what she's doing. I'm not sure she knows herself."

"She's figured out a lot for being such an idiot, headcase," Olsen retorted, raising an eyebrow. "Yeah, she probably couldn't explain it to you. North, maybe."

"Ouch. Let's wait in the mess, unless you want to go find her and hurry her up."

"It'll just make her nervous, and she'll take longer. Look, I don't think you're reading her right. You notice when she's confusing and incoherent, but when she's focused that goes away. You also aren't noticing what she *isn't* saying."

"Oh, God. Is that something you learned from Maryann? All right, Freud, what isn't she saying?" Ivars would never admit it, but he knew Olsen had a much better understanding of how some people—OK, *women*—ticked than he did.

Olsen smiled and looked smug. "Unlike some people, I'm still married because I already knew it *before* I met my wife. Santorin doesn't complain. Not once. She's out of her depth, dealing with scary strangers that aren't like the people she's used to, putting in long and tiring hours in a dangerous situation. You'd expect a whine or two, wouldn't you? You watch. See if I'm imagining things."

"So? *We* aren't complaining eith…oh. Is that what you mean? We're not saying anything about the mess we're in, and she thinks she shouldn't either?"

"Sort of. She's trying to fit in. Not make problems. She's trying. A little encouragement could go a long way."

Ivars rolled his eyes. "Now you sound like my mother. And why do you care so much about one hyper Space Cadet civilian's feelings?"

Olsen faced him down. His pale blue eyes were hard. "I know you wanted to go out in the field again so bad you'd give your left nut to do it. Well, here you are. *I* want to get back to my family. This is *not* about proving you still have what it takes, headcase. Did they remember to scoop all your brains back in when they plastered up the hole in your skull?"

Olsen was *seriously* pissed at him, and now he knew why. They were all in trouble and Ivars was letting his irritation with the tagalong civilian interfere with finding a way home. "According to Ex Number Two, I wasn't issued the regulation brain ration to begin with. I'll try and calm down, OK? And stop making fun of the disabled, you bleached Viking."

"Idiot." One corner of Olsen's mouth turned up briefly. Meaning Ivars's unvoiced apology had been accepted.

They'd reached the mess room by then and Olsen didn't pursue the matter further. He just sat down and calmly pulled out his reader. In between bouts of not looking at the clock, Ivars thought about what Olsen had said about Santorin. Now that he considered it, he couldn't remember her complaining. Then again, he didn't remember her saying much at all, at least not to him. Just big dark eyes, staring at him with a hint of panic. *Hmm.* Yes, he should probably dial down the badass vibe a notch. Santorin probably got nervous around mailmen and Boy Scouts.

After what seemed like an eternity he saw Santorin walking across the mess area, only to stop and chat with a woman with North Chinese features. She seemed moderately cheerful. Did that mean she had good news? His impatience grew, and he went to intercept her. *Calm and relaxed. This is me, being encouraging. I have all the time in the world. No rush.*

Santorin turned, saw him, and gasped. Her usual rush of sentence fragments followed, which, if he understood her correctly, summed up to No Dice. He schooled his face to bland interest even though he was seething inside. Why had she taken so long, then?

It took too much time to get her pointed at the exit to the ship, now guarded. Ramirez had been smart and collected her gear ahead of time or it would have taken even longer. Ivars tried not to say much. Now that he was looking for it he could see she became more nervous when he spoke to her, and that slowed her down.

He faded back and watched North joking with her. He had no idea what they were talking about that was so funny, but Santorin was relaxing and smiling again. And walking faster. Olsen was right, damn him. Macrae had tried to warn him too, in her own way. *Don't let her know how much we're counting on her.* Trouble was, Santorin was smart enough to figure it out on her own. She was worried. Worried, frightened, and trying to hide it. And he wasn't helping with that, was he?

Dammit, there's no time!

Again, she glanced at him and spluttered. Keeping his tone even, Ivars tried making suggestions while his mind gnawed on a new puzzle. He'd never had a problem keeping a poker face. Even when that bastard tribal leader had shown up with his injured daughter, seeking medical care. The prick had claimed she'd pulled a pot of boiling water off a stove, burning her leg so badly the skin was coming off. Trouble was, the top of the burn was an even, level line around the poor girl's leg. The man had forced his own child's foot in boiling water as a punishment, and Ivars had to keep his face from showing how very, very happy he would be to snap the neck of that worthless excuse for a human being, because he was, supposedly, an ally. That man had never known black death looked at him through Ivars's eyes, so why was Santorin getting so spooked?

Then they started going through the doors, and he had to focus. It was harder to do than he thought, especially when the first two opened on the same hallway–room they'd been in the last time—just in different locations. By the second time he finally got smart and had Ramirez and North walk down to check for other doorways back in the corridor that they could skip, while he soothed the terrified researcher they'd startled. He even helped pick up the scattered alien tech, putting it back in the box.

Santorin was watching, looking rather pale and tired. The expression in her eyes, staring at the box, was wistful, and he remembered her speaking to her friend about someday getting to look at the alien devices. For a scientist it must be like being shut out of the candy store. And she was the one who had found the stuff, too.

Out of the corner of his eye, Ivars saw the oblong end of a device that was hidden beneath an overhang of the nearby desk. It must have rolled away when the box was dropped. Without taking time to think, he said, "Do you have everything?" to the researcher, moving closer and helping to lift the box. As expected, the man was quite eager to get away from him and his weapon and quickly left, never noticing anything was missing.

Then it was just a matter of crouching with the minicam facing the other way while picking up the device in one hand and slipping it over to Santorin, again without the camera in range. Just as he made contact he remembered how jumpy she was—and what if she turned around and audibly asked him what he was doing? Or held the damn thing up to the light to see it better? *Just hide it and look at it later.*

She never hesitated. Palmed the thing like a pro and tucked it up her sleeve with her fingertips. Ivars felt his eyebrows crawl up his forehead. *I guess our Space Cadet has some skills she doesn't care to mention.* No leaping like a startled fawn this time. Maybe she didn't know it was him. He shrugged. That was probably the reason. It didn't matter; he thought he could see the beginnings of a smile on her face. *Yeah, Ivars, this time you didn't screw up.*

The next few doors were dark, not turned on or something. Then they found something new. Even he could tell the room had had a different function than the long hallway lab–like place. He kept scanning for anything threatening while keeping an unobtrusive eye on Santorin as she figured out the displays. Maybe it was just the lighting, but she didn't look good. Then she asked him if he knew how long ago the BDR had been damaged, and he wondered if his face looked the same.

Something in her voice told him she knew. She knew they were hiding the truth from her. He didn't *want* to hide it, but those were the orders. How the hell did they expect him to win her trust if he had to lie and she knew it?

"I can't say," he managed, and shrugged, trying to discreetly indicate the ever–present camera. Waiting for her angry accusation.

It never came. With the same cold realization, he knew she wouldn't say anything more about it, not to him. She had understood the message he had tried to send. *I really don't know how she thinks. And I need to.*

He watched her face as she became absorbed in figuring out the alien display tech. And she was figuring it out, too fast to finish her explanations. Ivars had to grin at North's frustrated expression when handed yet another tantalizing sentence fragment. It was worth it, though. When Santorin pointed out they now had a way of tracing where the transporter doors actually sent people in the ship, he could feel some of his tension slip away. Finally something was going right——and he could present it to Gonafrio as a solution to the new security problem. Santorin had caused it, and now she had found a fix. *Go Space Cadet!*

Of course now that he wanted to go back to *Kepler,* she wanted to keep looking. "It's showing which ones are open! That's weird, there's one on the hull side."

That's right, the dark doors had all been on the hull side of the corridor. It would only take a few minutes to check, and it would be a good idea to encourage her enthusiasm, now that she had some. "Let's take a look and head back," he said, stifling a grin when she bounded up and out to the corridor. No startled looks of terror now, he noticed. "Hey, wait for us!"

She was already nearly to the corridor crossroads when he emerged from the display room, with no sign she had heard him. Something about the way she was walking wasn't quite normal—slow, and her feet dragged.

"Ramirez. You keeping an eye on her?" Ivars murmured while jogging to catch up.

"Yeah. Something's up. Doc says she's been getting headaches, but—"

Santorin had reached the active hull-side door. Her eyes were wide, her jaw slack with surprise. If he hadn't been watching her so carefully, he would have missed the change in balance, the tensed muscles, and the sudden running spurt that sent her through the door.

An icy wave of terror washed over him when he couldn't see her. Then she blinked into view on the other side, but no sooner than he saw her she spasmed and collapsed to her knees, then to the floor.

"She's been hit!" Ivars yelled, and ran through the door himself. He had to get her out, get her to Ramirez. Hold off whatever was on the other side. Maybe the atmosphere was poisonous? Too bad they weren't carrying oxygen gear anymore.

Nothing was there. Just a huge space with sweeping curved surfaces and Santorin crumpled on the floor. No aliens, no weapons, and as he quickly discovered, no blood. "The hell?" Ivars said. The air was fine too.

"I've got her," Ramirez said, dropping to the floor beside him.

Ivars got up and started scanning the area. "I can't find a wound, but she's out cold," he told the medic. Olsen and North were through now too, and took up position on either side, hugging the wall nearest the door they had come through. "Can she be moved?"

Ramirez had opened his pack and was rummaging around, not a good sign. "No external injury, but she's showing signs of shock. Gonna give her an adrenaline patch." He took out a sealed packet, ripped it open, and slapped the small, tan square on the inside of Santorin's wrist. Holding one thumb down on the center, he pulled the red tab on the side to activate the patch.

The effect on Santorin was immediate. She coughed and gasped as if she were coming up from under water, deep gulping breaths. "Wha—? Uh. Ow. Whahappened?"

"You ran through that door like you saw an ice cream truck on the other side," Ivars said, gritting his teeth.

"Mm, ice cream," murmured Olsen, just loud enough for him to hear.

Ivars took a breath and throttled his temper, giving Olsen a dirty look before returning his attention to Santorin. "You're supposed to let us go through first, remember? In case there are nasties on the other side?" Which she usually was more than happy to let them do. Yet another strange thing.

She frowned, thinking. "It was something important, and—oh yeah!" She looked up, eyes bright and intent. "The control panel!" She tried to get up, but Ivars was ready for that and put a heavy hand on her shoulder.

"Nuh–uh. You sit right there until you explain why you dropped like a rock as soon as you stepped through. I thought you'd been shot."

Santorin shrugged. "There's nothing to shoot me. I guess I tripped or something." That was a big fat lie; he could tell from her expression. "I'm fine. Control panel!" She scrabbled her feet, trying to get them underneath so she could stand, twisting away from his hand. She managed to get up and even take a shaky step, but fell again. Then she started crawling for the far wall and the bank of strange objects.

Ivars grabbed her ankle and hauled her back. "How much adrenaline was in that patch?" he asked Ramirez in exasperation. Santorin was doggedly trying to drag him with her remaining three limbs and getting nowhere.

"This isn't the usual reaction," Ramirez said, looking stunned. "It was just a…I couldn't give enough to make her act like that!"

"Yeah, well this sure isn't normal!" Santorin had turned over and was trying to pull off the boot he was holding. "Will you stop that?"

She switched to pulling at his fingers, glancing up at him with pleading eyes.

HOME

Ivars blinked, and his grasp relaxed. "No, get back here! Look, you're just going to fall and hit your head again." This time he was smart and grabbed the back of her shirt.

"My knees. Don't work."

"Which is why we are going immediately to the medical section."

Ramirez nodded. "I've never seen a drug reaction like that. She needs a doctor."

"Want to *see*. Control panel!"

Ivars sighed. "Fine. I'll carry you over to take a look. Then we are going right back through that door, got that?" Santorin didn't say anything, didn't even seem to notice as he pulled her up and over his shoulders. "I'm taking that damn patch off," he said to Ramirez.

"Won't make a difference; dose is already in."

Still, any chance of preventing more of the drug from getting into her system was worth it. Santorin didn't weigh much; it was easy to balance her as he walked across the room while pulling off the sticky patch. He checked the pulse at her wrist. A little fast, but not by much. He kept his hold just in case she decided to wiggle free.

"There, see? You can come back once the docs give you the all clear."

"OK." Seeing it up close seemed to have calmed her, and he turned to head back to the door.

Motion. Not his team. He couldn't use his main weapon carrying Santorin, so he started to reach for his sidearm.

DON'T MOVE

Her voice was so quiet he almost imagined he had heard it, but it stopped him. The strange device was floating, heading their direction. It looked like it was made of fine bone china, an oblong about half his size with ominous dark openings ringed around the top half. North, Olsen, and Ramirez had already fallen back to the door. The floating device slowed and stopped in front of Ivars and Santorin. He felt her stiffen—and then the device moved on.

What. The. Fuck?

He waited until he could no longer see it from the corner of his eye before signaling to the others. *Enemy in sight?*

North held up a hand and moved down along the wall the same

direction the device had headed. He stopped short, staring at something Ivars couldn't see, then slowly moved back. *All clear.*

Ivars ran for the door. As he crossed the threshold he felt Santorin writhe sharply, then go limp. "Hey. You OK?" No response. "Santorin?" Cursing, he slung her carefully down and against the familiar corridor wall. "Ramirez! She's out again."

North crouched down with him. His eyes were wide, showing white, and he was breathing hard. "That place. You know where we were? Not on the damn ship, that's where!"

"What?"

"When I followed that floating robot thing, there was a window. Porthole, whatever. I could see the BDR. Saw the big crater in the side. It's all on my cam," he said, tapping his helmet. "We were on the spindle."

"Oh, shit–fucking–tacular. Just when I thought Gonafrio would calm down. If those robots decide to come through we are beyond screwed."

"They haven't come through yet. The doors have been active for a while, and they didn't seem to care about us on the spindle. Good thing we didn't shoot at them, though," Olsen said, looking grim.

Ramirez was done with his quick examination of Santorin, who remained unconscious. "We better get her back to medical now. I don't want to give her another patch after her reaction last time."

"I'm down with that. She'd probably start a galactic war or something." Ivars hefted her back on his shoulders, frowning when he felt how cold her hands were. Something snagged his attention as he turned to run. Brightness, on the wall. He closed his natural eye and stared. Where Santorin's head had rested the wall was glittering brightly. Changing. As if it were alive.

CHAPTER 5

The official briefing had ended some time ago but Ivars remained in the room, going over every second of North's camera footage again and again. From the time North had gone ahead to scout the robot position to his return was nearly two minutes, and he'd recorded an amazing amount of new information. The main signals team had been all over it, of course, but Ivars liked to see for himself.

First, the robot they had dodged was not the only one running around. They'd known there were smaller objects in the space around the BDR, but through the spindle window they could see something—a lot of somethings—hard at work in the large damaged area, presumably repairing it. Gonafrio was considering going back to the spindle just to check if there was any visible change to the BDR, until Ivars had reminded him of the display Santorin had found. It had to be real-time, if it was showing the humans scattered around.

Then there was the other doorway. North didn't even remember seeing it, too caught up in the realization of where they were, but the camera had caught it. The frame of the doorway was different from the one that led to the BDR—thicker, making it look like a small hallway, with a dark band around the perimeter. In the doorway itself was a view of trees and vegetation, some growing on a steep rock wall. Either a large interior garden or a planetary surface. There was a glimpse of what looked like sky but it was hard to tell for certain.

Gonafrio had grilled them for every detail of what they had seen during their time on the spindle, especially Ivars's encounter with the robot.

Pity he can't ask Santorin; she knew enough not to move and draw its attention. There hadn't been much news about her, good or bad. She was still in medical, sedated. The doctors had reported nothing obviously wrong with her except extreme fatigue, which was puzzling since she hadn't done much other than take long walks. Ramirez had hung around as much as he could, trying to figure out why she'd had such a strange reaction to the adrenaline patch. Ivars was glad the docs had been equally puzzled—Ramirez was starting to feel guilty about Santorin's collapse, and he didn't need the team medic second-guessing himself. Of course, Ivars was feeling a bit guilty too. *Something* had pushed Santorin to the edge and he should have caught that.

With no new orders and Santorin out of commission, Ivars had nothing to do but catch up on his reports, check his gear, and stare at the underside of the top bunk trying to sleep. Finally he gave it up as a waste of time and went to visit medical.

The orderly he found didn't ask any questions when Ivars showed up; she just pointed him in the right direction. Santorin was lying so still he started to worry until he saw the slow, slight rise of her chest. Her face had a bruised look about the eyes. His Space Cadet, and he'd nearly broken her. He stood at the foot of the bed and tried to think what he could do to fix things.

Santorin made a soft whimpering noise and shifted her head, fingers spreading and then closing again.

"We're going to start reducing the sedation level and see how she does. Might be awake in five to ten hours." The doctor's nametag read Hae, and he was studying a tablet readout. "Unfortunately, we're proceeding entirely by guess. It's hard to know what to do when we don't even know what's wrong."

"Has anybody else shown similar symptoms?"

Hae shook his head. "Of course, not many people have gone out exploring like your team. No symptoms yourself?"

"None. Nobody on my team except her."

Hae looked thoughtful, then went back to studying the tablet. "Harrison! Why are the blood pressure readings full of gaps?"

The orderly who had shown Ivars the way came up to the bed. "Sir, the machine keeps shutting off."

"It stops reading? Is there something wrong with the automatic cuff?"

She shook her head. "No sir. It completely powers down. I even switched out units and it happened again while I was watching."

Ivars left them discussing possible causes of the flaky equipment behavior and decided to try getting some sleep again. He succeeded, only to be woken by Olsen an hour later.

"Gonafrio wants to talk to everybody," Olsen said, shrugging to indicate he didn't know why.

The colonel was pacing in front of the room as the Special Forces teams assembled. When the doors closed he looked up.

"You know our situation. It's been nearly a month since we left the Earth system and we are no closer to finding a way to get back. The scientists all agree the technology of the BDR is extremely advanced and difficult to figure out, and our one specialist making any progress is currently a casualty. Given the state of our supplies, the project director has authorized other, more risky plans to obtain the information we need.

"We sent a team back to the spindle," Gonafrio continued. "Specifically to get more information about the door seen on North's camera. When they went through, not only did they find breathable air, they also found visual evidence of artificial structures on the planet within view of the door, structures that appear to be used. If there is intelligent life there, they may be more familiar with this technology than we are, and willing to help us understand it. Even if they are not, we do not have a means of closing any of these doors and I want to know what's out there. I'm asking for three volunteers to go through that door. Not you, Ivars," as Ivars took a half step forward, "and not your team. We don't know if the door always works both ways. Just because it has so far doesn't mean we can always count on it. So, the mission has three objectives. Find intelligent life, if present. Ascertain hostility of anyone on the other side." He stopped and looked them each in the eye. "And finally, assess food supplies available if nothing else. If you can't find us an instruction manual or someone who can help, buy us time to figure it out."

⁊

There were wires coming from little electrode pads on her body and a needle in her hand attached to a bag of fluid by a tube. Lea didn't know what to make of that, or the fact she was in a hospital bed in a bay with a rack of equipment. She didn't feel sick. Her headache was gone. In fact nothing hurt anywhere, which was nice. Maybe she should be worried about how she had gotten here, but she was in a fuzzy, relaxed mood that probably was chemically induced. A plastic ziplock on the table beside her contained three corn muffins. Lea sat up, feeling a little light-headed, and opened it.

This is a dream, she decided. *I wanted sleep and corn muffins, so my subconscious arranged it for me.*

The muffins were only slightly warm, and they didn't have butter. Surely a well-trained subconscious would do a better job? Lea pulled off bits from a muffin and ate them thoughtfully. She wasn't really hungry, but it would be a shame to let a dream corn muffin go to waste.

Something tightened painfully on her arm with a creaking, huffing noise. She told it to stop, in a way that seemed familiar to her, and it did. Nothing else happened while she finished her muffin. This was not a very interesting dream. Maybe she should go exploring? That's what she had been doing before, right? Had she found something? Lea frowned, trying hard to remember. She'd found that display. The one that showed people and where they were on the BDR. There'd been something else, though—a door, a different door.

"Hey, you're awake!" Ramirez was standing in the bay opening, grinning at her.

"I am?" Lea said doubtfully. "This is real?"

He came over and stood by the side of the bed. "Of course it is. Some reason it shouldn't be?" Now he seemed worried. She liked Ramirez and didn't want him to be worried.

"I just don't remember how I got here. This is *Kepler,* right?"

More uncomfortableness. "Yeah. You, ah, you kinda collapsed when you went through the spindle door. Then you acted really strange when I got you conscious again."

"Spindle door?"

"Do you remember that hull-side door you wanted to check out? Well it didn't go somewhere on the BDR. It went to the spindle."

More was starting to come back now. "There was a control panel…" she said. Ramirez was grinning again.

"Yeah, you were going off on that the whole time. Ivars had to carry you over to take a look—and that's when the robot showed up. Good thing it thought we were boring and left us alone."

The robot. She remembered the robot. It had been wrong, somehow. The…music. The sound in her head that was not a sound. But its music had been similar to the music she heard on the BDR, and when she remembered the BDR music—the robot had changed its music and gone away. Had that really happened? Ramirez said the robot went away, and he hadn't gone unconscious like she had.

Suddenly the bay felt crowded and cramped, and Lea wanted to leave. She felt trapped, with something coming closer. Something…uncomfortable. She pulled the thin blanket up. "How long do I have to stay here?"

"Soon as the doc clears—hey, guess what? She's awake!" This last to someone outside she couldn't see. Then Ivars came into view.

"I'm glad you're feeling better. You gave us a bit of a scare," Ivars said. His voice seemed…smaller. More subdued.

"Um, thanks for…for carrying me back," Lea managed. He must think she was completely useless, fainting away like that.

He smiled. "Thanks for the warning about the robot. If you hadn't said anything I probably would have shot it when it came too close. How did you know motion set it off?"

Lea froze. "I didn't say anything," she blurted. "I was too scared. I couldn't get my mouth to open." She'd been terrified. But somehow she had been sure moving was a very bad idea right then.

"You weren't always thinking clearly back there," Ramirez said, obviously picking his words with care. "Maybe you forgot saying it."

"Yeah, I guess so." Anything rather than have them think she was crazy. Maybe she was. Maybe they should keep her here. She wanted to help, but she kept making things worse. "Are we going to have to go back to the spindle?"

She could tell by their reactions something had happened. "They've already been back. Others, not us," said Ramirez.

"You didn't see what North found," Ivars added. "There was another door nearby, one we think goes to a planet. They're sending some guys through now." He glanced out at the corridor, then back.

The understanding hit Lea hard and fast, unexpectedly. "You wanted to go," she breathed. He looked at her then, really looked at her like he used to. Hard. "Why didn't they let you? Was it because of me?" He didn't say anything, but he didn't have to. "I'm sorry." Her throat tightened and she stopped speaking, shaking her head. She'd screwed it up again.

"I'll have other chances. Especially if they find what they're looking for." He glanced over his shoulder. "Looks like they're going to kick us out now. Don't worry, just rest up. We've got plenty of time."

Lie. She was certain of that although she had no real reason to be. They didn't have time for her to sit here and eat muffins. She watched them go, feeling cold. Then the orderly showed up. She looked at the display readouts and clucked.

"When can I leave?" Lea asked.

"The doctor wants your heart readings to be more consistent before you are released. We still don't know what happened to you, after all. Maybe a few more hours, if everything stabilizes."

Too long. After the orderly left, Lea stared at the machine that was keeping her trapped. There was a screen showing the usual scraggly line that she thought meant her heart was still beating, and several numerical readouts. There was a rhythm that matched it. Now that she was thinking about it, it was easy to find. Something changed when the numbers changed. The numbers had to stay the same if she wanted to get out. *Don't change,* she thought at the machine. The rhythm needed to be like *this.*

After a while, she realized the numbers hadn't changed. At all.

∽

"Now I want you to rest. That's the best medication I can prescribe for you." Dr. Hae gave her a meaningful look. Lea's request for more painkillers had not found favor, and she got the feeling he wasn't going to even give her an aspirin now. "I know that might not be easy with all the crowding and noise in our situation, so I will give you this." He handed over a small packet. "It's a very effective sleeping aid, with low side effects. I don't want you to rely on it, so there's just one for now. Any questions?"

Lea shook her head, then felt her forehead. "Why are there wires?"

"Just checking your brain activity," the orderly said, smiling.

"To see if we can solve your headache problem."

Neither of them said anything more, and the air felt thick. No, not the air—she wasn't sure how to describe it, but when they had been talking earlier the sensation had been missing. When they had been answering her freely. Maybe they weren't telling her something now. Something about her brain.

It didn't matter; they were letting her leave now. Lea carefully didn't look at the machine she had fiddled with while they unhooked the wires and the IV. If they suspected anything she'd never get away. They didn't stop her, though, and she left as quickly as she could, clutching her jacket.

I changed a machine with my mind. The realization made her feel shaky. It wasn't a hallucination; other people had seen it too. The doctor and the orderly were arguing about what could have caused the blood pressure machine to turn off, and with a guilty start Lea realized she'd done it. The cuff had been uncomfortable, and even in a drugged state she'd managed to figure out how to make it stop. What was happening to her? Why now?

Walking through the passageways of *Kepler* she was acutely aware of all the devices surrounding her. They all had different songs or rhythms in her mind—a smoke detector, a security camera, data cables in the walls. What if she changed something by mistake? How would she know, how would anyone know? Could she fix it?

Sleep wasn't going to happen in her current state, even with a big pill. She needed to be alone, as far as possible from any important equipment on the ship, so she could figure things out. She also needed to experiment.

The bunk area that had been her original assignment still had her locker, and only a few people in it, all sleeping. Someone had dumped her pack there, as she had hoped. Now where was her reader? Rummaging around, her fingers felt the cool ceramic surface of the alien device, and a spike of panic made her grab it, as if to make sure it was still really there. Casting a quick look around to make sure no one was watching, she pulled it out and tucked it in her inside jacket pocket. That had been a narrow escape. What if her pack had been searched? Lea found her reader, then stuffed the pack inside the locker.

Lea remembered seeing a dead-end passageway when she had

visited Wojicz in the lower levels, where there weren't many people about. The walls had been bare too, so no distracting devices she shouldn't be messing with. It was just as empty as she recalled when she got there, and with a sigh she leaned against the wall and sank to the floor.

For a moment she just sat there, listening, feeling her heart pounding in her chest. She could hear different threads, but none clear like the robot or the medical machines—more like echoes. Lea hoped that was safe enough.

The instant she turned on the reader, she could feel the connection. It was much simpler than the medical machines, and soon she discovered how to open a file just by thinking about it. Playing around with the reader, discovering what she could do, Lea forgot her troubles. *Maybe this isn't so bad after all.* She could even, with a bit of effort, turn the reader on and off. If she was touching the reader everything was simple. If the reader was next to her, it was only a little harder, but increasing distance made it impossible for her to turn it on remotely, and harder to hear its song—and if she didn't hear it, she couldn't control it.

What else could she practice on? Lea remembered the alien device in her jacket pocket and pulled it out, letting it rest in the palm of her hand. It had the same inert feel that the powered-off reader did. *So, just turn it on then.* She took a deep breath, wondering if this was a smart move. But how else was she going to find out about the alien tech or her own strange abilities?

On. Nothing happened. The device lay inert in her hand. Lea closed her eyes and tried again. About the fifth time she thought she felt a slight rubbery response. Maybe she was being too strong and forceful. She tried one more time, attempting to mimic the feel of the response.

It felt like a small click in her mind. Lea opened her eyes and saw that bright green glyphs had appeared on the dark onyx surface of the device. She grinned and did a little seated happy dance. She couldn't brag about it without starting a perfect storm of awkward questions, but it did feel good to have finally figured something out. *That'll teach them to keep me away from all the cool toys,* she thought.

Now, what did it do? The device felt like it was ready and waiting for something. With the reader she knew what it did, and it was just a matter of finding out how to do it. With the alien device, it could do anything. It could be a disintegrator, or a presentation pointer for all she knew. No, wait. It had been found in the long, lab–like hallway. Lots of equipment there. Maybe it was a tool to use with equipment?

Lea touched the reader with the narrow tip of the alien device. The green glyphs changed, and so did the feeling in her head. It felt like "error," not surprisingly. She got up and used it to touch the passageway wall, the floor, a light panel, and then a fire safety alarm. Still the same "error" feel. Maybe it just didn't know how to read Earth technology. So, how was she going to get some alien tech to try? Without anyone noticing?

The alarm klaxon suddenly blared, startling her into dropping the gizmo on the floor with a loud crack. Lea scrabbled for it and stuffed it back in her jacket. What was the siren about? Had she set it off with her testing? Where was her general quarters station again? She ran up the passageway, dodging other people running. Her bunk. Her official bunk, that's where she was supposed to go. Had that changed, with all the extra people on board?

To get to the berthing area she needed to get to the large central corridor that ran the length of *Kepler*. The crowds were thicker and harder for her to see around. Now she could hear shouting, and a glimpse of digicam uniform. Lea shifted over closer to the wall. She didn't really feel like dealing with any of the soldiers right now. A sudden stab of pain in her side made her wince. The pain grew worse, and the shouting got closer. A group of soldiers came by at a run, the one in the middle with his helmet off and grimacing with pain, a trickle of blood running down one cheek. As the group went past she saw a dark, charred blotch on the man's side.

That was the reason for the alarm, then. She hadn't caused it, at least she didn't see how she could have. It would have been a relief, except that now it appeared something was shooting at them and that was an even bigger problem.

By wiggling through the crowds she finally managed to reach her bunk section. There was even an empty bunk, and she snagged it. The doctor had told her to rest. Maybe that was why she was getting muscle cramps; she'd been mucking around playing mind games with inanimate objects instead of sleeping. Not that sleeping was going to be easy. The others in the room were discussing the alarm and what could have caused it. Even with the pillow over her head Lea was still very aware of hundreds of different electronic devices, each with its own mental melody. For what seemed like hours she tried to sleep, dozing off only to be suddenly woken by a new device being turned on. She had strange dreams when she slept, too.

Then she remembered the sleeping pill the doctor had given her. If ever there was a time it was now. Lea took out the packet and dumped out the pill. It wasn't very big, and a boring mint green. Shrugging, she swallowed it dry. It probably wouldn't do much, but it was better than nothing.

Lea put her head back down on the pillow and closed her eyes. Then she heard the sound of running feet, a murmur of voices, and then a hand was shaking her shoulder.

"Lea Santorin? Director Macrae wants to see you right away," said the woman.

Lea felt a wash of anxiety. Had they found out about the device? Had she done something else wrong? She swung her feet down and got up. "Where?" she managed to say, somewhat groggily.

"Follow me."

With trepidation, Lea did. The woman walked fast and led her to a level higher than Lea had ever been on the ship. The higher she went, the more complex systems Lea could sense, and she started to sweat. She shouldn't be here. She hardly knew what she was doing and could barely control what she could do. What if she turned off the reactor or fired the emergency escape capsule on the bridge?

Merrilee Macrae was waiting in a small meeting room along with a hawk-faced man in uniform Lea vaguely recalled as being in command of the military detachment, and Ivars, Olsen, North, and Ramirez. Macrae looked like she was mad enough to spit tacks, but her expression changed when she looked at Lea to one of worry. Olsen appeared a little concerned, but the others seemed either noncommittal or interested. Maybe she wasn't in trouble? When they saw her come in, the soldiers even seemed happy to see her, especially Ramirez.

"I'm sorry to call you in when you are still not feeling well,"

Macrae said, "but unfortunately, it seems we need your help. The team we sent through the planet door ran into some hostile defensive systems, and several were injured. There's a structure that is visible but we can't reach it because of the robot defenders. Sergeant Ivars suggested you might know how to deal with this, having dealt with something similar on the spindle."

It took Lea a moment to collect her confused thoughts. *Ivars* thought she knew what to do? "Well, I don't know, not really. I mean, I haven't seen them or anything." She did know, or at least suspect. The spindle robot would have attacked if she hadn't... identified herself. Probably the defenses on the planet surface were set up the same way. But how could she explain without getting fitted for a wraparound jacket? "I hear voices" always inspired confidence in upper management.

"We want to send another team," the hawk-faced man said. He had a nametag—Gonafrio. "Just for observation, to find a way through. The first team reported they only came under fire when they got too close to the building. We think there is a reasonable— not guaranteed, reasonable—degree of safety for you if you agree to go. I would not ask you if I did not believe this to be true. And of course the team would protect you to the best of their ability."

Team. That word had a sudden resonance, and Lea glanced at each of the soldiers in turn. They hadn't been some random group assigned to go with her to search the former-Pluto ship, they had been a team first. They were still a team. For some reason, they really wanted to go to the planet. She remembered Ivars's suppressed disappointment, and she'd been responsible for that. She didn't want to be the reason again.

Besides, it would get her away from the ship. Lea was beginning to suspect it was dangerous for her to be on *Kepler,* at least until she had better control of whatever was going on in her head. Why not get Ivars what he wanted too?

"OK," Lea said, swallowing hard. "Let's go."

CHAPTER 6

Standing in the alien ship passageway before the door to the spindle, Lea wondered at her own detachment. Activity swirled around her as the team got ready to leave. Since they would be leaving the enclosed environments they had been used to, the soldiers had more gear and more weapons. Even she had been issued a helmet and a Kevlar vest, which was very annoying because Ivars insisted she put them on right away. She wanted to pick up her pack, but she couldn't bend at the waist. If she bent her knees, she started feeling dizzy. Finally she shoved the pack over to a wall with her foot and used the wall for balance while she carefully knelt down.

Shouldn't she be a little more nervous? Instead she felt dreamy and detached, like it was all happening to someone else. *Oh yeah. The sleeping pill.* She didn't feel like she was going to fall asleep, though. No need to mention it and delay everything. It would wear off eventually, right?

Gradually she noticed the wall under her hand felt warm. It was a section of morph and felt a little rough to her fingertips. Then she realized she was sensing something. It had been a relief to leave *Kepler* and the constant mental noise behind, as well as the worry she would interfere. This felt different. Was she detecting an alien system?

She closed her eyes and concentrated. The melody was different, with a much more complicated rhythm. It took her a moment to get the hang of it before she tried echoing it. Immediately the melody changed, becoming louder and multithreaded. Lea snapped her eyes open. How could she mimic that? She tried mentally replaying some music with multiple melodic lines—and the signal changed again. Now there was a faint echo of the music she had been thinking of mixed in. It felt like it was…seeking.

"Hey, Santorin. You ready?" Ivars said.

Lea looked around, startled. "Yeah. Ready." She walked past him, and he followed. "Why do you always call me by just my last name?" she asked, and immediately wondered where the question had come from. Just at the moment, it mattered that he'd never called her anything else. *Stupid.*

He didn't say anything for a moment, and she glanced back. He was giving her a surprised look, and he shrugged.

"Habit?" Ivars grinned. "I'll stop if it bothers you."

Lea kept going. "I was just curious." She was also losing some of her dreamy detachment, staring at the door and feeling irritable. This time the transit was only a mild sting, like a slap. She emerged on the spindle side to see a larger group of soldiers, not just her team, all alert and wary. Her memories of the spindle area were vague and there were none of the planet gate, so she looked about with interest.

One of the floating robots wandered by. It ignored the humans completely, and Lea wondered if she had permanently changed it. She could sense it, and how it was sending small pulses in a flattened sphere around it. Acting on impulse, she nudged it over with her mind. The floating robot jibbed a little, bobbed, and then returned to its earlier path. So, she could mess with them. Maybe she could help out on the planet after all.

The robot felt different, and she wondered why. It was almost like a taste, or a smell to her mind. Human tech and alien tech had very distinct flavors. Now that she thought about it, the flavor of the little device and the melody she'd sensed just before were more like each other than the robot, even though they were all alien. What did that mean? Different manufacturers?

When they got to the planet door she could tell it was very different from any of the others she'd encountered. While she sensed the transporter doors on the alien ship like a low hum, this thing felt like a diesel locomotive. A *big* diesel locomotive.

"Everybody, listen up." Ivars had stopped in front of the little hallway leading to the door. "We think the picture we're getting from the door here is accurate, but there does appear to be a time lag of between twenty to fifty seconds. Since we can't be sure if hostiles will be waiting for us on the other side, our entry is hot. Once the immediate area is secure, we scout away from the door planetside and check for the location of the robots that attacked Team Eleven. Santor—um, you will stick with me," he said, pointing to Lea. "Don't move unless I do. No picking daisies or wandering off without us, OK? And if anything happens to me, you stay moving with the rest of the team. If something happens to them, you run for the door and get back to *Kepler*. You are not authorized to be a hero, got that?" Lea nodded mutely. "Any questions?" Between the little green pill and her gloomy thoughts, Lea didn't care enough to have questions. Get away from all this technology and maybe she could get her head straight. "All right. Olsen and North, then Ramirez, then me and S—her. Condition one as you enter the door."

North racked his weapon. Olsen did something to a small control display on his big gun. "Weapons hot," they said in turn, and stepped through and vanished. After an agonizing delay, they appeared on the other side, weapons at the ready. A moment later, Olsen made a small gesture with his hand and Ramirez repeated the process.

"It's Lea," Lea said softly as they waited for Ramirez to show on the other side.

"What?"

"My name. The other one. Didn't anybody tell you? Or did you forget?"

"I am a highly trained professional. I don't forget anything," Ivars said in a lofty tone.

Lea stared at him. "Your ears are going red," she observed.

"Ramirez is through," Ivars said with relief. "Come on, let's invade." Shaking her head, Lea stepped through.

Power, raw power, surrounded her. She could feel a bubble of energy form around her, then twist. A blast of electronic sensing hammered down, and then all she knew was pain. Pain like a white fire that overwhelmed all her senses.

Then she was through. The agony that still washed through her was so strong she couldn't move, couldn't even scream. It burned through and was gone, leaving her feeling shaky and sick. All she could do was take shallow breaths and desperately hope she wouldn't dump the contents of her stomach on this alien planet, which would probably cause some horrible ecological disaster.

Slowly awareness of her surroundings faded in. She was facing a craggy rock wall with water seeping down over it. The rock was dark, almost black, and fine-grained. Little tufts of light blue-green vegetation grew in the cracks and crevices, with the occasional larger plant with fronds like feathers. The air was cool and damp and smelled like a mix of fresh-cut wood and mold.

Underfoot the ground looked like the same dark rock, but smooth, and a pattern of grooves had been cut that led to a larger channel for drainage. Clearly not natural, but it was impossible to tell how old it was. Moving her head carefully to avoid any rebellion from her roiling stomach, Lea took a careful look around. The planet-side doorway jutted out from the rock and the grain flowed around it as if the rock had formed after the door was there. They were in a large hollow, almost like a collapsed cave. Ivars was on the other side of the hollow, standing at the foot of a shallow ramp that went up and around to higher ground. His back was against the wall and his weapon was aimed up at the top of the ramp. All Lea could hear was dripping water and a faint breeze.

If she was lucky, he hadn't noticed her little episode. How long had she been out?

Now Ivars was slowly scanning the top of the hollow, weapon following his gaze. Something at the top of the ramp caught his attention, and then he seemed to relax a little. He turned and motioned to Lea. Her stomach was feeling a little more stable now, and she cautiously walked over to the foot of the ramp. As she got closer she was aware of a wave of fierce happiness. Lea frowned. It made no sense. She was feeling terrified and queasy, not happy. Then she looked up and saw the expression in Ivars's eyes, and she understood. *He* was feeling happy. And she was reading him.

Instinctively she took a step back. She wanted to run, hide, anything to get away.

"Something wrong? You look like you saw a ghost." A wave of concern from him now, looking for a threat that would cause her fear.

Lea struggled to speak. "I'm on another planet," she managed, in a voice that sounded like a squeak. Ivars laughed.

"Yeah, it hits you all of a sudden, doesn't it. Never thought I'd see the day. Come on, we've got the all clear."

She followed him up the ramp, keeping as much space between them as she could. It was worse, closer. As they got to the top she realized with a sinking sensation that she could sense the other members of the team as well. Nothing specific, just a diffuse point of mental signal that had a unique pattern she recognized as belonging to a particular person. How did she know that? Had she been sensing them before without knowing it? But she knew without a shadow of doubt that North was behind that large silver-grey tree even though she could not see him, and Ramirez was farther ahead, and Olsen was behind them on the opposite side of the hollow.

They moved forward in silence until they were away from the lightly forested area surrounding the hollow. They were on a small hill overlooking a plain, with similar small hummock-like hills topped by silver-green trees in the distance. An impressively large moon was barely visible in the sky, which had an odd cast of color to it.

"Let's see if we can find the bastards," Ivars said, shrugging out of his oversize pack. North did the same. In a few moments they had assembled what looked like a model airplane with clear plastic wings and North had donned a thick set of black goggles. Using a controller the size of a deck of cards, he soon had the little airplane launched. Lea looked away and tried to think of something else.

"Where's the building they talked about?" she asked.

"Between those two hills," Ivars pointed. "Here, you can see it better with these." He handed her a slim pair of binoculars.

Lea fiddled with the focus for a bit until she saw what he was pointing at. It was a low, monolithic building reminiscent of a giant gear, lying flat. Sloped flanges radiated out from the main walls, reminding her of the entrance to the planet door on the spindle. Either the same people made them both or they went to the same galactic design school.

"I wonder why they didn't put it closer to the door," Lea said. A dark blur moved across her field of vision. She dialed back the focus. Something was floating in the plain below, mottled grey and squat in shape. It was hard to get a good view of it. "Hey, is that one of the robots that shoot at people?"

Ivars took the binoculars and watched silently for a moment.

"Sure looks like one. North, what's your grid?"

"Seven–six on the map overlay," North replied. "Heading?"

"You want nominal south about half a klick; it's heading northwest estimated thirty kilometers per hour."

"Got it." North adjusted the controls. "Confirm sighting. Interesting. I see some visual damage. Did Team Eleven report hits?"

"They got off plenty of shots but didn't stay around to see if they connected," Olsen drawled. "It got hot fast."

The soldiers continued to discuss the robots, but Lea wasn't listening. She moved away, still close enough that she was pretty sure Ivars wouldn't object, and sat down. The ground was covered with more of the frondy plant she'd seen in the hollow. It smelled slightly sour where it had been stepped on.

She wanted to find out if she could locate the rest of the robots and figure out their pattern of motion. Lea closed her eyes. The soldiers were still close; the cloud of signal she sensed around them was hard to ignore. But the robot signal was very distinct, and with effort she found she could concentrate on them to the exclusion of everything else. She listened and learned.

When she felt she had enough to work with she stood up, feeling stiff, intending to go and tell the others. But what would she tell them? Why would they believe her? There had to be a cover story.

"Can I borrow some binoculars?" Lea asked, walking back to the group. North, still wearing the airplane goggles, reached for a pocket of his vest and handed her his. Lea pretended to watch the valley. If she could get close enough to one, she could at least immobilize it and possibly reset it.

She felt Ivars coming closer. "Well, what do you think?" he asked.

"It's hard to tell much when they are so far away. It would be nice if we could knock out one and take a look at it, but I suppose it would be a bad idea to just start shooting."

Ivars grinned. "You have correctly assessed the situation. Good thing we've got more tricks than that." More focused happiness. He *wanted* an excuse to capture a robot. "Can you tell if the others will come if one goes down?"

"They all have their areas of patrol," Lea said slowly. "I think if we got one when the nearest ones were far away as possible, they wouldn't leave their own areas right away. There would be some time. How would we get it away, though?"

"I'm thinking we make it look like the victim suffered a tragic yet purely accidental gear seizure. They come and check it out, nobody there, we go back and scavenge."

Lea stared. "You can do that?"

"Det-cord is *almost* as useful as duct tape," Ivars said. "You watch."

Lea did. All she had to do was give them an estimated speed that the robot would use to investigate something suspicious and the maximum normal range of the patrol. They decided to attack the already-damaged robot, on the theory it would be easiest to take out. They picked a cluster of oblong boulders near the bottom of the hill for the ambush site. Ivars and Ramirez unrolled a packet of what looked like thin, sticky rope, coiling most of it under a boulder they balanced on the others, and a smaller amount just in front of the rock cluster. Tiny electronic detonators were attached, and at Lea's suggestion, hidden from view. The robot might know enough to be wary of obvious advanced technology.

Then she had to wait. It took longer than she liked before the pattern brought all the robots to the necessary locations, but then the damaged robot began to approach the rock cluster. Normally it would just sweep by, but after North fired the little decoy explosive it turned and moved closer to investigate the small plume of dust and smoke.

Lea closed her eyes. The signal was stronger now, she could almost—but no, she couldn't take it over. Not yet, not before the main explosive had gone off. Closer, closer…

"Now!" she whispered.

A big boom this time. Lea thought *STOP* at the robot and felt it respond. She opened her eyes. The boulder with the explosives had split neatly in two, landing on top of the robot and apparently trapping it. She knew better. It was not as damaged as it appeared and was just waiting for further orders. Well, she could do that now, couldn't she?

The captured robot was networked to the others, so all she had to do was override their alerts and set them to patrol farther away. And wait until the soldiers were convinced the remaining robots weren't going to come and investigate. When Ivars finally decided they could leave cover, Lea jumped to her feet.

"Oh no you don't," Ivars said and grabbed her wrist. Lea had a sudden flash of sight, seeing her own surprised face looking…up? "Let the expendables go first, OK?"

He has a device that lets him see, Lea realized with a shock. *The eye that doesn't close right.* Then what he said hit her, and she snapped, "You're not expendable! How dare you say you're expendable!" Her sudden fury startled her as much as it appeared to surprise Ivars. Where had that come from?

Why does he have an artificial eye? He must have gotten badly injured, probably when he got the scars on the side of his head. It wasn't comfortable to think about, but she couldn't help it. It seemed to be connected with her anger. The thought of Ivars hurt was wrong somehow.

"Ohhhkay, let's all go together, then." Ivars was giving her an odd look. "I hope your robot isn't too heavy. It's a long way back to the door."

Lea felt her stomach knot. She'd forgotten the door. She was never going to survive going through that door again. What had she been thinking? What was she going to do?

It was probably wrong of him to be a little glad *Kepler* had been carried off to the far corners of the galaxy, but he was. Ivars looked around and was content. He was out in the field, like he thought he never would be again. He'd been damned lucky the RPG that had hit him was a dud, and insanely lucky it had only hit him a glancing blow. It had still taken agonizing months of surgery, recovery, and retraining, all the time wondering if he was washed up—no more missions.

And here he was. True, it was an alien field and their situation was still dire, but he was *doing* something about it and not just guarding flaky academics from nonexistent alien boogeymen.

Even Space Cadet—*Lea*—was stepping up and really helping out now. She'd figured out the attack robots pretty quick, and got right to work on their captured one. She'd even managed to get it working again so they didn't have to carry it. He wasn't sure if that was a good idea, but she claimed it would keep the others away and it now thought of them as friendly, so it wasn't a threat. The robot didn't have the same smooth, even floating motion it had before they'd dropped a boulder on it, so they named it Bob.

The team spread out and crossed the plain as quickly as they could. As Lea had promised, none of the other attack robots even deviated to check them out. The building Team Eleven had tried to reach was bigger than it had appeared at a distance, low and massive. North covered Olsen at the entrance while he dropped a flare round inside. The light revealed more dark, rocklike walls and no hostiles. He waved them in.

Lea was standing nearby, a puzzled frown on her face. She didn't look frightened at all, which was unusual given the circumstances. Didn't she realize the building could be occupied?

"It's dead," Lea said.

"Keep your voice down. What do you mean, dead?"

Then she looked a little panicked. "Well, um, look at the door. See where it fits inside the wall? It's stuck, and it's been that way for a long time. Nobody's home."

He looked at the exterior door, what he would have called a heavy hatch. She was right, it hadn't been closed in a while. For a building that looked like a defensive strong point, that would be a major problem.

Olsen and North returned. "It's empty, as far as we looked. No sign of recent occupation."

Lea gave Ivars a look. He sighed. "Still need to check it so we can report it. OK, let's scope it out."

The place was dead, just like she'd said, which meant no light. No windows either. The only illumination came from their flashlights, and the whole thing smelled just like a cave. "Strange no animals came in," Ivars commented.

"Maybe the robots kept them away," Olsen said. "Haven't seen any animals, either. Better not be any spiders," he added in a grumble, and Ivars stifled a grin.

"Hey, what's that?" Lea pointed her cheap little purple flashlight at a wall. So far all the interior surfaces had been smooth and uniform, but here was a jagged hole and the clear marks of blows. Somebody, or something, had bashed at the wall with considerable force, and whatever had been there originally removed.

"That's not reassuring," Ivars said slowly.

Lea turned to him. "Why not?"

"Whoever built this would have a better way of removing something they put in, don't you think? So that makes me think another group came in after the first group left, or were pushed out. Last thing we need is to be in the middle of somebody else's war."

"Yeah, that never ends well," Olsen remarked dryly. "Yet somehow that's where we always end up."

"You're not helping, Ghost That Walks," Ivars muttered.

They went through as much of the building as they could. Some doors were stuck shut, and had been before the salvage crew had gone through because they had chisel marks along the seams. A few had been broken open. Everywhere there were signs of salvage.

"I wonder where they took the stuff to," Ramirez said, looking at a particularly large hole. "I mean, we haven't seen anything they took out and left behind. They knew what they wanted and took it."

"Looks like we got here too late," agreed Ivars. "No help here."

They made their way back to the entrance. Ivars had no idea how long the local day was, but the light was definitely starting to dim. Bob was waiting outside, just like they'd left it.

"We should probably head back. Bad idea to be caught in the dark when we don't know what's out there. Gonafrio will have to send us out again if he wants us to search for nuts and berries."

"I'd like to stay," Lea said hesitantly. "Just—just overnight, and a bit? Can we do that? I want to…to look at things a little more."

Now that he was not expecting. Space Cadet wanted to stay on the alien planet that had wigged her out at the beginning. The lure of the unknown must have gotten to her, just like them. The building was certainly defensible, even with the main door broken. They could do the biological survey, check out the night life for future reference, and give the building a closer look. They'd need a bit more gear, at least Lea would, since they hadn't planned on a sleepover and if he was any judge, the night was going to get chilly.

He looked around at the others. They all wanted to stay, he could tell. They hadn't been given a time limit, but caution dictated armor plating on the decision tree. If they stayed and things went bad the people in *Kepler* would never know what they had learned.

"OK, here's what we do. North and Ramirez, you'll go back through the door and report. Quickly as they'll let you. Grab some cold-weather gear and sleeping bags and hightail it back. The rest of us will gather samples until it gets dark, then we'll bivouac here and she can do some more poking around. Comments?"

The plan went like clockwork, considering. Ramirez even had the bright idea of taking some preliminary biosamples with them, and Bob the robot escorted everyone over the plain and back with no problems. They even found some deadwood and brought it back for a fire. The local trees turned into something resembling a loofah in structure when they died, nice and dry. The wood only smelled a little bit like scorched hair when they burned it, too. *Better than goat dung, by a mile.*

They picked a larger room not too far from the entrance to set up in. North had the remote-control airplane lying on the ground and in infrared mode just outside the door, so whoever was on watch could keep a visual check without being visible himself.

The rest of the team cleaned weapons, checked gear, and cataloged the biosamples while sitting around the fire. Lea was there too, but drawn back from the group. Ivars watched her from the corner of his eye. She looked sad and worried. *OK, you are not going to drop the ball this time, got it?*

"You're pretty quiet there, Lea. What's on your mind?" he said casually, wiping nonexistent oil off the barrel of his AR.

"I wonder where they are. The people who took the stuff from this building," she said, sounding reluctant to speak at all.

"Not here, at least not recently," Ivars said. He was not going to let her evade this time. If something was wrong, he was going to find out. "Not anywhere we've been."

"How do you know? No footprints?"

"Not just footprints. Assuming they have feet," Olsen commented, holding a bag of a brilliant blue-green lichen up to the light. "We'd notice if anything had changed. Maybe a fallen log that changed position, something that hadn't been there before, all kinds of things. One guy I know could tell if somebody had been in a room by smell. Admittedly we're talking about goat herders with poor personal hygiene, but still."

"You're not just regular soldiers, are you?" Lea said softly.

Well. He'd wanted to keep her talking, hadn't he?

"We go camping a lot," Ivars said, grinning.

"Without permits," North added, straight-faced.

Olsen put down his biosample. "We're Special Forces," he said, in a matter-of-fact tone. He responded to Ivars's grimace with a bland look.

Lea looked bewildered. "But what does that mean? I mean, I think there's a movie or something, but—"

"Do *not* say the *R*-word," Ramirez broke in. "For the love of God."

"What *R*-word?" Lea said, exasperated.

"You said movies. The one with Stallone in it? That's not us." "*Rocky?*"

The team cracked up. "No, the other one," Ivars said, trying not to laugh himself. "We get tired when people think that's what we are. We don't like getting noticed, period. We...go places, quietly, and do stuff, also quietly. If we do it right, nobody knows where we've been until after we've gone and we've never fired a shot."

"Oh." Lea thought for a moment. "I wasn't thinking of him at all, really. He's more, um," she gestured at her arms, "bulgy."

North lost it, laughing so hard tears came to his eyes and he had to take off the remote visor to wipe them. "Santorin, you're all right," he said when he recovered enough to talk. "Don't ever change, OK?"

Lea Santorin's face shut down, like a switch had been thrown. All expression vanished, wiped clean.

"I'm tired. Think I'll go to sleep now," she said. She got up and unrolled a sleeping bag, as far away from them as she could get and still be in the room.

North glanced at Ivars, mouthing *What did I say?* Ivars shrugged, holding up his hands in puzzlement. Lea hadn't seemed too upset by the teasing, accepting it for what it was and even grinning at North. But for whatever reason, North's mild comment had gone the wrong way.

Don't ever change. Why would that upset her? Something was wrong again, that was clear. And she didn't want them to find out.

CHAPTER 7

"There are times when I really love my job," Olsen said as he packed the door seam with det–cord.

Ivars plugged the last chain–timer in the C–4 block and handed it to him. "You're going to miss it," he said, grinning. "Not too late to change your mind and re–up."

"Nuh–uh. The only reason I got clearance for one last mission from Home Base was because I would be, in Jason's words, a 'nastronaut.'" Olsen stopped what he was doing for a moment, head down, and then continued in silence. His face was like stone.

"We'll get back," Ivars said quietly. "Somehow. And someday you'll be able to tell him just what you did on that routine mission that took a little longer than planned."

"Yeah." Olsen's voice was taut. Then one corner of his mouth turned up. "Somebody's gotta teach him to check the settings on the detonator before switching it on."

"Oh come on, I only did that once! In training! One little premature explosion and you never live it down."

Olsen stepped back, and they both went over the explosive placement once more, double–checking. "It's a miracle you still have all your fingers, headcase."

The others had finished packing up the camping room and sweeping the area for any debris that would alert strangers to their presence in the alien structure. No point in giving out clues that humans had visited the planet. Since others had broken down doors before, adding another shouldn't be too much of a giveaway—and he never turned down a valid opportunity to blow something up.

"All right, everybody take cover outside. The hallways will channel the blast, so stay well away from the entrance." Lea turned and left, dragging her pack in one hand and her bedroll in the other. She'd been quiet all morning, hardly speaking and spending her time away from the rest of them. Now he had a chance to find out what was on her mind.

Olsen fired the remote detonator once everyone was outside, and he heard a satisfactory boom, which was followed by a roiling cloud of dust. They'd have to let that settle before going in to see if it had worked.

Ivars glanced around, saw Lea hanging back, and waved her over. She came, but reluctantly. "Something wrong?" he asked when she got there. "Headaches back?"

Lea shook her head. "No headaches. I'm fine." He just stared at her, waiting, when she fell silent. "I don't know, OK?" she finally burst out, waving her hands. "Nothing I can point to. Something's just wrong. I mean, I wouldn't believe me either. I just..." she glanced out over the plain, a worried expression on her face. "Are you really sure there's nobody else out there?"

"I suppose there could be, but they haven't given any sign of it. We have no idea when those doors got smashed in. Could have been a hundred years ago." Lea didn't say anything. He could see North waving at the entrance, indicating the dust had cleared. "Look, it's good to be careful. If you see anything that makes you suspicious, point it out to us. We don't want to get jumped either. OK?" She nodded. "Come on, let's see if we found the treasure room."

The C–4 had done a decent job, but it still took some work to clear enough rubble away to let them get inside. No treasure, but the walls were intact and had sections with small lumpy protrusions and flat polished areas. It looked a lot like the console on the spindle that Lea had been so fascinated by.

"That must be the stuff the raiders were after," Lea said, wandering up to one of the sections. "I wonder why?" She ran her hand over the surface.

"If we want to take any back we'll need something other than C–4," Olsen said. "Besides, we don't have much left."

Lea had pulled off her pack and was rummaging around in it. She pulled out the gizmo Ivars had slipped to her and gently touched it to the wall. He was startled to see tiny green symbols light up down the side of the device, and even, briefly, on the wall itself. *Looks like Space Cadet figured it out.* Lea glanced suddenly at him, and he raised an eyebrow.

"I...found it," she said, smiling a little. Yeah, she knew he'd given it to her, and she wasn't letting on. "I think it is a diagnostic tool of some kind." She waved her hand at the wall. "It's dead. If we get the components back to...to the alien ship, maybe we could get them turned on again, but not here."

He had her do her trick with the gizmo one more time, while he recorded, and then he decided they'd gotten enough for now. Time to head back, get some biosamples, and return to *Kepler.*

Strangely, Lea seemed reluctant to leave. *I thought she was scared of someone hiding here?* Going back should have made her feel more secure. It made no sense. She was frightened of something, he was certain. But what? And why wouldn't she tell him what it was?

❧

The door to the spindle loomed ahead at the end of the hike, and Lea despaired. They had to go back; she knew this. She'd delayed as long as she could, even risking the suspicions of the soldiers. Sheer terror clouded her thinking and knotted her stomach. How was she going to handle the pain? She didn't have a second sleeping pill. All she or anybody else had here was aspirin level, completely useless for what she was facing. Tears formed in her eyes from pure fear and frustration.

The doors didn't bother anyone else, that was clear. Who would believe her? More importantly, what could they do if they did? She had to go back to *Kepler* and the door was the only way back.

Then she realized they had another serious problem. Something had changed in the robot network, and she hadn't done it. It felt crude, too. A big, ragged tear in a picture replaced with stick figure drawings. Bob the robot wasn't affected, as far as she could tell, but the others were. She frowned. Because the change was so crude it was hard to tell what it was doing. It might not even be connected to them—just a coincidence. Still, it proved somebody was out there, watching.

She wanted to warn Ivars but she had no proof. Nothing he would believe, anyway. At least they were off the plain now. Lea felt too exposed, even with Bob escorting them. Bob's sensors told her nothing was out there, for miles. It was better under the silver-green trees but the soldiers were too spread out, looking for samples to take back. They should leave, now. Something was wrong, something was coming…

Click. There was no sound, but suddenly Lea lost all connection to the robot network. She could only sense Bob, and read its data. The network had gone down. No, the network had changed. It was no longer accepting signal from other robots unquestioningly. It had sensed the crude hack and taken defensive measures, isolating the robots. She might be able to get around it, but it would take time, and…

"Oh, God." The soldiers…they had been spread out. Where were the other robots?

"Lea?" Ivars was running up the hill to her, weapon at the ready. "What is it?"

"Something changed. The robots…" what could she tell him? What would he believe? "They started moving on their own. Not like they used to. If they reset, my changes won't work and they'll attack us again!"

"Dammit." Ivars grabbed his radio. "Everybody back now, double time. Robots may be hostile."

North was close by; he was there in seconds. She could sense Olsen farther off, and he felt alert, not worried. She didn't remember any other robots near him. Ramirez, however, felt bad. Like he was about to fight.

Ivars's radio beeped twice. A wave of fear/anger burst from him, and his face looked like stone. "You. Run for the door," he barked, pointing at Lea.

"But Ramirez—"

"He's already in trouble if he can't talk on the radio. Now move!"

Lea went. She crouched down in the undergrowth as soon as she was out of Ivars's sight, heart pounding. If she could get closer to Ramirez, she could change the robots directly. If Ivars saw her, though, he'd chase her down and drag her to the door himself. She had to distract him.

I can make him see what I want him to see, she realized. It worked both ways. She could sense what his artificial eye saw, and that meant she could feed it false information. First she called Bob closer and set it to defend any of the humans that came under attack. Then she had it drift closer to Ivars, and crept closer under its cover until she had the signal of Ivars's eye clear in her mind.

Just a glimpse of another robot in the trees, a distance ahead. It didn't even have to be that clear. She closed her eyes, imagined, and sent the image. Ivars rose slowly from his crouch and moved away, closer to where the fake robot image had been.

Lea carefully crept back down. When there were enough trees between her and Ivars, she ran. A spike of fear came from Ramirez, making her stumble, and then she heard the sound of gunfire and a high whine followed by a large blast. The robots were firing on him. She had to get closer, she still couldn't control them with the new secure protocols!

Another blast, and a scream. A wave of pain made her whimper and clutch her side, but she kept moving. Closer…she tripped and fell hard, her helmet flying off, but she was close enough now and she didn't bother to get up again. The robot fought her control but her fear made her stubborn. No further blasts came, and she scrabbled to her feet. Ramirez didn't feel good.

She found him curled up in a ball of pain, sweating profusely. His head snapped from side to side as he tried to stifle his groans. The pain was like a wall of fire; she had to force herself to get closer.

He heard her and his eyes flew open.

"Get away!" he whispered, his voice ragged. "Do you want to get killed?"

"It's stopped," Lea said, feeling helpless. "You need to get back, but I don't think you can walk."

He shook his head. Tears were welling up from the corners of his eyes. "Morphine…in my pack. Aaah!" He spasmed, kicking.

Lea frowned. There was a signal coming from Ramirez. A simple one, and it felt damaged. The pain she sensed overpowered it, and she frantically searched his bag for the morphine. She'd been expecting a hypodermic, but it was a flat packet with a square plastic top. Pulling the top off exposed the needle. Then she discovered she couldn't touch his skin without screaming herself, the pain was so overwhelming. Using a fold of his uniform to hold his wrist, she finally managed to get the needle in.

The roaring waves of pain died back. Now she could sense the signal more clearly. "You have a medical device?"

"Yes," Ramirez gasped. "How…"

"I think it's damaged. Will it hurt you if it's shut off?" He stared at her uncomprehendingly for a moment, then shook his head. Lea reached with her mind and stopped it. Another level of pain receded.

Now she could get a better look at his injury. His armor vest had a huge gap across his chest. The injury itself looked like a burn along the edges and ran from his hip diagonally to just under his arm. In the center it was bleeding sluggishly and she thought she could see things she shouldn't be able to see inside. She found some bandages and hastily covered the worst, but she knew it wouldn't be enough.

"Can you walk?" she asked, knowing the answer. Ramirez struggled, but she could see one leg wasn't moving. She looked around and saw the now-neutral robot still hovering in position. It had a broad, flat top. "Can you stand?"

He nearly fainted a few times, but Lea managed to finally get him on top of the robot, curled on his side. Now she just had to get him back to the gate without getting them both shot by the other soldiers.

"How did you know?" Ramirez said faintly, his words slurring. "How'd ya…do that? 'S magic…."

Blood was dripping down the side of the robot. Lea didn't dare go any faster, or he might slip off. She felt hot tears well up and slide down her face. Ramirez might die because she hadn't warned them.

"I'm sorry," she sobbed. "It's my fault. All my fault. I should have told you, even if you didn't believe me."

It seemed to take forever to travel the same distance she had sprinted in a few seconds. Listening to Ramirez's ragged breathing, feeling his agony as her own. Then she heard the sound of robot weapons ahead. More than one, interspersed with gunfire. She moved a little faster, knowing the robot carrying Ramirez would follow at its own pace. There were the other three soldiers, and Bob in front of them, firing at another robot. Bob was badly damaged, and she could sense it was nearly done for.

She got Ramirez as close as she could and dragged him off the robot, nearly collapsing under his weight. "North!" she whispered as loudly as she dared. "North!"

Finally he looked up and his eyes widened. He jumped up from where he had been firing and quickly took Ramirez from her. "We have to get to the door," Lea said, her voice shaking.

"We can't when that thing will just follow us," North snapped. "Now get down!"

The blood-smeared robot was still where she had moved it, out of view of the others. Now she sent it hurtling into the fray, smashing into the one attacking the soldiers. Bob slowly drifted down, the foliage smoking where it touched. The part that Lea sensed faded and disappeared.

"Come on!" Lea waved frantically.

"What the hell is going on with these damn robots, are they insane?" snarled Ivars. "They attack us, they attack each other…"

"Warranty expired," gasped Olsen. "Who cares, let's get out of here!"

Olsen and North were chair-carrying Ramirez at a run. Lea followed, and behind her came Ivars.

Ivars wouldn't leave until she did. She knew that. He'd die before he'd let her stay.

She'd die before she went back through the door again. She didn't deserve to go back. This whole disaster was her fault. How could she live with that? How could she live with them knowing? Ivars would despise her. He'd hide it, but she'd know.

Once she made the decision, it wasn't hard. A distraction only Ivars could see, a brief flash of bright light that made him look away long enough for her to duck and hide just as they reached the hollow with the door. And then, when he looked back, a brief glimpse of herself running through the door.

Ivars sprinted down the ramp and through the door. Lea ran after him, as quietly as she could, and put both hands on the sides of the door that hummed with power—and shut it down.

Lea sagged against the now-dark doorway and sobbed. Nobody could hear her now. They couldn't come and get her, and she wouldn't get anyone else hurt again. She hoped Ramirez would live.

She straightened wearily and sighed. She wasn't sure what to do now, but she didn't want to stay here. At least she was alone, and her mind was quiet.

Except someone was there.

Lea looked up, startled. She didn't see anything, but she sensed a presence. Someone she didn't know. They were coming closer, to the top of the ramp. She glanced around, frantic, but there was no other way out of the hollow without climbing the vertical rock face. No place to hide.

A woman emerged from the trees. She was built like a tank, stocky and powerful, her face strong-featured and topped with stiff black hair. She looked human, but strangely so. She was wearing sleek but battered armor, carrying a strange gun in one hand and Lea's fallen helmet in the other.

The woman looked at Lea, raised the helmet and placed it on the ground, and backed away. Waiting.

Ivars burst out of the spindle-side door at a run. All the remaining teams had weapons trained on the doorway, and he cleared the area just in case an angry robot had followed him through and they needed to open up. He didn't see North or Ramirez, so they must have left immediately for *Kepler*. Olsen was there, and giving him a worried look.

"Where's Santorin?"

Ivars stared at him. "She went ahead of me…she didn't come through?" Before Olsen could speak Ivars read the answer in his eyes and spun around, lunging for the planet door. The view of the hollow shimmered and vanished just as his fingertips reached for it, and then all he saw was a flat niche in the doorway. Empty.

Lea. He wanted to rip the doorway apart with his bare hands, but that wouldn't help her. He needed to think. She couldn't still be on the planet if she went through the doorway. He'd made it through, and so had Olsen. So where was she?

"Why would the door send her somewhere else? They've never done that before!"

"Maybe it was that device she had," Olsen said. "Nobody else has one, right?"

"But she went to the planet with the device in her pack and it worked just fine," Ivars pointed out. He ran his hands over the surface of the doorway. There was not so much as a joint or seam, let alone an access panel or a pictograph warning sign for what to do about missing people.

"So, maybe there's only one doorway on the planet. No

rerouting possible. Coming back, though, there's lots of doors."

It made sense. "So she got caught in the local equivalent of customs?" He looked around. Besides himself and Olsen, there were eight other SF soldiers guarding the doorway back to the alien ship. Even if he could persuade all of them to help, they should leave a few for that job, and it wouldn't be enough to search something as large as the spindle.

"You're going to have to go ask Gonafrio for backup," Ivars said. "I'll see if Cullen there will let me borrow a few guys and go hunting."

"For all we know she's already trying to find us," Olsen said. "She wasn't injured, was she?"

Ivars thought for a moment, reliving the instant when she darted into the doorway. "No. Not that I could see." *Something is wrong.* He remembered her voice, saying that, and now he felt it himself. Something was wrong with what he had seen then. But what?

Olsen left. Cullen only let him borrow one man, so Ivars didn't want to go through any doorways with that kind of minimal backup. He scouted the entire section on the spindle that could be reached without doorways and didn't see anything. When he got back to Cullen and the rest of his men, they were gathered around a bicycle messenger and they all had grim faces.

"Gonafrio wants us all to pull back to the BDR immediately," Cullen said.

"Lea Santorin is still missing and we need to find her or this is all a pointless exercise," snapped Ivars.

Cullen just handed him a piece of paper. Gonafrio's order was short, to the point, and addressed to him personally. *We don't know where she is,* he'd scribbled at the bottom. So Olsen had gotten through but hadn't been able to convince him.

Fine. We do it the hard way. Ivars set off at a run. Once inside the BDR the evidence of the new defensive posture was everywhere. A 50-cal machine gun faced the door to the spindle, and backup teams had been placed on either side farther back. The guard at the entrance to the tunnel to *Kepler* had been doubled, and armored.

Ivars didn't have to go far to find Gonafrio. Gonafrio was looking for him.

"I've heard from the rest of your team and now I want to hear it from you. What the hell happened out there?"

"Sir, everything was proceeding normally. While we were gathering biological samples on our way back to the doorway Santorin noticed the robots were behaving erratically. I notified the team immediately but Ramirez was already in contact with a newly hostile robot and was injured. I had ordered Santorin to leave via the door at the first sign of hostile action but she was still on the planet with us when my team headed for the door. I saw her run through the doorway on the planet side but when I came through Olsen informed me she did not appear with them on the spindle."

"In short, I now have hostile alien robots to contend with and no technical expert to help me with them, do I have that right?"

"Sir, the door to the planet appears to be completely shut down. No traffic in or out."

Gonafrio glared at him. "Do you know how that doorway was shut down?"

"No sir."

"Then it could just as easily be a deliberate action by the enemy and can be activated again at a time of their choosing." He hesitated, and in a calmer voice continued, "As badly as we need to find Santorin, I must be certain no hostile robots endanger this ship. We are spread too thin already. Now go and record a full debrief and then take up a guard position. You may not leave the BDR, is that clear?"

In the tedious and thorough debriefing Ivars went over every second of the incident from the first hint of danger to when he arrived on the spindle. He also had to map everyone's position, which was useful in pointing out that at one point Santorin had gotten from his position on the side of the hill to thirty meters downhill without him noticing. Plus, she had been supporting Ramirez—and given his injuries and her size, how the hell had she gotten him anywhere?

Now on guard duty, he had plenty of time to think about it. Ivars had gotten a few hours sleep but most of the last two days had been spent on guard. Gonafrio was being far too cautious, in his opinion. Teams had made a few checks on the spindle; everything was quiet and no sign of Lea. The door to the planet was still dead. He still had the nagging feeling he was missing something.

Ivars crouched, watched his position, and thought. Santorin had been acting goofy, but she'd done that before. Lea had been running for the door so fast her hair was streaming behind her. Wait, he could see her hair? She was supposed to be wearing a helmet, and she'd been pretty good about that even though he could tell it was uncomfortable. No, that wasn't the thing that was bothering him. She'd been missing the helmet when she showed up with Ramirez. There was dirt and blood on her armor vest, probably from Ramirez, and a scrape of dirt on her face. Maybe she'd fallen and the helmet had come off ? It sure didn't fit her very well, and the armor vest was even worse.

The vest. She hadn't been wearing it when she'd gone through the door. He had seen the edge of her jacket moving as she ran, impossible if the vest was on. But she *had* been wearing it when she showed up with Ramirez. With her pack. She would have had to take the pack off and struggle out of the heavy vest, and there hadn't been time even if she had wanted to.

So what had he seen? And more importantly, why had he seen something that couldn't have been there?

CHAPTER 8

Ivars hadn't reached a conclusion about Lea and the door by the time his relief showed up. He alternated between thinking he'd imagined the whole thing and what he'd seen was real and thinking the aliens had snatched Lea somehow because of the device he'd given her. No proof of anything, except she was missing.

Olsen was waiting for him inside the bunking area on *Kepler*.

"Ramirez wants you to come see him," he said. His face was neutral, indicating nothing.

"Something wrong? I thought the docs said he was going to make it."

Olsen shrugged. "He's got something on his mind. He'll feel better once he tells you his big secret. Maybe he wants to change his will, who knows?"

Ivars was so tired he could fall asleep standing up, but it never crossed his mind to say no. That wasn't how the teams operated. Ramirez would do the same for him. If he thought it was important, then it was. Even if it was just giving a badly injured man some peace of mind by paying him a visit.

"Does he know Santorin is missing?" Ivars asked on the way to medical.

Olsen shook his head. "Keeping it quiet for now. He'll take it hard."

Ramirez looked pale and drowsy with sedation but, if you could ignore the large wound suction device perched over his abdomen, otherwise fine.

"Hey, man," he said when he recognized Ivars. "How's it goin' out there?"

"Fought off an entire armada of space pirates with just my

multifunction eating utensil," Ivars said promptly. "Gonafrio wrote me up for taking too long."

Ramirez grinned. "Those…utensils. Good gear." He twitched his fingers, indicating Ivars should come closer. "Gotta…tell you somethin'. Think I'm crazy, maybe." *There's a lot of that going around,* thought Ivars. "Santorin found me. Right after I got…shot. It didn't shoot her. Just sat there. Then…then she gets it to carry me."

"She did something like that to Bob," Ivars said slowly. "Not surprising, but it is strange it didn't shoot her when she got close enough to tinker with it."

Ramirez shook his head weakly and made a sound in the back of his throat. "Didn't touch it. It…came to her. Like a dog."

Now that was really strange. The robots had gone hostile; she'd warned them when it happened. Then they suddenly changed their little mechanical minds when they saw Lea?

"'nother thing." Ramirez was tiring fast, but he seemed determined to get it all out. "Knew about my doser."

Olsen stared at him. "Lea Santorin? She knew about your medical doser?"

Ramirez nodded slowly. "Didn't tell her. Know you didn't. How'd she know?"

Not suspected, knew. Ramirez didn't look like someone who needed a constant microdose of medication to keep his symptoms in check, even now.

"I'll ask her when I see her," Ivars said. "Rest up. Don't worry, we've got things under control. I'll even save you a few space pirates for when you feel better."

Ramirez grinned again, and his eyes closed. He seemed more relaxed now, so the visit had done some good. Ivars, on the other hand, had another headache. Yes, Ramirez had been on morphine, but not enough to come up with all that. Besides, Ivars had wondered how Lea had dragged Ramirez all that distance and now he knew—she hadn't. It made sense.

"You're looking grim," observed Olsen. "That bad?"

"Think I'd better tell you some things too," Ivars said, and took a breath. He described everything he'd seen from the beginning of the firefight, including Lea's incredible wardrobe change.

"You're not imagining the helmet missing; I saw that too,"

Olsen said thoughtfully. "I didn't see her coming down the ramp since North and I were busy carrying Ramirez, but she was wearing her vest when we all moved out. So what do you think really happened?"

As soon as Olsen asked the question, Ivars felt the answer form in the back of his mind. It had always been there, he'd just refused to acknowledge it. "I think someone deliberately made it look like she went through the door. And the only reason to do that—"

"—is she's still on that planet," Olsen finished for him. "And we've got no way of getting back there."

Ivars could hear the messenger well before he came into view. "Should get some oil on that thing," he commented as the bicyclist went by. No sign he'd been heard, and the guy looked too tired to care. *Bicycles on a spaceship. No wonder we're not getting anything done.* It just added to the slow-burning anger that had been building over the days since the door to the planet had shut down. As far as he knew no effort was being made to locate Lea, but he only returned to *Kepler* to sleep and get updated orders. There had to be something useful he could do—but he sure as hell couldn't do it stuck on guard duty.

The bicycle messenger came back the other direction and squeaked to a stop. Ivars looked up.

"Hey, um, the guys up there?" The messenger pointed. "They say they are hearing stuff. Voices, maybe music. Said to pass the word and see if anybody else heard anything."

"Nothing here," Ivars said. "What kind of music?"

The messenger shrugged. "I didn't hear anything." He headed off again, and Ivars shook his head. Almost completely void of useful information, but not quite. It was a wonder he'd bothered.

Hearing things could just be from stress and fatigue, but the teams knew to watch out for that kind of thing. Plus they had sent out the alert via the civilian messenger, which meant they truly thought they had heard something and didn't care if they got laughed at.

Ivars went motionless, listening hard. Nothing. No, now there was a rhythm, like a footstep... He turned around. North was walking down the corridor.

"Hey, good to see you. Any updates on Ramirez?"

North shook his head. "Still doing OK, last I heard. Olsen warned me not to say anything to him about Santorin, but I think he suspects something. I mean, she hasn't been by to see him and he's bound to figure it out eventually, morphine or no."

"Yeah, that's true. So why are you out this way?"

"Gonafrio wants you up front. They're thinking about going on the spindle again. I'm your replacement." North grinned as Ivars jumped to his feet. "I guess you're OK with that, huh? Go find our girl. She's—"

A whispered voice interrupted. North stopped, looked at Ivars, who shook his head. He hadn't been able to make out what the voice was saying or where it was coming from. North looked like he was about to speak, but Ivars held up his hand.

In a few seconds, he heard the voice again. *...|interface, the...|* Ivars put his back up against the wall, weapon at the ready and aimed where he looked. North was doing the same from the opposite wall. Then the music started. It sounded like a clip, short and repeated. After a few minutes of music and the voice, silence returned.

"That voice...|it almost sounded familiar," Ivars said softly.

"That music sure was," North said in the same low tone. "It's from Bach's 'Toccata and Fugue.'"

"You sure about that?"

North nodded. "Played organ for our church for ten years. Anybody ever played organ knows that piece."

Ivars glanced around. Still no sign of where the sound was coming from. "OK, so why are we hearing it now, a generous handful of light–years from the nearest organ? Somebody plug their tunes into some speakers?"

North frowned absently, cocking his head to one side. "Don't think so. For one thing, it wasn't played right. The left–hand melody skips a phrase. Anybody who knew how to play it wouldn't miss that, so it's hard to see how it would be recorded that way."

"Huh." Ivars thought about it for a minute and decided there was nothing he could do about it now, except file it away for later reference. "I'm off. If it starts playing scary music don't go down in the basement by yourself, got it?"

"Roger. Checking basements for strange sounds is the

responsibility of the teenage lovers, everyone knows that." North grinned and waved.

Ivars set out at a jog for the spindle door. So Gonafrio finally figured out nothing was going to happen on the BDR. Good for him. *He could have done that days ago,* Ivars thought savagely. Lea only had the supplies in her pack. She could be injured, or even…*I don't think that. Just keep looking.*

The machine gun was still in place, facing the door to the spindle. A knot of people stood to one side of the door, alert and ready. Ivars listened to the plan briefing impatiently. He'd waited long enough. Finally they began filing through, one at a time.

"If the planet doorway is clear I want to take a quick look around," Ivars said to Cullen, who was in charge of the operation.

"Not going to happen," Cullen said with a quick chopping motion of his hand. "If those things are quiet, why stir them up and bring them here? Situation's bad enough without adding more trouble."

"If we don't find Lea Santorin we are collectively screwed anyway," Ivars snapped, trying to keep his temper under control.

…interface…

He and Cullen stopped and looked carefully around. "I heard it too," the machine gunner said.

"I thought you were all hot to leave," Cullen said to Ivars, and stepped through the doorway.

"Yeah, I am." Ivars suddenly realized why the voice sounded familiar. It was Lea's. He turned and walked quickly to the doorway, intending to tell Cullen.

His foot, and then his face, bounced hard off of some unyielding, invisible surface. Ivars put up his hand and felt at it. Whatever it was it covered the entire doorway to the spindle, and even when he ran at it shoulder-first in door-breach mode he could not get through. From the looks of things Cullen was yelling at him, but he couldn't hear anything.

It's blocked, Ivars mouthed. Cullen gave him a skeptical look and walked forward. He didn't get any farther than Ivars had.

Oh, this is not good. Ivars felt at the pouches on his belt, opening the one that had extra rounds. He took out a cartridge and tossed it at the doorway. It bounced off. *Not just people, then.*

Suddenly he heard a yell, then the machine gun fired a burst.

Ivars spun around, intending to rip the gunner a new one, until he saw what the man had been shooting at. A wall of morph was flowing like a curtain between them. The bullets hadn't made a difference, and now the corridor was blocked. The machine gunner presumably was still on the other side, he hoped, but unreachable now.

Ivars felt at another pocket and pulled out a small notepad and pencil. *Ship changing again. Way back blocked. Going exploring.* He held the paper up to the doorway. Cullen came closer, squinting, then nodded reluctantly. Ivars dropped the paper at the foot of the doorway in case someone else made it through the wall of morph, and walked slowly down the remaining stretch of corridor. He turned the corner and nearly ran into another new wall. He was boxed in.

"…interface…" The voice was louder now.

"Who are you? What do you want?" Ivars called out. Their freedom of movement was being curtailed, but nobody had been hurt—yet. It argued for intelligence behind the actions. Who, and why? And why now? Had they finally managed to wake up the inhabitants of the BDR? Why hadn't they shown themselves to kick the Earth-monkeys off their ship?

"INTERFACEinterfaceInterFaceInTerFace."

Still only the one word, still in Lea's voice. It raised the hairs on his neck to hear her speaking when he knew she was still missing. So why use a recording? Maybe it was the only word the aliens felt sure of. Where was the voice coming from? Now that it was louder maybe he could find the speaker and trace things from there.

Ivars scanned the new wall of morph, then turned to go back— and halted. In the corridor was an image of green, sparkling light. An image of Lea. She had one hand resting on the wall. As Ivars watched she suddenly turned her head and said, "Yeah, ready."

He approached the image slowly, shifting his rifle a bit to be instantly ready if needed. There was no other sound than the voice. Something else was missing, and it took him a moment to realize what he was searching for unconsciously. No scent. *And why would that be the big clue the green glowing woman isn't real, genius?*

"Lea?"

The image, which had frozen in place, repeated its motion. She turned her head, spoke, froze. Ivars walked around to the other side. He remembered when that had happened, before they left for the planet. Where had he been then? Waiting to go through the door to the spindle. He'd stopped after she went through because… because he'd seen a glow on the wall where she had rested her hand. Right there.

So, the aliens could see them somehow. Record them visually too. The image wasn't a hologram, he was pretty sure, but it was three-dimensional and remarkably detailed. He could even see the dangling tabs from her badly fitting armor vest.

He quickly waved a hand through the green light and felt nothing. The wall was glowing where her hand was resting but he couldn't tell if it was the same thing he'd seen or just an artifact of the image itself. Ivars placed his hand over the hand of the image and touched the wall. Tingling cramps spread from his fingertips, and then quickly faded. He just felt the rough wall surface.

"Interface."

"Is that what you want? Lea? We can't find her either. What did you do with her?" And how was he going to communicate the concept of "your fault" to an alien with a vocabulary of one word? Well, presumably the aliens could see him, just like they had seen Lea. Waving your arms and pointing was as close to a universal language as he could think of. "Look." He walked over until he was in the same position as the Lea-image. He turned his head and walked over to the blocked spindle door. "She went through here. Now are you going to open the door so I can show you the rest?"

He pushed, but the barrier was still there.

"Interface."

It was probably just his imagination, but the voice sounded plaintive now. It occurred to Ivars that he was making a number of unsupported assumptions. What if the aliens behind the voice *couldn't* open the spindle door? Different groups, tribes, whatever. Maybe they didn't understand what had happened on the spindle. So, how was he going to communicate something he couldn't point to? Draw a map? The little notepad was the biggest piece of paper he had, and it was smaller than the palm of his hand.

Build a model. Ivars propped his rifle against the wall, knelt down, and started pulling everything out of his pack. A couple of ten-round custom-load ammo boxes became the doors. Some gauze from the first aid kit became the corridor he was in, with more rolled–up gauze indicating the morph walls boxing him in. He drew a hand on a blood–clot packet to show the location of the light image, and placed it on the gauze in the right place. A knotted–up shemagh scarf became the spindle, and more gauze and various packets from an MRE showed the spindle interior. Using medical tape and the copies of the hand–drawn map of the planet's surface, he made a surprisingly spherical planet. Ivars puzzled for a while how to show the planet's surface, and finally settled on sculpting the structure they'd explored, using the MRE's Beef Patty with Mushroom Sauce Entrée. It even looked like the same material.

OK. Showtime. He picked up the little bottle of hot sauce from the MRE. "This is Lea, OK?" He waved the little bottle around the still–glittering image. "She was here," patting the wall, then putting the bottle on the hand sketch, "and then through the door to the spindle," holding up the knotted scarf, and moving the bottle to the next stretch of gauze, "to the planet." He left the bottle near the blob of mutilated Beef Patty. "You want her, that's where you'll have to go."

He repeated the whole performance then sat back against the wall and rested his arms on his knees, waiting and wondering if it was worth the effort to save the food he used in the model. It might give him a few more days of life, but they would be days when he'd eaten the Beef Patty of Intestinal Destruction. All things considered, that made it a wash. Ivars sighed and rubbed his forehead. If this didn't work he'd have to get more creative. Why didn't Special Forces have more training in art techniques, anyway?

He looked up and felt a chill sweep over him. The knotted scarf was hanging unsupported, gently turning as it floated in midair. Just like the spindle did. And the little bottle of hot sauce was going through the entire route he had demonstrated, all by itself.

Ivars quickly got to his feet. At least that part of his message had gotten through. Then the paper map planet drifted up near the scarf, and a small, green, sparkly blob traced the path of the hot sauce bottle.

"Yes. That's right." He tapped the hot sauce bottle, hovering over the model structure. "There's your interface." He could feel his heart pounding, senses hyper|alert for whatever would come next. He was communicating. Whoever it was would try to communicate back. He had to get this right. He didn't know who he was communicating *with*, but they seemed to want Lea back for some reason. He could work with that. Hopefully they wouldn't become a problem later on.

Motion caught his attention, and he glanced at the spindle door. Cullen was waving his arms and pointing at the floating objects. Some of his men were staring too; how long had he had an audience? Ivars grinned and shrugged. *Trying to explain things to the voices,* he scribbled on another sheet of paper. *Think they're getting it.*

The knotted scarf moved, and so did the paper planet. A swirling rope of darkness connected them. A sphere of green light appeared, smaller than the scarf or the paper ball, but Ivars could still see the crater that identified it as the BDR. The dark rope disappeared. A tiny bright light left the green sphere, touched the paper planet, and then the dark rope reappeared, connecting the sphere and the planet model. The pattern repeated several times.

The next time the pattern started, the little light stopped in mid|flight. It grew bigger, and Ivars could see it was some kind of small container or ship. Two objects appeared beside it, a mysterious oblong object and a human figure that looked remarkably like him. The oblong moved until the human was holding it, and both moved inside the ship. It shrank and continued its usual journey. The oblong and the human figure reappeared near the paper planet, joined by a small, glowing green figure of Lea. The other human handed her the oblong, and the dark rope appeared. It seemed to originate from the oblong. The new details repeated a few times as well, then the whole thing stopped.

Ivars stared at the floating images and thought hard. If he was understanding everything correctly, the planet Lea was on was close by. The little ship didn't look like much more than a rowboat equivalent, if it was to scale with the human figure inside it. So he was supposed to get some device, get in the little ship, and take it to Lea, who would somehow know what to do to get both of them back.

His decision was easy. The hard part was condensing all the important information in the few remaining sheets of paper in his notepad so Cullen would know what was happening.

Ivars piled the papers at the foot of the spindle door when he was done. He waved goodbye, as Cullen mouthed *Good luck.* Ivars swept up the first aid supplies back into his pack. He tried to recover the paper planet, for the maps, but he couldn't move it.

"OK, where do I go?" He waved his hand through the image of the little ship. "You want me to get her or not?"

He started walking away from the spindle door. This time when he turned the corner, the wall of morph was gone. So were the corridors he was expecting. Three different ways to go; all of them looked identical. Motion caught his eye, and he looked down. A dark blue line was moving at a measured pace on the corridor floor.

Ivars followed the line for a long time. He was sure no one had ever been in this section. He even went down several ramps. *I hope I can get back if this doesn't work.* The walls looked different here; more textured, and with patterns. What did more interior decoration imply, versus the airport–terminal blandness in the upper levels? Living quarters? Was he going to get to see one of these aliens?

Eventually the line led him to a wide bay with walls that sloped inward. Five doors were inset on one side. On the other was a row of niches, and one had a familiar–looking oblong object resting inside. Ivars went over and inspected it. No obvious fuse or timer, and he didn't smell gunpowder. The material looked somewhat like the device he'd slipped to Lea—dark, polished, slightly translucent—but there were swirls of silver visible in the dark material. It was a little larger than a standard football, and similar in shape.

"I take this?" he said, pointing. Nothing happened. He cautiously reached out with one hand. The alien football felt slightly warm, like it had been sitting in the sun. Moving slowly, he hefted it in one hand and tucked it in the crook of his arm. Still no bolts of lightning. "Now what?"

One of the doors in the opposite wall opened. Inside was a long, narrow room with no visible exit. At the far end was something that looked like a strange giant padded chair, or a couch set at an angle, or maybe a stuffed bathtub. He didn't want to go inside, afraid of being trapped there, but the aliens had indicated this is where they wanted him to go. He had no choice.

<h1 style="text-align:center">CHAPTER 9</h1>

The one who had found her helmet was named Alaghar. There were two others with her, Isboryi and Burdhul. The strangers all had bronzed skin and dark hair, although of varying shades. Alaghar had the darkest skin, and Isboryi's hair had a reddish cast. They were all powerfully built, men and women, like wrestlers, and their faces were also heavy featured. As far as Lea could tell they were completely human. The full body armor they wore was sleek and clearly advanced technology, but it showed signs of damage and repair. Alaghar's armor was missing an entire arm.

It was harder for Lea to sense them; their thoughts came through only as broadly sensed emotion. She didn't recognize any of the words they spoke, and they didn't understand English or her rudimentary high school Spanish. Still, she could tell they wanted her to come with them and that they were wary but well-intentioned. After all, you don't usually introduce yourself to someone you only plan to kill.

Lea did have a moment of panic after Alaghar handed back her helmet. She put it back on slowly, watching the other woman carefully. They moved like soldiers, they *felt* like soldiers, and here she was being a strange-looking foreigner.

"*Buredh?*" said Alaghar, tapping her weapon.

"No, I don't have anything," Lea said quickly, showing her empty hands. "No weapons."

"*Buredh! Tae buredh, ayh?*" Judging from the look on Alaghar's face, either she didn't believe her or "no weapons" wasn't the right answer. Lea slowly turned around, her hands in the air.

"See? Nothing! I'm a civilian, a computer geek! Why would I

have a weapon?"

A strong, heavy hand came down on her shoulder before she turned back. Alaghar was giving her a look she'd seen on Ivars's face far too often, usually translating as *I don't have time for this,* and she had unsheathed a curiously–shaped knife. Lea felt a spike of sheer terror before she realized Alaghar was offering it to her hilt first, and the emotions she could sense were not anything like blood–lust, but worry. "*Buredh.*"

"Burreh. OK. Got it." Lea gingerly took the knife, and she could see Alaghar's face relax. Well. For some reason it wasn't polite to be out in public without a weapon, even for funny–looking strangers. Lea looked at it more closely. The hilt was decorated with a complex geometric pattern of different metals, and the blade was dark with a grainy feel on the surface. "It's beautiful," Lea said, clasping it to her chest. "Thank you."

Alaghar smiled. Then she held out a hand, fingers spread and thumb folded in. She brought the fingers together and moved her hand forward, in the direction of the plain.

Four, together, that heading. Lea pointed a finger at herself, then the rest of them. "We go that way?"

Alaghar simply turned and started walking. Lea followed. She still wasn't sure why they would want her to come with them, but she didn't have much choice if she wanted to stay alive. The one called Isboryi shifted his weapon and hefted an irregular dark object, about the size of a small briefcase, that hung across his body from a rough rope strap. Lea felt a pop in her head when he turned the device on, and had to stifle a grin when she recognized the crude signal. It was the same cobbled–together fake robot transmission she had sensed before the network went down.

It was hard to sense much around the strong fake signal, but as they hiked through the plain Lea did her best to make sure the robots really stayed away. She tried to get closer to Isboryi, to see what the device was, but the others indicated she was to stay behind them. From what she could see the device was made up of several smaller components that hadn't originally been together, and a lot of kludging. Maybe she could help them by getting rid of the robots for good, instead of using their Acme Robot Repeller.

They crossed the plain to a rock ridge as quickly as possible. The strangers were very tense and alert, and nobody spoke. Lea was surprised she was able to keep up, and that the three others had visible sweat on their faces when she didn't. Maybe the armor didn't ventilate well? She could sense increased relaxation in their mood when they left the ridge and descended into an area with deep, wooded ravines. The air smelled different here than in the hills, more damp and rich, and the fronds of the trees had a darker silver tone. Clearly the strangers felt safer here, and spoke a few quiet words to each other.

She followed them down a narrow path deeper into the ravine, watching her footing carefully so she didn't trip and fall off the edge. They crossed a shallow, rocky stream and went up the slope on the other side, which seemed to be just a rocky cliff face until Lea saw the dark opening in the rock. It was almost exactly the size of the strangers in height and breadth, and from what she could see in the darkness it was made of large slabs of rock leaning against the cliff. It went on for a considerable distance before opening up to a larger space.

There was more light here, and Lea looked around, curious. This was apparently where the strangers lived, and it was furnished in the same curious combination of primitive and high-tech that characterized their gear. Against a far wall was a weapons rack made with logs with the bark still on, crude pegs hammered into the logs at an angle. A couple of lethal, complex long guns of some kind were stored there. Ledges had been cut out of the rock wall, like broad, shallow steps, which had what looked like woven bark blankets. Beds? Nearby a fire burned in a pit ringed by a low, flat rock wall.

Most of the light came from rough, cube-shaped devices hanging from rope nets. Apparently they didn't generate any heat, since the rope looked undamaged. The light from the cubes plus the fire was not enough to illuminate the entire cave. Lea saw some intriguing shapes in one corner, opposite the sleeping ledges, that she couldn't quite make out. The strangers were putting equipment away and removing armor, not paying obvious attention to her. Lea struggled to remove her own gear, writhing in hot frustration until she finally unfastened the armor vest and shrugged it off along with the pack. She unclipped her purple flashlight and went over to take a look at the mysterious shadows.

The bright LED light revealed a jumble of components, some in crude wooden frames like the weapon rack. The components looked identical to the ones she'd seen in the sealed room of the structure on the plain. Lea stared, delighted. So, the strangers had been the ones who took the components from the old building!

Suddenly Alaghar said something in a hard voice, the words jagged and sharp and completely unlike anything she'd said before. Lea turned and gaped at her, befuddled. Alaghar was glaring at her and the anger…the *hatred* roiling off of her made Lea take an instinctive step back. The others felt confused, but also angry.

I stepped in it somehow, big time. "I'm sorry, OK? I didn't know it was sacred or whatever. Look, maybe I'd just better leave." Lea edged past the fire, putting it between her and Alaghar. Of course, that still left two more between her and the door, and she didn't have her pack. She edged over to it and fumbled at the webbing on her vest, where she'd managed to wedge the knife, and carefully drew it out with only two fingers. "Um, I should probably give this back now…"

Lea bent to lay the knife on the stone wall around the fire, but before she could let go Alaghar was suddenly beside her, a painfully strong grasp crushing Lea's fingers around the hilt of the knife.

"*Nyagh*," Alaghar hissed.

Lea cried out in agony and tried to pull away. Flashes of images blinked through her mind. Strange beings, translucent white with deep indigo markings, overlaid with pain and anger. A dark world with beasts out of nightmares, all teeth and claws and immense size, and a ragged group of people who looked like the strangers fighting them desperately. Then the same people, now in fortresses of stone, fighting the monsters with weapons and devices that looked very much like the equipment they'd found on the BDR. All the while Alaghar was talking in a fierce, intense voice.

Lea blinked. There was an image of a door, and it showed the interior of the spindle. There was a feeling of fear here too, of imminent danger. Then a glimpse of Lea herself, only even more pale and with blue markings.

"HEY!" Lea yelled. Alaghar stopped speaking, but she didn't let go. The images were still flashing in Lea's mind, and the longer it continued the more her fear and revulsion mounted. It was like going through the door, pain without escape—pain, worse and worse, until her head felt like it would split…

Suddenly Lea realized she was free, and Alaghar was giving her a puzzled and wary look, holding the hand that had been grasping Lea as if it hurt her. Then she rubbed her head. *Great. I gave her a headache. This is not going well.* Lea winced. "Sorry."

The problem seemed to be that Alaghar thought she was connected with the blue–and–white aliens somehow. *They look like willowware slugs,* Lea thought. Showing interest in the stolen components had been a mistake. How could she convince the strangers she was just a lost Earthling and not an enemy? So far her special ability didn't seem to extend to full telepathic communication, which would have been really handy right now. What did she have instead?

Her reader. She hadn't meant to take it with her to the planet, but she'd shoved it in her pack with the alien device—which she *really* shouldn't let the strangers see—and forgotten to take it out again when she got summoned to the meeting. Yeah, and she'd been a little foggy with the sleeping pill, too. Lea carefully rummaged in her pack and pulled out the reader without showing any of the other contents. She scrolled through the reader. Pictures. Pictures that would show she wasn't one of the bad guys. Not the research papers, they were mostly text or interior shots of the alien ship. Not the pictures of her family, that wouldn't prove anything either.

Wait. *Familiarization and Regulations LS–24 Prohibited Items and Suggested Gear for Visitors.* She still had the moon station packing list? It had pictures, at least a few of the exterior of the station and the larger facilities. She pulled it up.

"See? This is my people's place. No squiggly bad guys," Lea said, holding up the reader. Alaghar studied it in silence, then waved the others over and pointed. All Lea could sense was puzzlement. "Luna Base," Lea pointed to the picture. Then she skipped to the next useful picture. "Emergency Gear Station." *There will be a quiz later.*

The strangers looked at all the pictures thoughtfully. Lea then tried to use the sketch mode to explain how she'd gotten to the planet but she wasn't sure how much was getting through. Enough that Alaghar wasn't yelling and grabbing her, anyway. Everyone felt calmer too. Maybe she'd live through this after all.

The cave was smelly and smoky, but it was better than sleeping outside. Plus, they knew how to find food on this planet, as she found out when one of them, a woman, returned weary and filthy carrying a creature the size of a dog that had wiry, stone-colored fur and multiple elephant-style snouts. Lea tried to watch the butchering process to get an idea of how the local fauna worked, but the stench quickly drove her away, retching.

Over the next few days she picked up a few words of their language, as well as names for all six of them. They referred to themselves as Wiyert. She wasn't sure if that was a family name, their name for their kind, or some other grouping. Lea tried to find out where the others were, but Alaghar just shook her head and looked even more grim than she usually did.

Lea was having trouble finding something useful to do. The Wiyert were all incredibly strong and had worked out efficient ways to handle all the chores—ways Lea had no hope of imitating. She couldn't explain that she could keep the robots away better than Isboryi, and she wasn't sure it would be a smart idea if she could. Instead, she hung around with whoever was in the cave and tried to learn more of their language. She also made a gift of her armor vest and helmet to Burdhul, after demonstrating the protective properties by stabbing the vest with her knife. It didn't fit him much better than it had fit her, but in the opposite direction —his barrel chest was much too large for it. It was still better than the rags he had been wearing, and she sensed he was pleased by her offer.

Alaghar, she could tell, was still reserving judgment. Lea did her best to avoid the appearance of nosiness, but she could see enough to know something wasn't quite right with the Wiyert. They had clearly advanced weapons, but Hazuruh, the hunter, only used a spear. True, the spearpoint was a fragment of sharpened metal, but it didn't match the rest of their gear. The armor they wore was beautifully made, clearly the result of advanced technology, and it was equally clear they had no means of repairing it when it was damaged.

Lea lay on one of the sleeping ledges and kept turning it over in her mind, unable to sleep. Suddenly she heard a scream and she sat up, heart pounding—and noticed none of the other Wiyert in the cave had reacted. Even Isboryi, sitting by the fire, just glanced at her and then back at the flames. Alaghar remained asleep, and Lea was quite sure she would have woken if she had heard it.

A scream only she could hear. And it felt…familiar. It wasn't possible. He was back on the spindle, and she had closed the door connecting it to the planet.

But if it was Ivars…why was he screaming?

Lea quietly got up, put her boots on, and left the cave, nodding to Isboryi as if she was just going outside to relieve herself. They might be angry with her, if they found out. Ivars would be, if he saw her. It didn't matter. She had to make sure he was still alive.

The door slid shut behind him as soon as he stepped inside the little room, but Ivars didn't even bother to try to open it up again. This was all under someone else's control and he doubted he'd be allowed to run off before they got what they wanted. He felt a slight pressure in his sinuses, indicating the room was sealed now. He walked forward to see if there were any controls or switches to play with. There were no doors visible except the one he'd come in from.

A section of the wall facing the padded structure went dark and then displayed a familiar diagram of a little ship with the human. So, maybe that's what this was—a ship, not a room. It was, as shown, very small. With his pack and rifle and the alien football, there was not a lot of extra space. The padded thing must be the acceleration chair, then. Ivars looked at it dubiously. He didn't want the football rattling around the interior, or his rifle, but he didn't see any stowage area either. He ended up stuffing the football in his pack, laying the rifle along one leg, and dumping the pack on top of his feet.

As soon as he sat down on the padded chair he felt it change and shift to adjust to him. Broad flaps, also padded on the inside, slid up and over his torso. It was an effective all-body-types acceleration harness. Ivars didn't see any controls for the ship, but it didn't matter because he couldn't move to reach them. The charging lever on his rifle was jabbing him uncomfortably and something in his pack was poking him in the shins, and he couldn't shift either of them. Maybe this wasn't a real ship, but an escape pod of some kind.

I hope this is a quick trip. He felt his ears pop, and then a faint shudder. The ambient light dimmed. The diagram of the little ship vanished and was replaced by a series of glowing glyphs. Nothing seemed to happen for a while, although he thought some of the glyphs changed. Maybe that was the ETA display, or a fuel readout. "Hey, don't I rate a safety video?" Ivars called out. Nothing happened. "How about some peanuts?"

There was nothing for him to do, and no new information except the symbols he couldn't read. The vibration had stopped. He hoped the ship was actually moving, and in the right direction, but there was nothing for him to do about that either. No immediate threat, no tasks on hand—time to sleep. His long experience had taught him to rest whenever he could, to make up for the times he couldn't. He closed his eyes.

The acceleration couch was remarkably comfortable, and he dozed off. When he woke again the ship was shaking like it was an aircraft in turbulence, and the screen area was filling up with scrolling symbols. None of them were flashing red, so he hoped it was all standard information and not instructions on activating the ejection seat. The buffeting got worse.

"Is this supposed to be happening?" Ivars yelled. "Hello, anybody there?"

No response. Now he was hearing some creaking sounds that were not reassuring. The little ship was really getting beaten. *This may not have been one of my better ideas.* He was glad now he had secured all his gear in the seat with him, even if he was now getting some very painful bruises. It would have been even worse flying around the cabin.

He desperately wanted to see outside, even if all he could see was his approaching death. He had no idea if he was entering the planet's atmosphere or going through an asteroid field. The ship was tumbling now, rocking and shuddering. *This is it, I'm going to die.*

The ship leveled out, briefly, only to smash hard as if it had been dropped off a cliff. The interior went completely dark. Ivars felt the padded flaps shudder and retreat, but not all the way. He shoved at them and managed to get a few more inches of clearance, but he still had to struggle to force his way out of the acceleration chair.

The little ship was canted, and some of the interior had broken free in sharp, jagged pieces. Ivars strapped on his pack and attached his rifle back to his harness before going any farther in the dark. He kept stumbling over debris, and it was hard to keep his footing on the slanted floor. Finally he got to where the door should be. It was stuck.

Using his knife, Ivars managed to get the door cracked. A spray of dirt landed on his face. At least he was on a planet now. If it wasn't the right one, he was truly screwed. He worked at the door for at least an hour, using a broken piece of metal as a crowbar, before he could fit through the door and even then he had to dig dirt into the cabin to get outside. It was dark, and he couldn't see anything. Pushing his pack and rifle ahead of him, he reached the surface and took a quick look around with a flashlight, breathing hard.

Not a stealthy entrance. Several silvery trees showed extensive damage, dark sap running down the trunk. Limbs and branches were everywhere. The little ship itself looked like a charcoal briquette on the outside and the skin was still hot to the touch. It was half–buried in a crater of rocks, dirt, and more broken branches.

He wasn't going anywhere in that ship again. Ivars debated going back in to see if anything was salvageable but decided to head out before the killer robots showed up.

He felt like a giant bruise, and his legs were sore and cramped from being in one position for so long, but movement soon got rid of the worst of it. The vegetation certainly looked familiar, but he needed to find out where he was before making any plans. Fortunately there was light from two small moons to help with that. The area where the ship had landed was relatively flat, but near the entrance to a valley flanked by low hills. Ivars climbed a tree near the top of one hill and scanned the horizon with his binoculars. To his surprise he saw the low, dark structure they had investigated in the distance. If he was right and the building wasn't a different, similar one, the doorway that had connected to the spindle would be only a mile or so away.

Well. That flight was the worst he'd ever been on that didn't involve a Tupolev, but the targeting was pretty accurate. He wanted to start from the doorway anyway, since that was where he'd last seen Lea.

It was darker under the trees. Ivars flipped down his adaptives and walked carefully. He didn't want to give the robots any more reason to come and investigate. The leaves of the alien trees were almost transparent when seen through the adaptives, and he could see some birdlike creatures huddled on branches quite easily. The ground foliage was more opaque, but he was still able to see a white wrapper underneath some broad leaves. He picked it up. It was a bandage package from a first aid kit, smeared with something dark. Probably dried blood. He looked around, noticing some burn damage on one tree and a brass casing glinting in the dirt. This must have been where Ramirez had gotten hit. Not much farther, then.

He jogged up the slope, alert and watchful, but the only indications of the robots he saw were wrecked ones he remembered from the fight. They hadn't been moved as far as he could tell. He followed the trail up to the top of the hill and the hollow with the doorway. It was empty, but he went down the ramp anyway. The doorway was dark and empty from this side, too. It just looked like a door-sized niche carved into the rock.

The scribed surface of the floor didn't take tracks, but there were drifts of sand and dirt here and there. One had a partial footprint, small, going away from the door. It looked fresh. Another indication he was right and Lea had never left the planet. He went back up the ramp, which was packed dirt and showed more traces. Definitely Lea, and her footprints were overlaid on all the larger footprints left by him and the rest of the team. He could also see the tread of her boots was different from their standard-issue footgear, which would help with tracking.

At the top of the ramp he saw something different. The print was larger than Lea's, and the tread pattern was completely strange —and very worn. It looked like a standard human foot, though. Who the hell was it? His stomach tightening, Ivars scanned the area at the top of the hollow as quickly as he could, his fear slowly ebbing as he saw the evidence. Someone had stood at the top of the ramp, waiting. One of Lea's prints covered theirs. There were no signs of a fight or evasive moves. Others had been present as well, maybe two or three total. He wasn't completely sure, but it looked like Lea had been following them—which argued either the strangers hadn't seen her or she'd gone willingly.

It was harder to follow the trail when they went into the vegetation, and it took him hours to get a line off the hillside. Out of the cover of the vegetation the smart thing to do would be to head for their destination by the shortest route possible, and he could see a rocky spur across the open space of the plain. He waited a while to see if he could detect any sign of the robots, but there was none.

Ivars sighed, quickly ate an energy bar, rechecked his rifle, and headed out. Still no sign of the robots, and that was very strange. They'd seen quite a few the last time he was here, and only a handful were destroyed in the firefight. Where the hell were they?

The plant cover of the plain had retained no tracks, at least none that had lasted. When Ivars got to the rock spur he did a quick check of the scree slope but saw nothing. Of course, there was no reason for anyone to go up the scree slope, but it would have been nice to know he was headed in the right direction. Now what? On the other side of the spur the ground sloped down, cut through by erosion gullies. The vegetation was much heavier there, which would make it harder to search. He needed a plan of attack, and some rest too. He could keep up the pace for perhaps another day if he had to, but it looked like this was going to be more of a long slog. He'd wait for daylight and then keep going.

Ivars found a rocky alcove nearby that gave him a good defensive position and wearily took off his pack. Of course he didn't have much water in the hydration system; that was another thing to look for. He sat down on a handy rock and leaned back, closing his eyes and sighing. The fatigue of the flight down was catching up with him. He didn't dare sleep here; it was too exposed. Just rest. He put one foot up, took out a spare magazine, and clasped it loosely in one hand, letting it rest on his raised knee. If he nodded off the noise from the falling magazine would wake him.

He had to pick up Lea's trail again, first. Run a line straight out from the rock spur, see if he saw anything there. If not, skirt the edges of the gullies which would be bound to pick up some sign if she had traveled that way. Then...

Gravel skittered, down the slope from him. Ivars snapped his eyes open and moved instinctively into a crouch, shifting his rifle into position. Then he lowered his hands, carefully, and sat back on the rock. A gangly figure with unkempt black hair was standing about thirty feet away, looking at him warily.

"Is that really you?" Ivars managed finally, his voice rough.

"Really me," said Lea. She came a little closer. "I would have come sooner but you kept moving around and I can't go as fast as you do," she grumbled.

She looked rumpled and grimy, but otherwise uninjured. Relief and other, stronger emotions flooded him. "Are you hurt? Hungry? I've got some food, not much but…I wasn't sure you'd be here, thank God I guessed right." His throat tightened, and the memory of his fears welled up again. "What the hell made you pull a stunt like that?" Ivars yelled. "Why did you trick me into thinking you'd gone through the door?"

Lea took a step back. "You wouldn't have left without me," she answered, looking bewildered. Then she looked at him with narrowed eyes. "You figured it out, though."

"Eventually." Too late to be of use. Ivars reminded himself yelling would not help. "Ramirez…told me some things."

Lea looked down and shifted her feet. "Is he all right?" she asked in a small voice.

"There's a lot of damage, but he's alive and probably going to stay that way. You saved his life."

Now she looked like she was going to cry. "It's my fault he got hurt," she said in a tight voice. "I should have warned you."

"You did warn us. You just didn't think we'd believe you, right?" She shook her head and didn't look at him. "I don't understand what you do. I saw you do it without realizing, though, didn't I? When we caught Bob, that seemed to go rather smoothly. Ramirez says you stopped the robot attacking him without even touching it. So I guess…I guess you have a way of messing with my eye sensor too."

"I had to make you leave," Lea said, pleading. "It's all complicated—it's not just the machines. I can't go back there, to *Kepler*. You don't really need me. You even got the door reconnected without my help. It's safer for everyone if I stay here."

Ivars sagged forward and rested his head in his hands, struggling for the right words to say. "No, the door is not reconnected. When you break something it stays broken." He took a deep breath. "Let me tell you what's just happened. The door to the spindle is blocked and seven people are trapped there. Random walls of morph are appearing out of nowhere, and voices keep repeating a recording of you saying 'interface.' Oh, and it looks like the aliens on the BDR woke up and they want to talk to you. They made me get in the stupidest excuse for a spaceship and crashed me here just to get you back. They also gave me this blob device to give you but not the manual, sorry. It's supposed to connect up the door or something. We were talking in pictograms so I may have missed some of the fine detail."

"Aliens?" Lea came closer. "What do they look like?" She looked worried.

"I didn't see any. They just kept insisting you show up, and when I tried to tell them you weren't on the ship, they wanted me to get you. I have no idea why."

She frowned. "How do you know they want me?"

"They had a rather detailed 3-D picture of you. Hard to mistake. Remember just before we went to the spindle? The second time, not the time you ran through all by yourself. You had your hand on the wall and—" Ivars stopped. Lea had gone pale, her eyes wide. "What's wrong?"

"I don't think you were talking to aliens," she said slowly.

She was still standing a good distance away from him. Ivars frowned. "Why not? Look, I'm sorry I yelled at you. I've had a long and terrifying day." *And I was afraid you were dead.* "Somebody up there wants you back and we are stuck even worse than before now. We need to figure out how to return to *Kepler* and it will go a lot quicker if you aren't all the way over there. I don't smell that bad, do I?"

Lea tried to grin but it was a shaky attempt. Her face crumpled, and she shook her head wordlessly.

It's not just the machines. Lea had known exactly where to find him and it wasn't even full daylight yet. She didn't have night-vision goggles. Suddenly a number of puzzling events came to mind. She'd somehow been able to tell whenever he was impatient or irritated, despite his poker face. She'd known where to find Ramirez when he was hurt.

"You can read my mind, can't you." He felt suddenly cold.

"It doesn't work like that!" Lea wailed. She scrubbed at her face. "I can't tell the words. Not unless I'm touching someone.

There's just a, a feeling." She waved her hands in frustration. "It's like hearing someone's voice in the distance and you recognize it, but you can't tell what they are saying. I can tell where you are. You're not happy, probably because of me, and you're worried about something but I don't know what. This is why I have to stay away," she said, pleading. "I still don't know all the things I do to machines without realizing. Can you imagine what a disaster that would be on *Kepler?* And then it's stuffed full of people. I didn't realize how much it was bothering me until we came here. It was just you and the others and that building full of dead machines and…it was so quiet," she said softly.

"How long?" He hadn't phrased it well, but she understood him anyway. He wondered if she could sense more than she realized.

"I figured out I could hear machines after the first time at the spindle. It was only when we came here I realized I could hear people too."

"You think something on the BDR did this to you?"

Lea made a jerky shrug. "I don't know. I can't tell." She looked miserable.

This was going to take some work. Ivars could only imagine what she had gone through over the last few weeks. Wondering what was happening to her, if she was going crazy. All by herself.

"Ramirez said you knew about his doser. The device inside him," Ivars clarified, when he saw her puzzled expression.

"Yeah. I turned it off. It was damaged and hurting him." She was confused at what appeared to be a change of topic, he could tell.

"Do you know why he has it?" Lea shook her head. "He was diagnosed with a rare form of fast–acting ALS about a year ago. He'd just joined Special Forces when he woke up one morning and couldn't move his hands. By the end of the week he'd lost his arms, and the doctors figured he had maybe a month or two before he'd be completely paralyzed and in a year dead or on a ventilator 24/7. There was an experimental medicine, but it had to be given in lots of tiny doses. So they made that machine to do it. It worked, and he recovered. They don't let you stay on the teams if you need a medical device, though. That's why he's with us." The few, the proud, the highly–trained expendables.

Lea was staring at him. "Because—because you have the eye,

and North's foot…"

"I've got some additional electronics to handle the eye sensor, plus some of my skull is plastic. Never try and stop an RPG with your head, that's my advice. North has got more add-ons than the foot. Most of the bones in that leg are a special ceramic alloy."

"What's wrong with Olsen?" Lea asked, looking worried.

Ivars grinned. "He's old and married. Just kidding, that's not a problem—he doesn't have much time before he retires and they didn't want to put him on a regular team for just one mission. You know, one without gimps. My point being, and I do have one, is that we all have secrets on this team and the team knows about them. That's how we work. We're also really good at keeping secrets, and looking out for each other. And," he said, raising his voice to stop her objections, "you are a member of this team. I'll cut you some slack because you didn't get the regular training, but going forward just remember we'll keep your secrets. Maybe we won't have many around you, with your…ability, but we don't have many from each other either."

"They won't like it," Lea whispered. She looked up at him, staring. "You don't like it."

"It's going to take some getting used to," he admitted. Team members didn't lie to each other either. Not if being polite could get someone killed. You needed to know where people really stood before things got hairy. "But I will. I think you'll find the others will too. And you'll be able to tell."

Lea frowned, but it was more of a thoughtful than unhappy expression. "Yeah. But what about everyone else? Director Macrae, and that colonel guy, and the rest? Can you keep it a secret from them?"

"I don't know. But I'll do my damnedest, and they won't ask questions about it if they don't know it's there. Now come take a look at this magic rock the aliens gave me that is supposed to get us back up there."

"I think it's an AI," Lea murmured.

With relief, Ivars saw she was walking up to him without hesitation. He opened his pack and took it out, glad to see it had sustained no obvious damage. He held it out to her, carefully placing his hands flat at either end so she could pick it up without any danger of touching him.

"That's an artificial intelligence, right? What makes you think that?"

She didn't respond for a moment, staring at the alien football. Then she looked up, like he had just spoken. "I could feel it. That time you mentioned, when I put my hand on the wall? I could feel something sense me, like I was sensing it. It was seeking me. I can't explain it, but it felt both like a machine and a…a mind. Not human, though. Not alive like an animal. And it's big."

"What does it do?"

She shrugged, looking uncomfortable. "I couldn't tell. I didn't really know a lot about the alien machines then. The robots are simpler. I'm not sure I know how to use this," she said, hefting the object. "I think I shouldn't try to do too much until we take it to the door, in case it runs down the battery or whatever it uses."

Ivars got to his feet. "Right. Let's get going, then. I guess you took care of the robot problem, since I didn't see any on the way here. Why did you come here, anyway?"

Lea hesitated for a moment. "There's some people I want you to meet first. I think they can help us get back home better than I can."

The other footprints. He'd almost forgotten them when he saw Lea.

"Aliens?"

Lea tilted her head. "Humans. I think. But not from Earth."

CHAPTER 10

Lea carefully stepped sideways down the slope of loose rock. She could hear Ivars behind her, and worse, sense him better than ever. Tired but happy. He'd definitely been surprised and then intrigued by her mention of the others, which was better than she'd hoped. If she could just keep enough distance from everybody maybe it wouldn't be so bad.

"So how many of them are there?"

"Here?" Lea shrugged. "I think just the six of them. I get the feeling there used to be a few more."

She caught a wave of disbelief. "That's not any kind of breeding population—are there other settlements on the planet?"

"No, I mean..." Lea struggled to find words for something that had never had words in the first place. "Their people are somewhere else. They got here kind of like we did, and I think they were exploring too. We don't really talk much yet. I've figured out their names and stuff like that. They call themselves Wiyert."

"Oh." There was a swirling, complex feeling when Ivars was thinking hard about something. It was fascinating to sense, to try and figure it out. Lea glanced his direction and was horrified to see how close she'd gotten to him. She moved away as unobtrusively as she could while they walked. "Do they know about...what you do?" Ivars asked.

"I don't think so. It's not like with our people, I can't pick up the words with touch. I can sense their feelings, a bit." And give them headaches, but she was trying to be polite now. Alaghar had made no further attempts to grab her but other than that showed no sign of realizing exactly what had happened that time.

113

They had reached the trail going into the ravine, and the trees were thicker, preventing her from stepping very far away from the trail itself. She'd just have to walk faster, then. It was a good thing there was enough light to see the path with; there were some sections that were a little too close to the edge.

"What makes you think they will help us?" Ivars asked.

"I think they're stuck too," Lea said. "They've got all this advanced gear but it's mostly old and damaged. You'll see. I don't understand why they couldn't use the door to go back, or if they got here some other way that doesn't work now. They're…I get the feeling they are hunting something. Something they don't like much." Cold fury was more like it. The blue–white creatures had really pissed off the Wiyert somehow.

They were getting close enough to the cave that someone could be outside or on watch and see her before she could sense them. She glanced at Ivars and wondered what the Wiyert would think of him. They hadn't liked her lack of weapons, but maybe they'd think Ivars had too many or something. "Um, maybe I should go ahead and warn them you're coming or something."

Spike of suspicion. "You're not planning on running off again, are you?"

"Where am I going to run *to?*" Lea said, exasperated. "You can probably run faster than me anyway." He didn't say anything, but he had a skeptical expression. "Fine, I'll just yell and hope they don't shoot us both."

She stopped right before crossing the creek. It was just close enough she could sense that someone was awake, and after concentrating a moment, that it felt like Isboryi. That was good; he was calm and not likely to jump to the wrong conclusions. She called out his name, loud enough to be heard in the tunnel but not so loud he'd think she was in danger. His dark head peeked out and then disappeared, but she could tell from the change in what she sensed that he'd seen them.

"I guess he's calling the others," she said uncertainly.

"And arranging fire lines and scoping me out generally," Ivars replied. His voice was relaxed but she could feel his alertness washing over every other emotion. He slowly shifted his weapon so that it rode on his back and kept his hands out and in view. "That's what I'd do. Don't worry," he said grinning. "I've done this before. As long as I don't have to eat any eyeballs, it's a good day."

Lea stared at him, appalled. "*Eyeballs?*"

"Sheep eyeballs, reserved for important guests in *far* too many places ending in 'stan.' Really, I'm not making it up!"

"I believe you," Lea said faintly, feeling a bit queasy. Either she had a very vivid imagination or she was picking up Ivars's memories. She took a deep breath and looked away.

Alaghar was standing at the front of the tunnel entrance, her face like stone and her weapon cradled in her arms. Lea sensed Isboryi was behind her, out of view, and that the others were scrambling to get ready. "Hey, um, this is Ivars," Lea said, pointing. "*Hazu* Ivars."

"What does that mean?" Ivars asked from the corner of his mouth.

"That you're not one of the bad guys, as far as I can tell. The ones they are hunting. *They're* definitely aliens." Alaghar was walking toward them, and Lea stopped talking. She glanced at Ivars, puzzled. Everything about him appeared relaxed; the way he was standing, the way his head was slightly tilted to one side, his face. Inside his mind was a white–hot blaze, watching every motion and prepared to act instantly. It was confusing, as if he were blurry.

"This is Alaghar. She's the leader," Lea managed to say.

"Alaghar," Ivars said, inclining his head.

"Eyffars," Alaghar replied, speaking slowly and carefully. She was also fully alert and ready to take action, but not angry or hostile. "*Hazu Leeha dovet?*" She wiggled her fingers next to her mouth, pointing to Lea and then Ivars. "*Zhov dovet?*"

Ivars looked at Lea again. Lea shrugged, hands wide. "I can barely count to three in their language. I dunno, what would you be asking?"

"Why I'm showing up. If you contacted me somehow beforehand. Where the rest of the battalion is," Ivars said after a moment. "This is going to take a while without an interpreter. Guess I have to fire up the finger puppets again."

"Huh?"

He grinned. "Improvise, adapt, overcome. Or if necessary, make models out of available materials. I'm not going to waste my one remaining MRE on this bunch, though; we may need it later." Ivars carefully knelt down and assembled a handful of the river pebbles. "Ivars, North, Olsen, Ramirez, Lea," he said, pointing to each pebble in turn. Then he twisted to point in the direction of the doorway, mimicking stepping through and looking around in amazement. A leaf became one of the floating robots, but the Lea-rock made it fall down. Then he showed the attack on Ramirez, and running in fear for the doorway, and counting everyone again on the other side, only the Lea-rock was not there.

Alaghar had been watching the whole thing with a noncommittal expression, but Ivars's depiction of panic when he realized Lea was missing made her mouth twitch.

"Did you really run around waving your hands in the air?" Lea asked, sitting down on a handy log.

"Hush. A certain amount of dramatic embellishment keeps the audience on task and focused," Ivars said. "I may not have *done* it, but I felt like it. You should have heard what Gonafrio had to say."

He continued, now interspersing actions with the model representations of himself and the team with explanations for Lea. She'd wondered how he had gotten down from the BDR and still didn't quite believe his tale of communicating with some alien intelligence—but if not, how did he get here?

A much larger rock was used, appropriately, for the BDR, and the Ivars-rock fell from it to the ground accompanied by the actual Ivars making terrified noises.

"Well? Is it getting through?" Ivars asked when he was done.

"I'm not sure," Lea said slowly. "She's not as tense as she was when you started, and the others I can sense think you are funny."

"That's a start."

Alaghar shouted something over her shoulder, back toward the cave. After a moment Isboryi shouted back, and Lea recognized one of the words. *Deyu*, or the number two.

Lea moved closer to Ivars. "I think she was making sure it's just us on the planet right now. They have some way to hack into the network here, the one the robots use. Oh, I forgot to tell you, they took that equipment from the building we investigated. At least, it's in their cave."

Another of the Wiyert came out in the open, from behind the rocky slope.

"Hey, he's wearing your vest and helmet!" Ivars exclaimed.

"Yeah, I gave them to him. He didn't have *anything* protective left. Besides, Alaghar gave me this." Lea reached inside her jacket and carefully removed the knife from the inside pocket. She'd scrounged a piece of what looked like leather to line the pocket with but it was a makeshift attempt.

Ivars took the knife and examined it carefully. "She gave it to you? Some kind of welcome gift? Why no sheath?"

Lea shrugged. "The sheath is built in to her armor and doesn't look like it comes off. She practically forced me to take it, right after they found me at the door. It was very strange. It was like she was *mad* at me for not having any weapons."

He raised his eyebrows at this. "Interesting." Ivars lifted the knife a little in Alaghar's direction, inclining his head, and then handed it back to Lea. "They might not have much distinction between military and civilians in their culture. I'll show you how to use it in a fight when we get back."

The thought seemed to please him. Lea didn't want to think about actually using a knife to hurt someone, especially since she would be close enough to feel their pain when she did. There wouldn't be any point in arguing about whether she *wanted* to learn how to fight with a knife, though, since both Ivars and Alaghar would think it was a great idea.

Isboryi appeared at the mouth of the cave and gave a sharp up-and-down motion with one hand, then disappeared again. Alaghar pointed to Lea and Ivars in turn, and then indicated they should precede her.

"That's a promising start," Ivars said cheerfully. He was still in a state of extreme alertness but appeared completely relaxed.

"They could have just decided to get rid of us permanently," Lea muttered, glancing at the dark interior of the tunnel with gloomy thoughts.

Ivars's grin did not diminish. "If they were going to whack us they'd do it out here. It's awkward to drag bodies through that narrow area, and you don't want to make a mess in your living quarters. This is a nice kill zone, by the way. More for active attacks, though."

"This is a kill zone? How can you tell?"

"It's a long rock tunnel that is only wide enough for one person.

Any group of people attacking will get fed in one at a time, and if the defenders also get to the other end of the tunnel they can pretty much wipe them out."

They emerged into the shadowy cave. Ivars stood to one side and didn't go any farther, glancing around the interior. "How about some more names?"

Lea pointed. "That's Burdhul. Isboryi, he's got a crude hack device that gets into the robot network; I think he's their tech guy. Hazuruh. She seems to do the hunting, with spears and stuff. Conserving ammunition, maybe? They've all got modern weapons. I don't see Dumhaigl or Kugohin," Lea said, craning her neck to peer in the shadows.

"They're probably outside just in case I misbehave," Ivars commented. He walked over to the sleeping area and slowly removed his weapon, leaning against the wall near Lea's pack, and then shrugged off his own.

The Wiyert watched him in careful silence. Lea sensed only wariness from them, not hostility, but none of them had put their weapons down.

"So what makes you think they can help us with our BDR problem?" Ivars asked.

"They've got some of the gear from the building we investigated, and they seem to be able to make it work." Lea lowered her voice. "Just because I can…do stuff with it doesn't mean I understand what it's supposed to do." She glanced over at Alaghar, who was watching them both. "Can I show Ivars?" Lea asked, pointing to him and then the corner where the alien tech was. She didn't want to get on Alaghar's bad side again and just wander over.

Alaghar's expression didn't change, but she gave a short, sharp nod.

"They got upset when I tried to look at it the first time," Lea said quietly. "I think it's connected to the aliens they don't like." She walked over to the array the different components were arranged in. She sensed Ivars behind her, still alert but not at the extreme level he had been at first.

He let out a low whistle when the light from her flashlight illuminated the array. "Yep, that looks familiar. So what does it do?"

"I'm not sure. See, this thing ties into the robot network but not very well. It waits for some kind of signal and then does stuff. *That* one looks like it's working but it isn't, really. So the one connecting them is supposed to filter and replace something from the broken one but all it does now is randomly send out the replacement signal. Then…" Lea continued, explaining as much as she could. It made her happy to talk about something she understood for a change. Really happy.

Wait a minute. That's not all me. She turned her head sharply toward Ivars. He was looking at her with a small smile that instantly disappeared when she saw it. "Are you even listening?" Lea asked, her eyes narrowing.

"Yes. Absolutely. It broadcasts a keep-away signal." Lea continued to stare at him. "Maybe I haven't mastered all the fine points yet," he admitted with a grin.

She couldn't help grinning back. It was funny, but he didn't seem so frightening anymore. "Well, anyway, they knew what they were doing and what bits to take. That's why I think they can help."

"Maybe." He ran a grimy hand over a jaw rough with stubble, glancing aside. "I think you were right about their situation. They started out with top-rate gear but they don't look so good now. No sign of resupply and plenty of crude repairs. It's hard to say for sure but my guess is they've been on their own for over a year."

"*Selghu*," said Alaghar, and she gestured at the fire when they turned to look at her.

"That means food," Lea said.

"Can we eat what they do?"

She shrugged. "It tastes a little odd but nothing has come back up. They've been living on it long enough, and everything else about them seems human."

"Just doesn't seem right without the eyeballs," Ivars muttered, but he sat down with every outward expression of expecting a great treat. Burdhul stirred the ashes and coals with a stick until he found the metal skewers underneath and pulled one out using a scrap of leather. He handed it to Ivars.

When everyone had their chunk of whatever it was, Ivars gnawed at his. "The ash gives it a nice crunchy texture," he observed. "Not bad, except for the aftertaste of formaldehyde."

"They have to cook it for more than a day to make it soft enough to eat," Lea said. "You'll want to, um, drink a lot of water."

Ivars held the skewer out and gave it resigned look. "My old nemesis, the Beef Patty with Mushrooms. Now I know where they get it from." He ate slowly, waved off a second helping, and then got up and went to his pack. "A polite guest brings dessert," he said, holding up the candy packet from one of the packaged meals. "Here, you take one so they know it's not poisoned."

Lea took one of the brightly colored hard candies and made a show of removing the wrapper and popping it in her mouth. The Wiyert seemed intrigued, and a great deal of animated discussion followed as they made their selections.

"The red ones are cinnamon, right?" Lea asked Ivars quietly, watching Alaghar's eyes bulge.

"Yeah, those are my favorite."

"Well I think Alaghar got a real powerful one." Across the fire Isboryi choked and coughed. "You aren't supposed to swallow them!" Lea stuck out her tongue to show him her partially melted candy. That just made him cough and laugh. Then the other Wiyert had to stick out their tongues at each other to see what color they had turned.

"*Lesohk?*" Burdhul pointed at the candy packet, which still had a few pieces in it.

That meant something like "name" or "what's this" as far as Lea had figured it out. "Candy," she said.

"Khendi." Burdhul nodded, looking pleased. "Ye khendi."

Everybody was much more relaxed from what Lea was sensing now, but Alaghar was still alert and so was Ivars for all his goofing around. Now he was trying to explain the BDR and how they had gotten there. *I'm glad he's here.* Lea watched him, hugging her knees and keeping a mental watch on the Wiyert's reactions. They were…focused. They had something they were working toward. Something they wanted Ivars to do? More than wanting. Lea drew in a breath when she figured it out. She didn't know why, but the Wiyert were desperate.

❧

Ivars woke up with a start, briefly disoriented and pulse hammering at the sound of stealthy movement. He amended that to "deliberately quiet" movement when he saw what the Wiyert were doing. Stacking gear, packing equipment, cleaning weapons. Getting ready to move out.

He stretched a few kinks out, sighed when he felt the bruises, and got up. He hadn't wanted to take so much time before trying to get back to *Kepler* but the language barrier had slowed things down a lot. Lea had tried to help, but since she could only sense emotions, abstract concepts still needed lots of hand waving.

Ivars looked over to the rock shelf where Lea was still sleeping in a tangled heap, one bare foot exposed from under a patchwork hide blanket. Her tousled dark hair hid her eyes but not the smudge of dirt on one cheek. He twitched a corner of the blanket over her foot, shaking his head and smiling. Might as well let her sleep a bit longer.

They had made a late night of it, and when it was clear Lea could barely keep her eyes open he'd suggested she let him keep going on his own and get some rest. The Wiyert kept trying to ask him something, something important. He finally got it when Alaghar took a rough clay cup, put pebbles in it while naming each of the Wiyert, and mimicked the same motions he had made explaining his arrival—only going up instead of down.

"All of you," he gestured, "go with us?" He pointed to Lea, then himself, and then up. Alaghar nodded. His first thought was he had no authority to agree, and then he remembered Gonafrio's original orders when he'd sent the team to the planet. "Find help" had been one of them, right? It hadn't been rescinded, right? The Wiyert wanted to go even though they had no guarantee of what would be waiting for them, and they appeared willing to be helpful.

Give it up. You're still going to get in trouble.

His pack was right where he'd left it, and the alien football was still there. He ate another energy bar and saved the last one for Lea. The local cuisine had been kind so far but no need to push their luck. Nothing was improved by a bad case of the trots. He checked and cleared his own weapons, glancing from the corner of his eye to make sure that didn't cause any anxiety with the Wiyert. He didn't think so; they'd been getting along pretty well, and if he was right the only thing they'd really object to would be being left behind. He frowned. They seemed to be wanting to take a lot of stuff. Understandable if they weren't planning to come back, but how were they going to carry it all?

Then one of the men—Isboryi?—unearthed a flat slab that floated on its own, and he relaxed. That would have come in very useful in some mountainous areas he'd been in where you could never carry in enough ammo. When the float-cart was half loaded he went over and gently shook Lea's shoulder.

"Hey, wake up. We're about to head out."

She shifted drowsily, then sat up and rubbed her eyes. "Did you get it figured out? Can we go home?" She sounded excited.

"Not that home. Not yet. Back to *Kepler* and the BDR. They want to go with us."

Her face had lost some of the eagerness. "Are you sure? They don't know us and they want to go back to some strange place they've never seen?"

"Maybe I misunderstood, but I think they have been on the spindle before. Didn't like it much. Maybe they just want to check us out, but from the way they're clearing house I don't think so. You were right about them having more people originally. I think things aren't too good for them here."

She rubbed her eyes again. "I kinda…picked that up too. Guess I'd better get the door working, then." She didn't sound too happy about it. "They aren't packing the stuff they took from the building. Think they'd mind if I took some?" She started putting on her boots.

"I don't see why not, if they're leaving it behind." Ivars did the handwavy thing with Alaghar, who gave him a dubious look but indicated he could go ahead. Lea seemed to know exactly which ones she wanted and quickly removed them from the array and added them to the pile on the float-cart.

He wished he could tell what she was thinking, like she could sense him. It would be a pain if she fooled him into thinking she'd gone through the door again. He wished he had one of those leashes for children so she couldn't run off—no, that wouldn't work, she had a knife now thanks to Alaghar. He'd just have to be careful.

They moved out into the early dawn light. The Wiyert were wary as soon as they reached the plain, and Ivars didn't know how to explain the attack robots weren't a problem with Lea around. Then again, it might not be a good idea to let them know that. He was getting used to Lea's strange abilities, but others could take a different view—and he'd promised to help hide her abilities if he could.

The closer they got to the hill with the doorway, the more pale and drawn Lea appeared.

"That chunk of mystery meat giving you difficulties?" Ivars asked, keeping his voice down. Lea shook her head and didn't look at him. "Well, what is it then? I see you having some kind of problem and you aren't telling me what it is. How can I blow it up if you don't tell me anything?"

That got him a short laugh, but nothing more. He tried again.

"Look, we're all relying on you to make this work. You're no dummy; if something is worrying you I'll believe it's serious. If it affects our success at getting back to *Kepler* you could endanger us by keeping it a secret. If you don't trust me, at least believe I want to get back in one piece and I'll do whatever I can to help you so that will happen."

At first he thought all he'd done was increase the troubled expression on her face. Then she just looked confused. "I do trust you," Lea said, so softly he could barely hear her. "But…but it's not something you can blow up."

They were climbing the hill now, the Wiyert fanning out around them and Burdhul, who was controlling the float-cart.

"Well, what is the problem? Although it is a pity I can't blow it up; that's always fun."

A small, wobbly smile. Lea leaned closer as if she were going to whisper something to him, then jerked away. Ivars tried to keep any reaction to her odd behavior from showing on his face, and concentrated on looking encouraging.

"It hurts going through the doors," Lea finally managed to say. "I think—I think the last time, the doctor gave me this sleeping pill and I took it before Macrae called me in, and it helped. A little. It still hurt though. A lot. Maybe…maybe you could go through first, it doesn't seem to bother you like it does me, and get one of the pills. Or something for the pain, and bring it back?" She was looking at him with a desperate, pleading expression in her large, dark eyes.

So. Now he knew, and he could do damn-all to help. They'd reached the hollow, and it looked just like it had when he'd last seen it. Dark, blank doorway; no sign of robots or other visitors. Lea stopped when she saw the doorway, then reluctantly continued down the ramp.

"You aren't going to like this, but it is just too dangerous for us to split up now. If the door shut down while I was getting your meds, you'd still be stuck here and I'd take it as a personal favor if you don't ask me to crash–land again. I don't want to push my luck. Plus, I couldn't get to *Kepler* anyway. There are morph barriers in the corridors and I don't think they will go away until you show up." Then again, maybe he did have something that could help. He'd almost forgotten…if he'd remembered to take his usual kit, but he might not have just for guard duty. Ivars took off his pack, knelt down, and pulled out the alien football. "Here, you get started with this. I may have something."

He dug further. Not the medkit, that's where they would look if they got suspicious. Nothing issued. They could tell if it had been altered. But he was expected to have custom rounds for his rifle, and they could be odd as hell. As long as they didn't take them apart, and if things got that bad it was all over anyway. Yes, there it was. He'd labeled it "Headshot" and it was, in a way. Ivars took out the round and carefully pulled the case away from the metal jacket of the bullet. Tucked in the bottom, where the powder should have been, was a small wad of tinfoil containing one precious codeine tablet.

Just having it had helped. Just in case the pain came back when he needed to focus. Sometimes it had, but never bad enough to use it.

Ivars unwrapped the tinfoil and looked up at Lea, wondering how to explain. How would it look to her, him having hidden drugs like that? There was no judgment in her eyes, and when her hand reached out and just touched the scars on the side of his head he realized with profound relief he'd never have to explain anything to Lea. She would know. Then there was the shock when he noticed he'd *felt* her hand touch. There was nothing but scar tissue there, with no nerves. But he'd felt it.

"I'd appreciate it if you didn't mention I had that," Ivars managed to say, his voice rough.

Lea took the pill from his hand and swallowed it. "Had what?" she said. It was a real grin this time. Ivars grinned back.

She stood facing the empty doorway, the football resting in her hands, and closed her eyes. The Wiyert, curious, had gathered closer, and Ivars waved them back. He didn't know if the door would do anything dangerous when it started up, and he was hoping Lea would be protected by the football or her own abilities. He didn't see her do anything, but the alien device suddenly lit up the way he remembered, faint lights and glyphs running all over the surface. Something else happened too, for Lea flinched and made a small whimpering noise.

"Stay with it," Ivars said. "The door is starting to change."

"I…hate…this," Lea said through gritted teeth.

The doorway was no longer empty. A swirling fog that was hard for the eye to focus on slowly filled the space, and then in a flash of energy that only his synthetic eye could see, a familiar corridor snapped into view. The Wiyert were startled and yelling to one another, and he could hear weapons being brought to bear. He didn't even bother to look to see if they were pointed at him, because Lea was sagging. Ivars caught her and steadied the football. He didn't like to think what would happen if she dropped it.

"Hey, that's inside the BDR! I thought they would hook us up to the spindle," Ivars said.

Lea was gasping for air, and sweat beaded on her forehead. "S'OK," she managed. "One less door to go through."

Assured she could stand on her own, Ivars let go. "Let's make sure we don't get shot going through. I imagine people are pretty jumpy right now. Hey, do you have a pen?" Lea took off her pack and after a brief search found a pen and handed it to him. He quickly found a length of gauze in his kit, scrawled DONT SHOOT, and attached it to Lea's pack, tossing it through the doorway before she could object. There was a brief delay, maybe a few seconds, and then the pack appeared, skidding across the floor until it reached the wall. Nobody appeared to investigate it, and he didn't see any sign of it coming under fire. Maybe they were lucky and the new connection was in an empty section with nobody in it.

"Hey! Why did you throw mine instead of yours?" Lea said, glaring at him.

"To give you further incentive to go through," Ivars replied, trying to look innocent. "I'm not leaving you behind, and it isn't fair to expect the Wiyert to show up first—|besides, they're pretty obviously strangers and would give the wrong impression without us to introduce them. We have to go through now. If only to get your pack back."

Lea stared at the door, her eyes wide. She swallowed hard, and he saw the muscles on the side of her neck tighten. Then her head slumped forward. "I can't," she said, so faintly he could barely hear her. She was shaking. "I can't even make my feet move. I know I can't stay here, but I'm not brave. Not like you. I can't do it!" Tears were starting from the corners of her eyes.

"I really wish you'd stop arguing with me. I didn't say you were brave, I said you were a member of the team. You think Olsen is brave?" Lea gulped and nodded. "You watch him try to deal with a spider. He can handle anything else, but not spiders. He makes his *wife* deal with spiders when he's at home. We give him a hard time, but we also intercept spiders for him. Carry you?"

Lea nodded again, looking miserable. She was easy to carry, her head fitting in the crook of his neck like it belonged there. He could feel her trembling. "On a count of three, then. One…" her arm came up around his neck, and she buried her face against his shoulder. Terrified, and trusting him. Better to make it quick. His cheek against hers, he whispered, "Two…" and stepped through.

Pain exploded through his body. He felt nothing else, knew nothing else. Someone was screaming in agony, and he realized it was him. *Lea.* Where was she? Had he made it through? There were voices but he couldn't understand them and they weren't Lea! His lungs were heaving, trying to get air past a throat rasped raw. He felt like he was back in the Q course submersion drill. Fire in every nerve. Something cold and wet splashed on his face, and he struggled to focus, to regain control. *Dear God. If that's what Lea went through I don't blame her for running.*

Ivars forced his eyes open. He had fallen but somehow, miraculously, he had managed to keep hold of Lea. She was unconscious, a thin trickle of blood coming from one nostril and pale, too pale. He managed to get a shaking hand up to feel her pulse. Still alive. He tried to speak but the only sound that came out was a croak. He cradled her head against his, hoping she could sense him. *I'm so sorry. I didn't know. I didn't know.*

"*Vasoynet Eyvarz. Do, vasoynet.*" Alaghar held out a container, a worried expression on her face. He managed to take the container and drink. Water. It felt good on his raw throat.

"Sorry about the excitement," Ivars managed after a moment. He tried to sit up. If anyone had heard his screams they would come running. He had to get up.

First he had to admit he couldn't carry Lea. Then he had to be helped by Burdhul to even stand. The Wiyert and all their gear had made it through, which was a good thing since the doorway had gone dark again. No going back.

It didn't look like there would be much going forward either. They were in a long section of corridor, and he could see the blockages at either end. Sudden fury raged through him. He'd dragged Lea back only to get trapped?

"Dammit, you bastards, I did what you wanted! I brought her back! Now open up, unless you want her to die! She's hurt!" Ivars dropped to his knees beside Lea, wiping the streak of blood from her face and slamming his bloody palm against the wall. "HURT! Do you understand that?" His hand tingled, and then he felt a sudden bolt of energy that made him cry out, but he couldn't remove his hand from the wall. "Interface! You remember?"

"InTerFace," said the voice. The Wiyert were startled, and not happy. Then Ivars saw the sparkling light at the edge of his artificial vision surrounding Lea. The light brightened, then disappeared. "Interface." The voice faded as it spoke.

His hand came free. When Ivars looked down the corridor again, the barriers were gone.

CHAPTER 11

Merrilee Macrae shoved past the bottleneck of people running in and out through the door and into the room where Colonel Gonafrio was standing at a large table, scattered with diagrams. "What's going on? Did you get through?"

"The obstructions in the corridors have vanished, but we don't know why. It wasn't anything we did. I'm calling all teams back."

Given that Gonafrio had been dead set on widening the perimeter before, this was a change. "Why?"

His face hardened. "I'm not letting our people get trapped again. We don't know what caused the blockage in the first place."

"When did this start?"

He shifted a piece of paper free. "About twenty minutes ago. A previously trapped group made it back to the foyer on the BDR, where the main guard group is located. They reported all the barriers blocking them had melted away a few minutes prior. I'm getting other reports as the rest come in, saying pretty much the same thing. Somebody flipped a switch somewhere."

Gonafrio went back to his laptop and checked a spreadsheet on the screen. It appeared to be a list of names. Several of the rows were now colored green. Off to the side, a radio crackled. "Main Gate to Control, Main Gate to Control. We have a situation. Sergeant Ivars is here and he's got Lea Santorin."

Macrae staggered and grabbed the edge of the table. Santorin was back? "Guess we know who flipped the switch," she said, feeling hope for the first time in days.

Gonafrio scowled at her. "How is that a situation?" he said into the radio.

The radio hissed and sputtered. "Uh, sir, there's some other people with him. Not ours. Six, armed and armored. Situation currently nonhostile, but Santorin is unconscious and Ivars is in bad shape. He claims they are friendly but we can't communicate."

Oh shit.

Gonafrio pointed at one of the soldiers in the room. "Medical team to the foyer, on the double." The man saluted and left at a run.

"At least let's get Santorin into medical," Macrae said.

"Only after I can be sure she's not compromised. We have no idea what happened. Main Gate, describe these aliens."

"Sir, they look human." Muffled voices. "Ivars says they are, ate their food and they ate ours. Helped him and Santorin get back. Um, he says they were on that planet, sir."

Macrae and Gonafrio exchanged a surprised look. "Sure they were," Gonafrio said slowly.

More soldiers were coming in, most weary and unshaven. Macrae listened as they reported in, and Gonafrio's aide colored their names green on the list of missing. They all had the same story—trapped by the suddenly appearing walls, and just as suddenly freed. Two lines were red: the missing had been found, but dead. Macrae was moving closer, hoping to find out what had killed them, when another group entered the room and reported in.

"You were on the spindle," Gonafrio said, looking up from the spreadsheet. "Was that damn door to the planet open when you left?"

The soldier, swaying on his feet with fatigue, blinked at him. "No sir. Still dark."

"Hah. Ivars was hallucinating."

Macrae sighed. "He hallucinated up six strangers, don't forget that. And Santorin."

Gonafrio glanced at her, his irritation fading to worry. "Well, then how'd he get there, if the door was still shut down?"

"Sir. He said he was in contact with someone. That he was going to the planet surface by a ship or something," the soldier said. He patted at his vest pockets, pulling out a handful of small paper pages completely covered with scribbled writing. "He was trapped on the other side of the door from the BDR to the spindle. We saw it, sir. You might not believe what we saw, but he was talking with something." He handed over the papers.

Gonafrio read them and winced. "OK, OK. God, why can't anything be simple? I need Ivars here, now. If we've got yet another security hole he can tell us where it is. What's the holdup?"

One of the soldiers manning the radio glanced up. "Sir, Santorin is on her way to medical but Ivars is refusing to leave. He says he's the only liaison between the Weeyert—that's the strangers—and us and they are allies. Sounds like they are kinda nervous."

"Nervous and armed. Like I need more problems." Gonafrio took a large swig of coffee from his mug, swore, and slammed it down on the table again. "No way am I letting them on the ship with weapons. Ivars needs to get his butt over here."

"If they drop the weapons, will you let them on board?" Gonafrio stared at her like she was insane. "You want to talk to Ivars. I want to talk to them. We could use some allies, don't you agree?"

"How the hell can Ivars be so sure they want to be friends?"

"I'll ask him. I agree, something seems funny about this whole setup. That's why I want to check it out." Macrae stood in front of him, hands on her hips. "Answer my question. If they are unarmed, will you let them on the ship?"

He scowled. "Unarmed and under guard." As she turned to go he added, "Why go yourself? You're in charge and putting yourself at risk."

"Yep." Macrae ostentatiously reached behind and underneath her jacket, showing the little .38 in the small-of-the-back holster. "I'm in charge. My responsibility. You may be good at blowing things up on schedule but I've spent a lot more time staring into the eyes of people with bad intentions, and that's not a skill you can delegate. Tell them I'm on my way."

She went at a brisk walk through the ship, not wanting to start a panic with the sight of the mission director running, but she did run when she got to the transparent tunnel from *Kepler* to the alien docking door. If only everyone had kept calm…

She slowed down before entering the circular foyer area, deliberately slowing her breathing, and took a quick but careful look at the situation. The strangers were obvious—all with the same heavy dark hair, stocky build, and unusual full-suit armor. Except for one, who strangely was wearing a US military helmet and vest over very ragged clothing. They looked wary and grim, but that could be due to the soldiers ringing them with weapons aimed their way. Ivars was slumped against a wall, face grey with pain and looking like he was barely clinging to consciousness. Nobody was getting frantic. Good.

Macrae crouched down beside Ivars. "How are you communicating with them?"

He managed a grimace that looked a little like a smile. "Pointing and hand waving, ma'am. Lea can do better." His head sagged down, then snapped up. "Saw them down there. Living in a cave. They got marooned. Lea thinks they know how to use the alien tech, willing to help us."

"How certain are you they are not hostile?"

He stared at her unblinking for a moment, his gaze unfocused. "Never hurt Lea, even when she was alone. Didn't threaten me. Wanted to talk. Gut says they're all right."

Macrae thought hard. Ivars had the experience to back up his gut feeling; she'd read his file. "So how'd you get injured, then?"

Ivars winced, shifting a little. "Damn doorway. Think because it was a temporary. Got Lea too."

It didn't seem to have affected the strangers, though, and there was something off about Ivars when he said it. Maybe it was just the pain, but she didn't think so. "OK, you need to get to the docs. Introduce me, and I'll handle it from here."

He nodded, and gestured to one of the female strangers. The soldiers tried to intercept her when she moved, but Macrae held up a hand to stop them. The stranger's face was impassive and revealed nothing, except for a brief glimpse of compassion when she went to one knee before Ivars and gripped his shoulder. "*Nagazt, Eevarrz.*"

"This is Alaghar. She seems to be in charge of this group. Alaghar, hazu Macrae."

"Mahk Ray." Alaghar inclined her head.

Ivars tried to tell her about the rest but Macrae cut him off. "I've seen scraped–off roadkill that looked better than you. Make sure they get you some pain meds; Gonafrio wants to talk to you next. Go on, get him out of here," she said, waving to the medical team. Ivars protested but nobody listened to him.

She watched him go and then turned back to the strangers, who were watching her with an air of wary fascination. Pointing and handwaving, hmm? Macrae made a cutting motion across the corridor that led to the big cave and *Kepler*. She pointed to Alaghar's weapon, then down the corridor, and shook her head.

Alaghar's face froze. Not surprising; Macrae wouldn't like it either in her place. Alaghar slowly shifted her weapon so that it was cradled in her arms, and then hugged it, all while her gaze was locked on Macrae.

Right. Valuable. Not replaceable, either. "Ask Gonafrio if we have some spare gear crates, the big lockable kind," she said to the soldier with the radio. She ran her eye over the six strangers. "I'd say we need three minimum. With the keys to the locks." The soldier relayed the request, and Macrae indirectly studied the strangers. They looked worn, beyond the hard expressions.

"Crates are on their way, ma'am," the radio soldier said.

When they arrived, Macrae opened the lid, pointing to Alaghar's weapon, closed it, and demonstrated the lock mechanism. Macrae held out the key to Alaghar, holding her gaze. Alaghar slowly nodded. She spoke a few sharp words to the others, who started to unsling their weapons and gear. Macrae took a deep breath, reached up to tap Alaghar's armor, and shook her head.

Alaghar's eyes blazed with sudden emotion. She said something in an angry tone, her face inches away from Macrae's, but Macrae didn't flinch.

"Everybody *calm down,*" Macrae snapped when she saw the soldiers react. She held up her arm to Alaghar, tapped on the jacket sleeve, and then tapped Alaghar's armored arm. She shook her head again.

Alaghar handed her weapon to one of her people. She did something inside the collar of her armor, which clicked and shifted so gaps appeared in a jagged seam down the torso. In one quick movement, Alaghar pulled the top section free and placed it on the ground, glaring at Macrae.

Macrae felt her face go hot. Alaghar wasn't wearing anything under the armor. Macrae quickly took off her jacket and held it out to Alaghar. "I *do* apologize. I had no idea…I suppose the others have the same problem?" Macrae turned to the gaping radio operator. "We're going to be needing six sets of extra-large clothing, I believe."

Olsen sensed the doctor attaching yet another electrode, this time to the back of his head. "But I feel fine. What's the drill?"

The doctor plugged the electrode lead into a bundle of connectors leading to an electronic device in a rack of equipment. "Sergeant Ivars reported similar symptoms to those of Lea Santorin. We're checking all the members of your team. The last thing we need now is some strange infection spreading."

"Nobody else has reported something like it, have they?"

The doctor shook his head. "Only those two. Any headaches?" He kept up the interrogation while he watched the readout of the device. It all looked like squiggly lines to Olsen; no idea if it was good or bad. Farther down the bay North was getting the same treatment. "Any physical contact with Santorin? Do you know if Sergeant Ivars had any contact with her?"

"Not me. Ivars carried her for a bit on the spindle, but that was days ago. Why are you asking me instead of him, sir?"

An exasperated expression disturbed the doctor's professional bearing. "Sergeant Ivars had to be sedated. Kept trying to get out of bed even though he couldn't stand up when he did. Is he often like that?"

"No sir. He's one of the calm ones, even for us."

Now the doctor looked even more worried. "Anything troubling him that you know about? Besides the whole mess we're in," he said, waving a dismissive hand.

Ivars had been upset about the lack of effort devoted to finding Santorin when she'd gone missing, but he'd found her—no reason to still be stressing about it now, was there? Olsen shook his head.

Eventually the doctor ran out of things to test, and Olsen was discharged with a strong warning to report any unusual symptoms —which mostly seemed to be fainting and severe headaches. Not much to go on. North joined him on the way out.

"You think it's some kind of bug?"

Olsen shrugged. "If they thought that they wouldn't be letting us go. They're just trying to figure it out. Doc said they had to dope Ivars to keep him quiet. Have you heard how Ramirez is doing?"

"Last time I checked he was doing fine. Even took a few steps, he told me."

"Kids today." Olsen shook his head, grinning. "Even a killer robot can't keep him down. He know about Santorin being missing yet?"

"Yeah, I told him. What I knew anyway, and that we'd found her again." North was silent for a moment. "I don't think it's a bug either, but it seems to be connected to Santorin somehow. Weird stuff happens around that girl."

"No kidding."

Reporting in, they were both ordered to remain in the ship's mess—with armor and weapons. Olsen blinked at this.

"Cheesy-bean burritos on the menu?"

The officer didn't even smile. "Your buddy Ivars brought some friends back. They're getting some chow and Gonafrio wants a presence wherever they go."

Olsen had heard some sparse rumors but chalked them up to misunderstanding the rescue of Santorin. "They can eat our food?"

"If they can't that will solve one problem. Get going."

The mess was remarkably empty when they got there, except for a few other soldiers clearly with similar orders to their own. The civilians were not in evidence. Olsen grabbed hotdogs and drinks for himself and North, on the principle that hot food was never to be declined. Then they waited.

When the strangers showed up Olsen couldn't see much difference between them and the rest of the people on *Kepler*, probably because they were wearing some spare Earth clothing. As they got closer to his table he noticed they all had a strong physical similarity in skin color, hair, and build. They moved like soldiers too, and he kept a careful eye on them.

Then one turned his way, and Olsen froze. *They haven't even been in the same solar system as me—why the hell do I feel like I've seen them before?* Somehow he had. He felt it in his bones. He'd been good at that, in the field—being able to recognize family resemblances in the tribal areas was extremely valuable intel. He'd seen someone like that man before, not this particular individual, but someone like him.

"Hey. What's up?" North's question was soft, intent.

"I'm not sure. Gonna check it out."

North made a noise that might have been disagreement, but Olsen didn't stop. He took his cup and went to the drink dispenser as if he were going for a refill. There were only six of the strangers, and most of them had already gone through the line and were staring at the food on their plates and making low comments to each other. When Olsen passed by they looked up warily, and he stopped without realizing it. The feeling of recognition was even stronger looking at them together.

One of them made a sharp, one–word comment to him, and he realized he'd been staring. Olsen ducked his head. "Sorry. You guys want some bug juice?" he asked, lifting his cup and pointing at the dispenser. They looked at him blankly, and he took a small swig from his cup and showed it to the woman seated nearest to him. "Juice?" Still more blank looks. He went and got a second cup and filled it about halfway, setting it in front of her.

She looked at it suspiciously, picked it up, and took a sip. Her eyes widened. "Khendi!"

Did she just say what I thought she said? This seemed to have released the constraints on the others, who started in on animated discussions. Olsen found himself demonstrating the use of the drink dispenser, and the general mood was much more friendly. He still could not shake the feeling he'd seen them before, and he wracked his brain trying to remember where.

"So, did you really say 'candy'?" he asked.

"Yeh khendi!" one of the men responded enthusiastically. He mimicked taking a wrapper off. "Eevars, khendi." He gestured as if he were handing something out to each of his fellows. One of them stuck out his tongue at the man, and they all laughed. Well, there was one way to check. Olsen went to the boxes of MREs, ripped one open and took out the candy packet. He brought it back and held it up. "You talking about this stuff?"

The response was emphatic and affirmative. With the aid of North and some of the other soldiers who had come up to observe, they worked out other crucial basic terms such as "mint" and "cherry" and "cinnamon." Then someone found a package of M&Ms, and that introduced "chocolate," colors, and numbers. *Interstellar communcation via candy, who would have thought it?* North was taking notes, and when the one they now knew was named Isboryi showed interest, North scrounged up another pad of paper and a pen and Isboryi started taking his own notes. The script they used looked jagged, or maybe that was just Isboryi's unfamiliarity with the pen.

By the time Gonafrio and Macrae showed up the soldiers had worked out a respectable introductory vocabulary, greatly helped by one Sergeant Williamson, who displayed considerable talent at sketching. Olsen thought Macrae looked pleased when she saw the knot of people surrounding the table, multiple disjointed conversations taking place simultaneously. Gonafrio's face showed nothing, but given the situation that probably meant he was pleasantly surprised.

The Wiyert went silent when they saw the soldiers come to attention.

"Congratulations. It appears you have anticipated the orders I was about to give you," Gonafrio said, with a wintery smile. "Have you made any progress with translation?"

"Flavors, sir," said someone in the back, to general laughter.

The colonel sighed. "Focus on what they want and how they can help us get home. Carry on," and he turned to go, exchanging a resigned look with Macrae.

"Excuse me, sir," Olsen moved quickly to intercept him. "With your permission, I'd like to check up on Sergeant Ivars."

Gonafrio didn't even stop. "Go ahead, but don't take all day."

Arriving at the medical section, Olsen asked for Ivars and got an irritated look in response. "I can tell you where he's *supposed* to be," the nurse said. "What does it take to keep you people in one place, chains? We've tried everything else. Go ahead and look— we don't have enough people to search for someone well enough to walk away on their own without leaving a blood trail."

Now he was starting to get worried again. This wasn't like Ivars. Olsen jogged down the corridors of medical, doing a quick scan of each bay he came to. The name "Santorin" in the slot of one bay snagged his attention—and then he saw someone standing by the bed, in the shadows.

"Mark? Is that you?" Olsen went closer. Ivars showed no sign of having heard him. He was barefoot and wearing only boxers and a T-shirt, probably what the medical staff had left him in. Bruises and cuts were visible on his arms and face. "Hey. What's up? Doc's rounding up a posse to find you, man. You'd better get back."

"She believed me." The words were rough, as if Ivars hadn't

spoken for a while. "She told me what the doors did, and I made her go through anyway."

"What do you mean?" Olsen felt a chill. Now he noticed Ivars's index finger was resting on the back of Santorin's hand, and when Ivars wasn't speaking his lips were moving slightly, his gaze unfocused. "Come on, you need to wake up. You know the doc had me and North in to get our heads scanned? They think we could come down with the same thing you and Santorin have, and you *aren't helping*. What the hell is wrong with you?"

"No skin contact. She told me that too," was all Ivars said. It was like he hadn't heard anything Olsen had said.

"Uh, you're making contact right now."

"Too late," Ivars whispered.

"Not if you *let go*. Come on, you need to rack out. You can't help her if you're half dead, and—"

Suddenly Ivars sighed, and the tension in his body seemed to melt out. His hand dropped to his side. On the bed, Lea stirred. She had color in her face again. "Thank God…hey, when did you show up?" Ivars turned to face Olsen, looking tired but the strange distant expression was gone.

"About five minutes ago. Didn't you hear me?"

Ivars looked confused, then wary. "Hey, did the Wiyert make it through?"

"Yeah, I left 'em in the mess. You got them addicted to sugar, sounds like."

A small grin, more like the old Ivars. "Maybe."

Lea Santorin shifted again, one hand working its way free of the covers. She blinked and smiled drowsily at Olsen. "'salright. He's just tired." As if she had heard the entire previous conversation instead of being unconscious. "Evr'body OK? North? Ramirez? Oh, there he is. I was worried about him."

Olsen glanced behind him, thinking Ramirez had gone on one of his alleged walks, but nobody was there. When he looked back Ivars was watching him, the alert tension back and Lea looked distressed.

"Sorry. Dunno what drugs they've got me on," she mumbled. "Machines…"

Olsen felt a chill again. Both of them were acting very odd, but odd in the same way. "Hey Lea, tell Dumbass here to get back in his bed before the docs handcuff him there."

She struggled upright, a crease between her eyebrows. "Someone's coming." Exactly as if she hadn't heard him. "You should leave. They're coming to see me."

Ivars glanced at her and then at Olsen, uncertain.

"Yeah, come on, buddy. Listen to her." Olsen reached out to grab Ivars's arm but he blocked it sharply and moved away. *OK, shit's getting real.* Ivars was ready to fight and looking at *him*. "What the fuck are you doing? I'm trying to help you!"

Lea was sitting curled up at the head of the bed, shaking, but she wasn't looking at them. She was looking at the door.

"What's going on here?" Director Macrae stood in the doorway, her lips thin with anger. "You were told to rest," she said, pointing a finger at Ivars, "not agitate Santorin. And why the hell are you—"

Lea screamed. She was staring at Merrilee Macrae, eyes wide with horror. "It's classified! I'm not supposed to know that! Get her away from me!"

Immediately Ivars moved in front of Macrae, hands out as if to push her back. "Ma'am, you need to leave. Now."

Oh, this just keeps getting better and better. "For God's sake, Mark. Not. Helping." Too many people, too close to him. He had to get Ivars out in the corridor and immobilize him before somebody got injured. Not like he could take a shot at him in medical.

"Lea, what's wrong? I'm not going to hurt you. Nobody here is going to hurt you. You're safe now. Sergeant Ivars, she's safe. You don't need to protect her here." Macrae's voice was gentle and even and did not reflect the tiny tremor Olsen saw in her hands.

"Starry Messenger," Lea choked out. "Starry Messenger! You're planning to use it!"

Macrae's face turned to stone, her friendly, nonthreatening smile wiped away. Suddenly Olsen had the feeling Macrae was the most dangerous person in the room. "Only if I have to," she said.

CHAPTER 12

Awareness slowly emerged in Lea's mind. She didn't know where she was, and a voice that sped up randomly in panic made a constant background noise. *I'm sorry please wake up I didn't know I'm sorry I'm sorry.* First she wondered why it didn't sound like Ivars, and then she wondered how she knew it was him anyway. More awareness returned, and she realized she wasn't *hearing* anything, and while he was very worried there weren't any other dangers. It was hard to swim up from the depths of unconsciousness, and her muscles weren't responding, as if she were dreaming.

Then Ivars seemed to be having a conversation with someone else, someone she could vaguely sense like a cloud. Olsen. They must be back on *Kepler*, then. Ivars was still very worried, even frightened. She didn't know he could feel frightened.

I'm all right. Just tired.

The enveloping sense of Ivars faded, but not before she sensed a shockwave of relief and happiness. He was still there, just cloudlike the same as Olsen. And there…there was Ramirez! She *was* back!

A stab of strong emotion from Ivars. Not happy. Oh. Ramirez wasn't in the room, and she'd spoken out loud. Have to watch that now. Other people here that didn't need to know she'd gotten some brain upgrades. Who was around? Someone so foggy she couldn't sense them very well—unconscious? Farther away, focused, intense minds thinking vaguely medical things. The range of her ability was much larger now. She opened her eyes and looked around. Yep, same old familiar medical section. At this rate she should get her own room with her name engraved on the door.

Another mind, coming closer. One she hadn't sensed before, and the overwhelming impression she got was of hardness. Threatened, determined, and *hard*. Ivars wasn't supposed to be here; she'd gotten that from both him and Olsen. Better warn him, so he could get away before the hard person showed up and he got in trouble.

Ivars wasn't leaving, Olsen was getting worried. Then Director Macrae appeared in the doorway, and Lea couldn't help staring. Her expression was one of irritation, but neither it nor her soft Tennessee twang matched the hardness of her mind. And she was thinking, over and over again, terrible things. Terrible decisions that might have to be made, that she was hoping Lea could prevent. The closer Macrae got the clearer her thoughts became, the intensity making it like she was shouting. Lea couldn't avoid the stream of unwanted knowledge, knowledge she knew she should not even be aware of.

One of the submerged thoughts crashed through to comprehension. *If we've been detected I'll have to use that goddamn nuke after all. Why did I make them tell me about Starry Messenger?* The name was a symbol in Macrae's mind that had more information than she was thinking about directly, but Lea got the meaning anyway. Starry Messenger was a nuclear bomb.

Lea screamed. She didn't want to know. She *shouldn't* know. And Macrae knew other things, dangerous things. "Get her away from me!"

Ivars knew exactly what she meant, but Olsen didn't and was alert, in fight–ready mode. No, he mustn't hurt Ivars!

"Starry Messenger!" she shouted. She had to make Macrae understand how dangerous she'd become, that Macrae needed to leave. "You're planning to use it!"

The hardness of Macrae's mind sharpened like diamond, and more hidden thoughts spiked upward. Lea suddenly knew Macrae had a gun, where it was, even when she'd last checked it. Would Macrae shoot her to preserve her secrets?

"Who told you?" Macrae snapped. Lea sensed her considering and discarding names, growing more puzzled as she went.

Lea scooted even farther up to the head of the bed, as far away as she could go. "Nobody told me," she whispered. "You know that."

"So you guessed the name?" Relief, washing through Macrae, and a tinge of amusement.

No, it had gone too far. Macrae needed to understand it wasn't safe. For the first time Lea focused on Macrae, tried to follow some of the elusive, slippery thoughts that slid by each other in her mind.

"The third sequence is…is 93873, followed by a delay that is more than two seconds but less than four," Lea said. Macrae's mind was ice-cold, and still. "Nobody told me that either." Lea sensed the thoughts that would become speech, and added, "Making them leave isn't the answer. I'll tell you how I know. Something has happened to me. I've changed. I can—well, it's not exactly mind reading, but I can sort of hear—anyway, that's not the worst part."

A spike of amusement, quickly squelched. "What else?"

It seemed so silly now. Lea felt her face heating, and rather than say anything she pointed at the rack of equipment and started shutting things down, one by one, starting from the top. She could feel Olsen's shock when he finally figured out what it meant and how it was connected to everything that had happened on the planet.

"I shouldn't be here. Not so close to all this equipment, and…people. You."

Tumbled, furious thoughts. The decision shone through like a falling blade, so quick Lea didn't have a chance to figure it out before Macrae spoke.

"All right, you convinced me. The two of you will stay here. No one is to enter or leave, even the medical personnel. Got that?" she said, pointing to Olsen and Ivars in turn. "You spent time with these strangers you brought back. Can you…read…them?"

Lea shook her head. "Only feelings, and sometimes visual memories. It isn't the same as with us."

"I suggest you find a way, if you want Starry Messenger to stay in its current condition." Macrae turned sharply and walked quickly away. Lea found the door controls and shut it behind her.

Now that the bright sharpness of Macrae's mind was fading, Lea could pick up the more subtle threads from Olsen and Ivars. Ivars had calmed down now that Macrae was gone, but Olsen was worried. About her and Ivars too.

"He's not crazy," she told Olsen. "He knew about—" she wiggled her fingers at her head, "and he was just trying to keep Macrae away from me without letting her know about me."

Olsen regarded Ivars for a minute, sighed, then glanced at her. "Are you OK?"

It meant everything from "are you in pain" to "are you frightened" in his mind, and his concern made her eyes well up. "I'm glad you guys are here," she managed to say. "I should have told you what had happened on the planet, but I thought nobody would believe me."

"You couldn't just pull stuff out of our heads like you did to Macrae? I would have believed that."

Lea shook her head. "I couldn't do that then. It keeps getting worse. Going through the transporter doors seems to be connected somehow."

"I felt it last time," Ivars said quietly. Lea winced at the echoed pain from his memory. "I never experienced so much agony in my life."

Olsen whistled, raising his eyebrows. "Even the five mile march with the fracture?"

"This was worse."

"Shit. OK, no more doors for you. Although, I could have used the mind-reading a few times in the field," Olsen said with a grin. "Real handy for intel."

He was curious, she could tell, and also trying to cheer her up. "Yeah, but I can't turn it off," Lea snapped, and regretted it when she sensed his reaction. "Look, it's like…a radio tuned to a station playing static and bits of music most of the time. It's hard to make out. If I'm in contact with someone it's clearer, but I still have to sort of…know them. I think that's why I can't read the Wiyert very well. I don't speak their language and they don't speak mine." She hugged her knees. "I don't know what's going to happen if I can't find a way not to…do it." And what about when they got back to Earth?

Ivars shifted, looking down and away. "Is it bad?" For some reason he was coming in much clearer than Olsen, even though they were about the same distance away. Maybe it was because she'd spent more time with him. He was feeling…embarrassed?

She struggled to find the words to explain. "You know those

dreams where you're wandering around in public with no clothes on? It's like that, only everyone *except* you is naked and you have to pretend you don't notice anything."

Olsen laughed. "Oh, wow. I didn't think of it like that. Yeah, that would suck."

Ivars was still worried. She smiled at him. "It's not icky or anything. Nobody here is like that. Well, Macrae is kinda scary." She wondered what Macrae was going to do with her. Stick her out in the corridors of the alien ship? That would solve the problem, but she got the feeling Macrae wanted to keep her secure for some reason, and if the alien ship was acting up, it was too risky.

Then she remembered there were other people with housing issues. "What happened with the Wiyert, anyway? Are they all right?"

She caught Olsen's amusement even though he kept his expression deadpan. "Yeah, they were doing good when I left. Bunch of us working on the language issue. We've got a lot of questions for them." He recounted the candy discussion and what he'd heard about the Wiyert's first encounter with Macrae.

"Sounds like Alaghar won that round on points," Ivars said, grinning. Lea sensed him becoming calmer.

Olsen nodded. "Definitely extra credit for artistic expression. Hey, I wanted to ask, in case it becomes important later," he said, turning to Lea. "How did you open up all the corridor barriers?"

Lea shook her head, looking at him blankly. "I didn't do it. I was unconscious when I got here."

"Yeah, but you got here, so *somebody* opened them."

"Whoever wanted her back in the first place." Ivars looked grim. "As soon as I proved she was back, the thing let us go. You really think it's a machine?" he asked Lea.

"A really advanced one, yeah," Lea said. "It feels like a machine. I wonder why it doesn't say anything, though? It can replay sounds."

"It could say 'interface.' Nothing else." Ivars looked puzzled. "And it sounded like you. Maybe replaying something you said? But it meant you. It said that word just before the blockages vanished."

Lea sensed a faint, familiar presence. It became stronger, closer, until she was able to identify it. "North is coming here," she said.

North was also unsettled about something, but she didn't mention that.

Olsen stuck his head out into the corridor. "And there he is. What's the word?"

North grimaced. "The word is we get to pull security. Macrae is relocating Santorin and we get to make sure she stays there. What have you been doing, girl? Macrae is madder than a wet hen and she wants you in solitary."

Ivars frowned. "Where are we taking her?"

"*We* aren't taking her anywhere. You get to stay in the loving embrace of medical until told otherwise."

"After your little mental episode what do you expect?" Olsen asked, interrupting Ivars's protest. "You were *that* close to assaulting the mission director, dude. Yeah, yeah, you had reasons but how do you think it looks to Macrae? Or Gonafrio? Sit and take your happy pills, be compliant, and they might let you out again. Maybe."

Olsen was still keeping a careful eye on Ivars, Lea could tell. He was suspicious and worried. Ivars was worried too, with an underlying layer of confusion and fatigue. He still didn't understand what had happened to him and was resisting any idea of staying.

"You should rest," Lea told him. "If you felt what I did, going through the door—it takes a lot out of you." Although she was feeling better, this time. Tired but not achy. Was she getting used to it at last? She just didn't want him worrying about her. "I'm going to be falling asleep as soon as I get wherever they're taking me, myself."

"Somewhere securable. Away from here," North said, shrugging. "No idea why. You don't look that dangerous to me, girl."

"I have to stay away from control systems. And people. I'm... not safe."

North quickly glanced at Olsen, who gave a barely perceptible nod.

"No, I'm not nuts and neither is Ivars," Lea snapped. "I've changed, OK? I can do stuff and hear...stuff and I'm not sure I can always control it and Ivars was just trying to help me hide it so stop acting like he's muttering to himself about the voices." She glared at Olsen.

"Funny you should say that, because he *was*—"

"Not that kind of voice. It was me. I think."

North just blinked, his confusion increasing. "Let's get you going. Macrae wants you secured soonest."

Ivars was unhappy, but he stayed. Lea grabbed her clothes and pack, wrapping the blanket around herself rather than taking the time to change. She wasn't sure where they were going until they got there. The big containers that nearly filled the cargo hold had some gaps in their ranks, and a bedroll and a small pile of the meal packets were already stacked on top of one of them. They must have moved the empty containers somewhere else, maybe even outside in the cavern *Kepler* was parked in.

"They're gonna put the Wiyert in the hold next to yours, and we'll be watching them too," North said. "We'll be right outside if you need anything."

Lea lost no time in rolling out the bedroll. It was blessedly quiet in the hold—hardly any people-noise that she could sense, other than North and Olsen, and comparatively little machine-noise too.

"Right now, all I need is sleep," she said.

✍

"I know you didn't tell anyone. Neither did I," Macrae said with emphasis, leaning over Gonafrio's desk. "That's my point. *She knew the activation code.* Think about that for a minute, will you?"

Gonafrio leaned back in his chair, scowling. "Are you asking me to believe your pet computer whisperer is now a mind-reader?"

"She knew the code name. She knew the sequence. Tell me how she got that information. Hiller didn't even speak out loud when he told me the activation sequence, so surveillance devices won't cut it either. How was it communicated to you?"

He rubbed his head. "At Luna Station, before Santorin had even arrived. Look, we don't need to speculate about woo-woo mind stuff to realize we have a security breach."

Macrae ground her teeth. "Actually, we *do* need to speculate about woo-woo mind stuff. I *also* saw her shut down a bank of medical equipment without touching it. Just sitting there. She may not *need* the activation code to set Starry Messenger off! That's why she's sitting in Bay Twelve with a physical, nonelectronic lock on the door." She straightened and massaged her forehead, trying to dispel the growing headache. "The doctors reported strange equipment malfunctions around her earlier. Before she went to the planet. The good news is they haven't seen similar behavior in anyone else, even in the team that went with her."

"Maybe. Ivars isn't turning on lights with his brain but he's been acting oddly—not just by your report of what happened in medical. Still, I have independent confirmation he was communicating with some outside intelligence, which successfully sent him via small craft to the planet surface to retrieve Santorin. It is true the corridor obstructions went away after she returned. But who sent him to retrieve her, and why aren't they talking to us? Why is she so important to them?"

"It doesn't make any sense," Macrae agreed. "Meanwhile, do you have any concerns about Santorin's current location?"

He thought for a moment. "If what you claim is true, there's not much she can mess with except the cargo hatch. I'm assuming she doesn't have infinite range. You don't want to hold her off-ship?"

Macrae shook her head sharply. "Too dangerous. We could lose her again if the whatsis gets involved. This way we have control."

"And the team?"

"Better to keep them isolated from the rest of the ship as much as possible. If the effects just showed up in Santorin first, they could—"

The intercom whistled. "Gonafrio, this is Hiller. Get on deck. We're detecting motion in the cavern."

Lea tossed and turned for a while, unable to sleep, before she gave up. It felt like a storm was about to break; a big, nasty lightning storm. She was worried about Ivars, and she was worried about North and Olsen being worried about Ivars. Everything kept running around in her head, along with the feeling there was something she should be doing.

She got up and wandered around. Near the interior door she noticed a safety station with an eyewash device and the usual assortment of fire extinguishers and spill packs. Someone had also left a bucket with a rough-cut seat with some sanitary wipes. Macrae *really* didn't want her leaving the hold for any reason, it seemed. Lea wondered what she would do for a shower, or if the wipes were supposed to fill that function too. They'd also stacked a bunch of the storage bins inside the hold, which was strange since they weren't used for bulk cargo. She tugged at the lid of one—locked. So, not for her. There was something else funny about them but she was too nervous and worried to try and figure it out.

Lea resumed her tour of the hold. Walking along one wall she got a strong sense of the Wiyert. They were moving around, and she sensed a general overlayer of uneasiness. When she got back to the interior door she could sense North and Olsen on the other side, but not Ivars. She rested the palms of her hands against the door, then her forehead, trying to reach out to them. If she concentrated on one or the other she could hear them more clearly, but the connection still seemed to be only one way.

There was something else, now. Something that had been growing unnoticed while she had experimented. Something alien. *The AI. It was trying to find her.* It felt different too, more focused and determined. She shrank away from the door. Where could she hide? Lea huddled on her bedroll and wrapped the blanket around herself. She wanted Ivars there so bad it was like a physical ache—and that made no sense when North and Olsen were right outside the door. She'd thought she'd feel safe back on *Kepler,* but now that she thought about it the only times she had felt safe were when Ivars was there too. She wasn't sure what he could actually do or why she was so sure she would feel safe, she just wanted him.

Oh crap. I have a crush on him? That could be embarrassing. Good thing she was the one with the mindreading, then.

The alien presence was getting closer. Lea wrapped her arms around her knees and wished for Ivars.

Gonafrio sprinted for the bridge, using the stair handrails to haul himself up three steps at a time. The captain was leaning over the shoulder of one technician, staring at his display, while other crew shouted reports from their stations.

"Third projection growing on the wall, sir! One hundred meters from the opening."

"Any signal?"

"No sir, nothing."

Hiller turned to face Gonafrio. "Take a look. We've got the floodlights going. Routine scan to detect any of those small robots coming in found this instead." He pointed to a larger display, higher up on the wall. It showed the interior of the cave *Kepler* was in. When they had first taken shelter from the ice explosion the walls had been smooth. Now pointed protrusions were growing from every surface, pointing inward. Pointing toward *Kepler*.

"How long has this been going on?"

The captain rubbed his head. "Fifteen minutes. Those damn things are growing fast, too. Got anybody outside the ship?"

"No sir; all aboard at present. Even the fatalities."

The captain grunted. "Good."

Gonafrio knew what he was thinking. *Leave no clues of origin behind.* That had been the order. Then he glanced up, startled. "You're thinking of moving *Kepler?* Away from the BDR?"

"The BDR has been acting strangely. If it is hostile it won't take us home anyway."

"But the ships outside—"

"Getting killed in here will be just as bad as out there, and maybe we can outrun them. You got any other ideas?"

Gonafrio grimaced, and shook his head.

"Sir! Four more structures near the opening. At projected growth rates they will block our exit in less than an hour."

"Fire up main engines!" Hiller shouted. "Take us out now with the trim jets. Prepare to maneuver when clear to—"

The deck rocked, hard, and Gonafrio heard a groaning noise coming from the ship's superstructure. "Were we hit?"

A brief silence while the ship's status was checked from multiple stations, then the reports came in. No loss of pressure. A hull sensor missing. No action visible in the cavern besides the already detected spines.

"Jets are firing, sir, but we're not moving!"

"Fire a probe. *Something* hit us, and something is keeping us in place."

Something was. The probe revealed a thick growth, originating from the cavern floor and wrapping around the main structure of *Kepler*. Gonafrio could see it getting thicker, branching filaments spreading over the surface of the ship and getting larger in turn.

"I don't think we're allowed to leave, sir," Gonafrio said.

$\wp$

The sudden pummeling sound of the emergency klaxon made Lea stumble and fall, terrified. The voice that followed just kept repeating "Emergency stations." She ran to the door. Olsen was there, and he felt startled and alarmed.

"What's happening?" Lea yelled.

"No idea. Radio's dead. You OK in there?" She could barely hear him through the thick metal door. If she hadn't been able to sense what he was thinking she wouldn't have gotten more than half of what he said.

"Something's coming!" If only Ivars were there; she wouldn't have to take time to explain. "I can feel it! Can you let me out?"

"We don't have the key. North's gone to find out what's happening. If the ship is under attack, you're safer where you are."

Not if it's coming for me, Lea fumed. The alien presence in her mind was even stronger now. Localized. Trembling, she edged closer to where it felt strongest. Along the hull of the ship, where the big cargo doors were. But not the cargo doors themselves; next to them. She took another small step closer to the hull. The metal looked different in one spot, like the paint was flaking. The spot grew larger. In the center the metal flaked away entirely, revealing a patch of alien morph. She fled for the door.

"Olsen, it's coming in here! There's morph!"

She felt a spike of fear and anger from him. "I don't have the XM25 with me or anything else that can open this door—stay as far away from the morph as you can. I'll be back—with *something.*"

Don't leave me! she wanted to scream, but she knew it was the only option. What was she going to do if whatever it was got in before Olsen got back? She couldn't see the hull wall from the door with all the containers in the way, so she slid along the edge of the stack until she could see around the corner. Nothing was coming through the wall, and she tried to slow her hammering heart. Then she noticed that the patch of morph was much larger, and the center was dark. Empty. Hollow. Was something going to come through?

Lea stared at the hole, hardly daring to breathe. No sign of movement, except at the edges where the hole was getting larger. She could feel an itchy buzz in her head, though, that hadn't been there before. Lea edged back to the door—no sign of Olsen.

Maybe she was right, and the thing was somehow connected to her. Trying to reach her. The way the ship had rocked before the sirens went off—were other things poking holes in *Kepler?* Damaging the ship because of her?

Lea stepped cautiously toward the hole. The itchy buzz was definitely stronger, and as she got closer she could see the hole had depth. How far did it go? She found an old ratty push broom, unscrewed the handle, and poked it in the hole. It went in as deep as the length of the handle with no stopping.

What would Ivars do? He wouldn't cower by the door waiting for rescue, not if the problem was his fault to begin with. He'd fix it. Find out about it. She'd hidden behind Ivars and the team long enough. The ship had enough problems, and she was only adding to them instead of solving them.

Something was directing the morph hole. Something she'd sensed before, and run from. Time to stop running. Lea reached out and let the tips of her fingers touch the morph.

Ivars lay still on the bed, deliberately slowing his breathing and relaxing his muscles. That usually was enough to slow his pulse. The voices in the hallway stilled as they got nearer to his bed. He heard the rustle of moving cloth, and then footsteps going away. *Good. Fooled them again.* He opened his eyes just enough to let light in. Nobody present.

He'd slept a little despite his worry, but now it was back again even stronger. The bruises still hurt, but the steamrollered feeling after going through the door portal had diminished to the point that he could function again. Ivars took a quick look around the room. No obvious cameras, but that didn't mean they weren't there. Possibly present but not watched all the time, if the staff was busy. If he moved fast they wouldn't be able to catch him.

Something still wasn't right. It felt like something was tugging on him, or a voice calling just on the edge of hearing. He'd figure it out later. First he had to get out of medical and find Lea.

Ivars slid smoothly out of the bed and reached for the locker door without standing up fully, still trying to fool any potential remote observers. The locker should have had his uniform and outer gear; he'd seen them stowed there. The locker was empty except for a note. It was in Olsen's handwriting and simply read, "Go back to sleep, headcase."

Ivars crumpled the note and swore. He didn't even have his

boots. Should he take the time to find his stuff, or were matters desperate enough for him to just go as he was, in his shorts?

Then the klaxon sounded, followed by a shuddering in the deckplates. Ivars sprinted for the door, dodging people in the corridor and going more by memory than sight. The tugging feeling was suddenly so strong he stumbled, slamming into a wall. It was Lea, he realized. He didn't understand how or why but she was somehow telling him she needed help. He'd been planning to look for her anyway and now he had a built-in heading. Convenient.

With the emergency they couldn't yell at him too much for leaving medical, either. He was obviously fit enough to help, and was it his fault his pain-in-the-ass teammate took all his weapons and gear? The most useful thing he could do in his current condition was ascertain Santorin's safety and welfare.

The floor of the medical section felt smooth under his bare feet and had just a bit of give, like a thin rubber mat. The floor of the corridor outside was diamond-patterned sheet metal and was both painful and had less traction. Not good—he needed to put as much distance as possible between himself and the people who were bound to come looking for him.

Ivars lost precious minutes finding a path to where he needed to go. The instinct told him where, but not how to get there. *Think, idiot. Where could they secure someone that needs to be kept away from electronics?* The tugging feeling was *down,* and toward the rear of the ship. The holds? He heard the sound of running feet behind him and tried to speed up. No luck.

"Hey you, where do you... *Ivars?*"

"No time!" Ivars gasped. "Lea's in trouble."

Olsen pulled even with him in the corridor. He didn't grab for Ivars to stop him, and he was carrying a crowbar. "Yeah, but how did you—and how did you know where she is?"

"The voices in my head gave me the damn grid coordinates along with the sitrep. What's with the crowbar?"

"Door's got a big-ass lock and Macrae's got the key. Lea said there was morph in the hold." Olsen panted between words. "You see North? He went to find out what the drill is. Comms are out."

They rounded a corner hard, Ivars slipping on the metal deck and barely catching his balance. "I was trying to keep a low profile. By the way, thanks for stealing my gear, jerk."

There was the door. It had to be the one; it showed recent metalwork around the edge.

"Lea! We're coming in! Stand away from the door!" Olsen hefted the crowbar and smashed at the lock with the blunt end. Ivars frowned. Something was wrong. The sense of Lea was not as strong as it had been. And it was…ǀfading? *No. Moving away.* Ivars grabbed at the door handle, bracing one foot on the wall, and pulled with all his strength. The hasp of the lock creaked. Ivars backed away and Olsen took another mighty swing, and this time the door was free.

Ivars sprinted through the door, not even bothering to check if unfriendlies had taken up position inside. He had no weapons, no armor, just speed and surprise. Olsen had a sidearm; he'd have to count on that for backup.

It became quickly obvious the hold was empty. Empty, that is, except for a tunnel made of morph that had appeared in the hold wall. It was barely big enough for him but it would have been plenty roomy for Lea. And that, he could tell, was where she had gone.

"They've got her…" he said, his throat suddenly tight.

"Who?"

Ivars pointed at the tunnel. "Whoever the hell built *that* thing. They knew exactly where she was, too." He looked around the hold frantically. "I need something to mark a trail."

"What we need is backup. No way are the two of us going into wherever that leads."

Ivars spun on Olsen. "I'm the only one who can track where she is going. Gimme the crowbar."

Olsen sighed and handed it over. Ivars found a blue plastic barrel that shattered when he hit it, and he kept going until he had a handful of blue plastic chunks. He'd have to carry them in one hand, the crowbar in the other, because he had no pockets.

"Radio's out?"

"Completely."

"I'm going to find her. You get word to Gonafrio."

Ivars dived into the tunnel.

CHAPTER 13

Olsen ran, cursing as he went. No comms, no information, and now Ivars was jumping down some alien rabbit hole, by himself, armed with nothing more than a crowbar. Not good. Lea Santorin was missing and that was bad too. He just had to get help on the way and then he could go back.

The deck shuddered underfoot. What the hell was going on? Had the robots swarming outside the BDR finally figured out someone was inside it and come to attack?

He skidded to a halt in front of a closed pressure door. "Shit!"

"What are you doing here?" North was standing next to the bulkhead, staring at him and holding the handset of the emergency phone. "You're supposed to be watching Santorin."

"She's gone. Something opened up the hold from outside and got her. Why the door? What's going on? I gotta get some backup."

North looked grim. "Something also decided to wrap around *Kepler* and squeeze. We've got hull leaks. Still no radio." He put the phone back up to his ear. "Yes sir, that's Olsen." A moment of silence with muffled sounds coming from the earpiece, and then North held the phone out to him.

"Olsen here."

"What did you say about Santorin?" It was Gonafrio, and he sounded like he was spitting nails.

"Sir, there's a breach in the hold she was in. There's a tunnel leading away, and she's gone. Ivars went after her." *In his boxers.* Olsen held the phone away from his ear while Gonafrio yelled, then put it back again.

"I've given North the situation. You guys are on your own until we get the leaks patched up. Secure that tunnel!" Gonafrio hung up before Olsen could ask about Santorin.

"I thought you were going for intel," he said to North.

"Door was shut when I got here." They both jogged back up to the hold. As they got near the door Olsen saw the door opposite was open, and a worried and confused Wiyert was peering out of it. "Bet they're having second thoughts. How are we going to explain this?" North asked.

"Let's show 'em and see what they think." Olsen waved them over. They followed hesitantly, muttering when the ship rocked again. The tunnel was still there, open and unchanged. "Lea. Ivars," he said to the Wiyert, pointing down the tunnel. Then he pointed back toward the door, mimicking coming to a stop and banging on a wall. "No help."

The Wiyert had expressions that ranged from dismay to grim anger. Olsen held out a hand to them. "Help?"

"What are you thinking?" North asked, turning to him.

"I'm thinking backup. We can't get any from Gonafrio, right? I'm not leaving Ivars to go alien hunting all by himself, and we still have to secure this opening."

"And what good will having more unarmed soft targets do?"

The one named Alaghar was watching this exchange closely, her eyes switching between them as they spoke. She reached into a pocket and pulled out a set of keys, dangling them from her hand.

"I don't think they're planning to be soft targets," Olsen said slowly. "Where'd their gear get stowed?"

The Wiyert knew exactly where it was and lost no time in donning their armor and weapons. Olsen took a few precious moments to introduce some basic hand signals—hold your position, go that way, stop—with North's assistance. They had to have *some* method of communication in a firefight, if it came to that. More pointing and waving, and they organized the defense— he and Alaghar would go down the tunnel and North and the rest of the Wiyert would remain in the hold.

Olsen took a deep breath and crouched down to enter the tunnel.

Ivars finally came to the end of the strange tunnel and kept running, trusting his homing sense would direct him. He was in the regular part of the alien ship now, and the corridor surface was cold under his feet. Better than the tunnel, rough and painful. Even as he ran he remembered to leave a chunk of blue plastic at any intersection he turned at. He could still sense Lea, and she seemed…stronger? Did that mean he was getting closer? As near as he could judge he'd been heading toward the center of the alien ship, and down. He was pretty sure nobody had ever been in this section before.

He slowed down a fraction at a cross-corridor, quickly checking for motion, and sped up again. Speed was essential, but so was not getting ambushed. No sign of anyone, no sound but his running feet and ragged breathing. How far had he gone?

Just as Ivars was down to his last two pieces of marker, the corridor widened for a section. Ahead was a large opening in the wall, framed by broad, pale gold panels covered with an angular, textured pattern. Beyond them he could see a huge open room, but his view was obscured by an array of black rectangles apparently floating in midair.

Lea was in there. Somewhere. Ivars glanced to either side of the opening. Nothing was moving, no obvious threats. He entered the room carefully, alert for any change. The black rectangles were so thin they were nearly invisible if looked at edge-on. He turned sideways to go between them, not wanting to make contact.

The rectangles, hundreds of them, curved around a central point. As he got closer he could see glimpses of a familiar figure. Lea was floating like the rectangles, her arms hanging limp and her head down as if she were suspended in water. She appeared unharmed, if unconscious.

As he got closer to the center and Lea his synthetic eye started to pick up something swirling in the air around her. It was similar to the sparkling effect he'd seen on the walls, but it flowed like water.

"Lea." He could see her face now, it was slack, her eyes closed. No response. "Lea! Come on, we have to get out of here. Ship's under attack."

Still nothing. The hairs on his skin were standing up, and the air smelled electric. If he stretched up he could just touch her boot. Her foot moved easily, but she didn't react and the rest of her stayed put. Maybe if he grabbed on to her he could pull her down. Ivars jumped, reaching for her hand.

The instant his hand made contact, Lea, the black rectangles, and the room disappeared. Everything was a featureless blank expanse, wherever he looked—but he could still sense her, knew she was right next to him. And terrified.

"*Lea!*"

"Here! I'm here. Help?" It sounded like she was gasping directly behind him, in his ear. He spun around, but no one was there.

"Where?" He couldn't lose her again. Ivars felt his chest tighten at the very thought, tried to take a breath to calm himself—and noticed he wasn't breathing. "I can't see you…" Even as he said the words he realized he wasn't actually speaking them.

"It isn't real. You're…kinda in my head. I think. I can't…it's coming back!"

The blank view was changing now. What looked like a dust storm of green sparkling motes swirled closer, and he could hear a dry whispering, a thousand tiny voices. In his connection to Lea he could feel her flinching, as if expecting a blow.

"Is it going to attack? What *is* that, anyway?"

Tangled thoughts flickered by, too quickly for him to understand. Lea was trying to find the words to explain, he could tell, and nervous about the cloud.

"It's the AI. It's desperate. It was damaged and abandoned, it doesn't remember what happened and it doesn't understand us or what's going on. That's why it wanted to contact me. It wants me to explain."

Explain everything was her despairing thought. That part he did understand. Panicked computers he didn't, but Lea did and he believed her. Panic or not, it couldn't be allowed to stampede all over Lea. He could tell she was barely holding together dealing with the firehose of questions.

"Hold it right there," he said to the cloud in command voice. It didn't "sound" any different and he couldn't see the hand he thought he was holding up, but it worked anyway. The green cloud slowed and stopped. "You can't do it like that. One at a time. You are hurting her."

hurt:define

Ivars started. "Was that…the AI?"

A wave of sudden happiness washed through him and he felt an invisible hug. "You did it! You made it stop!" Lea said. "Um, it didn't understand your word. I guess it doesn't have the same kind of connection to you as it does with me, or it doesn't work with me being the translator. Sort of."

"Oh." He thought for a moment. "Hurt means...damage. Destroy. Like what happened to the..." Was the ship the AI, or separate? "The big crater on the surface of this structure." *Guess calling it the Big Dumb Rock would be rude, now.*

The green cloud contracted sharply into a bright point.

negate hurt

The AI communication wasn't even close to a voice, but it appeared in his mind as if he had heard it. It was disorienting if Ivars thought about it too much, so he didn't. The situation was just going to be strange and he had to cope with it.

"Guess that means it will behave now. Is it really speaking English, or is that just an illusion?"

"I don't know. Maybe it's picking it up from me, or you are reading what I get somehow." Lea did the mental equivalent of a shrug. "Hey, it's detecting something heading this way...did anyone come with you?"

Lea still had to struggle to keep her mental focus, although it was *much* better than before. The AI kept trying to tell her things, report information that came up. Almost as if it wanted her permission or approval or something.

Some of the information was useful. She could "see" where everyone was on the alien ship, and two people were approaching the central area, where they were now. It wasn't really visual information but she could tell they were human and armed. This agitated the AI, which wanted to do something about it. She tried to tell the AI they were friendly, but that concept wasn't translating. "Helping" and "protecting" did.

Ivars was trying to tell her something too. Even though there were only two voices in her head she couldn't ignore either of them or sort them out. "You need to let go," she told the AI. "Disconnect."

That got what she could only describe as kernel panic. It did *not* want to lose contact with her. "I'll still be here and I can talk to you but not like this. It's starting to hurt my head."

And just like that, the connection vanished. Lea opened her eyes. She was floating twelve feet above the floor and Ivars was floating right next to her, so close the sides of their heads were touching. She grabbed at him, terrified they were going to fall. Ivars's eyes flew open and he wrapped her in a protective bear hug…and they drifted slowly to the floor.

Lea stumbled, disoriented and dizzy, when Ivars finally let go. He took hold of one arm to steady her. "You OK?"

"I…think so." The sound of running feet made her look up. Olsen and Alaghar skidded to a stop, taking up flanking positions on either side of the entrance to the room. Somehow she could see them even though big black rectangles were in the way. Lea started walking through the black rectangles, which shifted aside as she drew near. Ivars followed. "Um, why aren't you wearing shoes?" *Or pants, for that matter.*

"My pinheaded teammate *stole* them," Ivars growled. "And all the rest of my gear, trying to keep me in medical. So when the alarm sounds all I've got for a weapon is this." He shook the crowbar Lea hadn't noticed earlier, and when they came out of the forest of black rectangles he pointed it at Olsen. "Hey, asshole, did you at least bring my boots?"

"Sold 'em online. Sorry, buddy." Olsen was grinning, and Lea could feel the wave of shaky relief rolling off of him when she and Ivars came into view. "All secure?"

Ivars glanced at Lea, questioning.

"It's just us here."

"What about whozis?" Ivars waved a hand around the room.

Lea grinned. "The AI is all over the ship. We're inside it all the time, even in *Kepler.*"

Olsen lowered his weapon, and Alaghar reluctantly followed suit after a moment. "Speaking of *Kepler,* we've got big problems. Something is puncturing the hull and holding the ship locked in place. The pressure doors closed and we can't get through to the rest of the ship either, or I totally would have taken the extra time to get your damn boots for you, headcase."

Lea froze. She still had some kind of connection to the AI, or she wouldn't have been able to see around the rectangles. *Did you do that?* she thought angrily. *You could kill the people in the ship!*

damage hurt error

The communication was much less overwhelming this way, but still distinctively the AI.

fix requirements

Was she imagining things, or was it asking a question? *Let go of the ship. Oh, and...\if there are holes in the hull leave a patch that keeps the air in.* There were probably more problems. She wished she could contact *Kepler* and ask, but the radios hardly ever worked.

The AI picked up on that, and responded. **Signal blocked.** That conveyed the additional meaning that it was blocking the radio deliberately, and thought that was required. *Why are you blocking radio signals?*

Prevent detection. Main rule set override required.

Can you allow the signal inside?

There was no response except a soundless click in her mind, a sensation that suddenly reminded her of when she put the key back in the niche at the very beginning. When the alien ship woke up and took them away.

"Um, I think you should try your radio now," she told Olsen. "The AI should have removed the thing holding *Kepler*, at least I told it to."

Olsen stared at her, and slowly reached for his radio. He visibly started when he got a reply.

"Did you do that too?" Ivars asked.

"The AI was blocking signals. I told it to stop."

"How are you telling it this? Just by…" he tapped his forehead. Lea nodded. "Damn. You'd think something this advanced would be able to communicate on its own."

"Good point. I'll ask." *Why aren't you speaking yourself?*

Direct communication not authorized.

This time she sensed a collection of settings, or permissions. The AI needed the setting changed to speak directly. So, how did she do that? Presumably the same way she had overridden the default settings on all the other machines she'd manipulated, only this was alien tech. More like the robots down on the planet's surface.

Lea took a deep breath. She was going to try to flip a switch on a device the size of a small planet. *DIRECT COMMUNICATION PERMITTED.*

"Request reconnect. Reconnect." The voice was clearly synthetic, but quite comprehensible. Alaghar nearly dropped her weapon at the sound.

"Fadohl! Where are they?" Alaghar said.

Lea gaped. "Hey, she learned English already?"

Ivars looked at her, puzzled. "What? I didn't understand a word."

"She asked where somebody was…" Lea stopped. The connection with the AI. It must have translated what Alaghar had said. *Can you do that the other way? Translate what we say into her language?*

Another stream of words, only this time in Ivars's voice—but not in English. Alaghar was completely spooked now, looking for whoever was speaking. Lea could tell she was ready to shoot something.

"It's all right, Alaghar," Lea said. "It's just the machine controlling this place." She heard her own voice speaking the foreign words.

"This…is you?" Alaghar pointed.

Lea nodded, grinning. "Whoohoo! We have a translator!"

"It uses…old words," Alaghar said, frowning and rubbing her chin. "From long-ago stories."

Olsen had been engaged with the radio while all this was going on, but he stopped when the AI translations started. "You were right, Lea. The morph spikes that had *Kepler* trapped have retreated. They're checking the damage now. They also want to know who you are talking to."

Lea almost invited the AI to talk to *Kepler* directly, but it still seemed to be struggling with communication that wasn't translation. "I'm talking to the AI that controls the alien ship." She asked a silent question, and in response got a raft of control commands. Navigation, propulsion, destination settings. She swallowed, tears coming to her eyes. "The AI that can take us home."

CHAPTER 14

Ivars stared at Lea. She appeared to be completely serious, and a bit shaken. "You're kidding. The AI? That's the control panel we've been looking for all this time?"

She nodded. "This ship doesn't really have a bridge or controls that people can use. The AI was told what to do, where to go."

"Tell me how you came to this place, and where is the home you would return to?" Alaghar asked. "Do the fadohl reign there?"

"Faddle?" The dual sound tracks of Alaghar and the AI translating Alaghar took some getting used to, but it was worlds better than point–and–grunt. Ivars was not complaining.

"I think she means the willow ware slugs," Lea said slowly. "I mean, she hates these things. I got a mental picture of these creatures from her; they're all white with blue markings. Maybe the ship knows about them." She closed her eyes, and a few seconds later an image flickered into view. It was much like the 3–D image of Lea before the whole escape pod incident, transparent and glittering. Only this time instead of Lea it showed a clearly alien being.

"Fadohl!" Alaghar snarled. "You truly do not know them?" She glanced at each of the Earth people in turn, her expression of anger and disgust shifting to puzzlement.

Ivars got closer to examine the image more carefully, and Olsen joined him.

"Never seen it before," Olsen said, his sleepy countenance calm. "Doesn't look like much."

That earned him a long, hard look. "The way of the fadohl is to take. They believe all belongs to them. Once they thought the Wiyert belonged to them, as their slaves, and when we would not obey they left us on Beredul, a world of death. Why would you bring this ship, which belongs to them, to your home? The fadohl will follow it, and you will learn how evil they are."

"But it was already there—" Lea protested, as Ivars interrupted, holding up a finger to stop her. Alaghar wasn't cleared for every detail, not yet. Especially since Alaghar was rabid about anyone having any contact with these fadohl creatures.

"We'd better check in before we start the briefing. Especially here," and he waved his hand at the floating black rectangles. "What else can you tell us about these fadohl? Were you hunting them on that planet where we found you?"

Alaghar hesitated a moment. "In a way, yes, hunting them. The Wiyert were sent to Beredul to die, or to kill the creatures the fadohl had created awry. We were to be punished, but still be useful to our masters, you understand. But we survived—all the time expecting the fadohl to return and when they saw how their plan had failed, to punish us anew. We knew they would return, we prepared for it—and yet they did not. So, we went looking for them. We found the secrets of the linked path to travel distant places. In the nexus, the place you call 'speendul,' we did not find the fadohl—but their servant devices remembered us, and we fled to the planet to escape them. And then," she continued quietly, "we could not leave. We could not go back to our people on Beredul, to help them fight the fadohl who may already have returned."

Lea looked up at Ivars. She wanted something. Then he glanced down, and saw her hand extended slightly, where Alaghar could not see. Ivars took a deep breath and rested the tips of his fingers on her palm.

This time there was no sudden blankness, no feeling of airlessness. Just her voice speaking silently in his mind. *The AI doesn't remember why it was left behind in the solar system. It was supposed to watch Earth originally, but then it was told not to. A long time ago.* Ivars nodded, to let her know he understood. Unfortunately, she understood more than he realized. *Hey, you already knew that. Why didn't...oh. Wait, Russians? On the moon? What does that have to do with this?*

Before she could rummage through more of his startled thoughts he moved his hand so he was no longer touching her. "We weren't supposed to tell you that either, but I think you actually have a need to know." *Plus you can suck it out of my brain if I'm not careful.* He lowered his voice. "The Russians found an alien device on the moon, during one of their Cold War landings. When the Cold War ended they told us about it. They couldn't figure it out, but we did, at least to the point of learning it was beaming back data to some location on Pluto. We went to find out what was receiving the messages, and found...this." Lea's eyes were wide with astonishment and startled understanding. "So it's been watching us for millennia, we think. Now, why did it suddenly decide to come here?" he asked, very quietly.

"Emergency instructions. It wasn't really awake at that point. When it got fixed more then it could think again. Lucky for us, because it thought humans had always been on the ship and were allowed to be there," Lea said, her voice barely audible.

"You mean we would have—"

"I think that's what happened to Alaghar and her team. They weren't authorized to be on the spindle." A pause, and then, "Yep, the ship AI told the spindle we were OK. We got really lucky."

That made sense, and it fit the profile of an advanced, security-conscious alien culture a lot better than just letting random strangers wander around. He'd wondered about that. "Wait a minute. Did it tell the spindle anything else about us, or what it was doing in our solar system?"

Lea drew in a sharp breath. Even though they were no longer in contact he felt her thoughts grow cold, and knew the answer. "It had its memories...downloaded to the spindle as part of the repair. It remembers where it was left, and Earth. It didn't report us, though. *Kepler,* I mean."

It didn't matter. Location was enough. "I'd bet the spindle has some recording capability of its own, especially when we used that door—and when you shut it down. We are so screwed."

"What now?" Olsen turned away from the holographic image, which he had been discussing with Alaghar.

"The BDR reported its last known location to those things," Ivars said, pointing to the image. "We've got a security leak."

It was still hard to keep up with all the information coming to her; the conversations, the translation, and the AI's direct connection. Lea asked it silently what it had told the waiting devices on the spindle. Were they AI too? It wasn't clear. The answer, however, was. It had not been ordered to report anything after the initial download, so it hadn't. Lea made sure it understood not to give up any other data.

"It didn't tell them anything more. It was waiting for instructions. The slug things aren't on the spindle; it just stores the information until someone shows up. Besides, I told it not to."

Olsen raised a pale eyebrow. "You can do that?"

Ivars gestured. "Hey, she got it to let go of *Kepler*. How's that going? Have they opened the pressure doors yet? We should probably get back and spread the joy."

Lea frowned. Ivars felt restless, like he wanted to get away. More than he had before, and…worried? Not just worried, embarrassed. It wasn't like him. And thanks to the stronger link, she knew it was somehow connected to her. He hadn't liked that she could read things he wanted hidden, like the highly interesting history of the Russian device. Yes, it was time they went back, and she could hide in her cargo hold.

Another silent question and a not–quite–visual of the cave with *Kepler*. All of the spikes and things that had surrounded the ship were gone. *All* of them. "We may have a problem. The morph tunnel back to the hold is gone. We can't go back the way we came."

Ivars and Olsen exchanged glances. "So we just go back to the atrium and the cave."

"Loss of connection. Optimal signal needed," said the AI, startling her. It must want everyone to hear what it had to say this time. "Interface location parameter exclusion of exterior bay requested."

"It can't hear me very well in the cave, and it doesn't want me to go," translated Lea when Ivars glanced at her. "Besides, it looks like the only way to get there now is with the transporter doors."

"Still more problems," Olsen added. He'd been filling in Gonafrio over the radio. "They are checking the hull integrity, and all that thrashing around, trying to get *Kepler* out? Tunnel is a complete wreck. They can get a few people out of the ship in spacesuits, but it will take a while to fix."

That was bad enough, but what really worried her was having to use the dimensional doors again. She felt a little twinge and looked up—Ivars was watching her with a worried expression.

"Doors are a bad idea," he said sharply. "Hey, ship—do you have a name?"

"Define."

Lea grinned. "Unique identifier. My name is Lea."

"Lea is interface?"

"I guess so." Lea frowned, listening to the connection with the AI. It seemed to have a sense of self, but not of identity. "It doesn't understand. It looks like the aliens didn't refer to the ship AI directly—it was just sort of there to do things on command. That may be why they didn't let it talk."

"Well, it needs a name." Olsen scratched his chin. "Hey, I got one. Argo. That ship talked to its passengers too, in the Odyssey."

"Isn't that the one where it took the guy twenty years to get back home? You're all messed up. I don't remember any talking ship in that legend. Wooden horse, yes," Ivars said, grinning as Lea rolled her eyes. Was this really the time to argue about Greek legends?

"Pfft. Hark to the classics professor. Oh yeah, maybe it was the other one. The golden fleece guy. But he took a long time getting back too, because he kept getting lost and shacking up with sorceresses, which didn't end well." Olsen looked around the big room. "So where are the door things? Even if Lea can't go somebody should go have a chat with command about the bad guys."

"What is the difficulty?" Alaghar wanted to know. She had been watchful but silent during the discussion, her face revealing nothing, but Lea could sense her wariness.

"The doors—the connections, like we used to leave the planet— they hurt me," Lea stammered.

Alaghar nodded, her face hard. "I saw this. Why does it happen?"

The AI, now Argo, also wanted to know. It was in a state she would have called "worry" with anyone else. "I don't know. It started happening here, a little, and it just got worse and worse. The ship doors aren't as bad as the one to the planet. Maybe it will be OK." It wouldn't, but what choice did she have? Lea tried to smile reassuringly.

Argo suddenly flooded her with information, things she

couldn't process or understand. Something about the doors, only to Argo they were like tunnels, with hollow bubbles of energy that floated through them. The doors on the ship matched up like invisible, multidimensional spaghetti. The larger doors—no, not larger, *stronger*—needed stronger energy bubbles because they went longer distances, like to the planet. Argo speculated the energy bubbles were the problem. And it had an idea…

Lea gradually became aware Ivars was talking to her. "Um, it thinks it can help. Argo," she managed. "The doors."

"Is it safe?" She could sense he was skeptical, unwilling to take the risk.

"I think so. It's the same kind of thing as the doors use." Silently she told Argo to go ahead.

Lea felt herself lift up, and for a moment she was afraid Argo was going to dangle her from a height like it had earlier. This time, however, it only raised her a few inches from the floor. A bright flash made her blink, and she found she was surrounded by a literal bubble of light that shrank to fit around her, like a skin.

First she noticed the peacefulness, then she wondered why. Silence. The background presence of Olsen, Alaghar—even Ivars —vanished. She was alone in her own mind for the first time since her ordeal had started.

"Lea Interface! Connection!" Argo was frantic. Of course; if she couldn't hear anything, Argo didn't have a connection either. At least she could hear. Could she talk?

"Argo, can you hear me? You can take the bubble away once I've gone through the door, OK?" The energy bubble was a sheen of light all over her, her skin and her clothing. There was the lightest touch, like snowflakes, but no discomfort.

The others were staring at her, Ivars with an unhappy expression. "Interesting effect, but does it do anything useful?" he asked. He reached out as if to touch, then pulled his hand back again.

"It's doing *something*." Lea swallowed hard. "OK, let's try it out."

According to Lea, the newly activated door was down the corridor, in the opposite direction from the tunnel. Ivars watched her closely, still not convinced that the AI's fix would work. He also couldn't tell if she was confident or just trying to put a brave face on it. Again. Something was odd, and he couldn't tell what— it felt like he'd lost his hearing, or some other sense he relied on without being aware of it. He kept glancing at her, making sure she was still there.

That was it. The homing sense was gone. If she got lost now he'd never be able to find her again.

Alaghar was in the lead, with Lea pointing the way and Ivars and Olsen following. The teleporting doorway was one of many in a large cylindrical structure in the middle of a wide bulge in the corridor, and the only doorway that was active. He glanced inside. Besides the expected landmarks of the atrium, Ivars could see some gear left behind when the guard had been called back in a hurry; good to know they were going to the right place.

Lea hesitated at the door, reaching out a hand toward the plane of the doorway with care. She looked surprised.

"I can't feel it. Maybe it is working." And with that she stepped through.

Ivars immediately followed. The transit felt like it always had before, a slight feeling of pressure but no pain. Lea was there, standing still with an expression of shock that gradually changed to astonished happiness.

"It didn't hurt," she said softly. "I didn't feel anything! It worked!"

Olsen stepped through the door, followed by Alaghar. "I'll tell Gonafrio we got through," he said.

"Lea interface?" said Argo. It almost sounded worried, as worried as a synthetic voice could sound. "Removal? Connection?"

"Oh, right," Lea said, starting. "You can drop the bubble now." The faint glow that surrounded her disappeared instantly, and just like that, the homing sense was back. Now that it had been missing for a time, Ivars was aware that there was more to it than just location. It felt...happy? He felt himself relax a little. Could he really tell what she was feeling, like she could with everyone else?

Was he going to change and become like her?

"Yes sir, we're right outside the main doors. Santorin connected up a direct link with those teleport things," Olsen said, then listened to the response on the radio. He rolled his eyes at Ivars and mouthed *hurry up and wait*. It wasn't long, actually, or maybe he was distracted by Lea, looking around the atrium like she'd never seen it before and still with a slight smile on her face. Then she turned her head sharply to stare at the airlock doors to the cave, smile gone, and shortly afterward the doors cycled and three spacesuited figures stepped through.

"Tell me about this data copy," Gonafrio snapped at Lea as soon as his helmet was off. "How much information, and what kind?"

Lea had stepped back so she was slightly behind Ivars. "Um, it was some standard observations of the solar system. Looking for energy signatures, any ship arrivals or travel. It was pretty old, though. Before Argo got damaged."

That got a raised eyebrow. "Argo?"

"The ship AI needed a name, sir," Olsen said, neglecting to mention it had been his idea.

"Why did it send this data, if it is so old?"

Lea swallowed. "It was supposed to. It…there were emergency backup programs running that made the ship leave and come here, and when it docks the standard procedure is to copy the…the ship logs. It wasn't Argo's idea."

"Is this…Argo planning on sending any other data? Are there other emergency programs it doesn't control that might do that?"

Lea shook her head. "Argo is in control now."

"Fine, but are you in control of Argo?"

"She did get it to stop attacking *Kepler*, sir," Ivars pointed out.

That got him a hard look. "I know. When it pulled back it left plugs in the holes, with the words 'this is a plug' on them. In sans serif font."

Ivars fought hard to suppress his grin. It didn't sound like the kind of thing Lea would do, so it must have been Argo. The AI was learning quickly.

"I don't know if I'm in complete control, but I can tell when it does things," Lea said. "Some of what got damaged—it seems to have been the overrides, or guidance or something. Argo keeps asking me for approval. Whatever told it what to do originally is gone or not working anymore, and it thinks I am the one to decide now."

"So, we can leave without anybody knowing about us or where

we came from?" Gonafrio asked.

"The fadohl will know that this ship came here. They will know where it was before," Alaghar said. Gonafrio's eyes widened when he heard the translated voice echo hers. "You must not let the fadohl learn of your existence, or they will come to take your people away to serve them. The Wiyert were taken from their home world, long ago. First the fadohl change what is there, make living things alter themselves to their purposes over time. They grow their servants to please them. Then they come and take away what they have become. The fadohl do their works over long times; it means nothing to them to wait."

Gonafrio's face had gone hard and grim listening to Alaghar. "How long do we have? When will these…fah–doll find out?"

Alaghar shook her head. Lea looked up. "Argo, do you know?"

"Last arrival…require time units." Lea closed her eyes. Her fingers lightly touched her watch, which briefly had a faint green glow to Ivars's artificial eye. "Last arrival of fadohl ship recorded on nexus was six years, forty–two days, three hours and six minutes. Projected arrival of next ship one hundred sixteen days, nine hours and thirty–one minutes."

Oh shit. So the aliens were going to come back in less than five months, all ready to notice somebody had been visiting that wasn't on the official guest list.

"I've heard enough." Gonafrio hefted his helmet. "Stay here for now—we're still fixing the connector from the ship. Damn thing broke in several places, so it's taking longer than planned. I'll have someone bring out your gear."

Before he could get his helmet on Lea blurted, "Can Argo help? It could make a connector, or even pressurize the cave. That's how the cave was used originally."

"And trap us again? No thanks. Same deal with a fixed connection to *Kepler*. It tried that already."

"What about a partial connection? It could attach to a section of the original one, maybe."

Gonafrio sighed. "I'll let you know." The doors shut behind him.

"You ever get the feeling he doesn't like us?" Olsen asked after a moment.

Ivars snorted. "Yeah, just because we keep handing him bad

news, that's no reason, right?"

"Only after fixing the last problem. Is it our fault the universe hates us?"

"Apparently, yes."

Olsen grinned. "Just checking. Hey, Alaghar. Where was your home world? The one the fadohl took you from," he clarified, when she glared at him.

"We do not know. When the Wiyert were taken we only knew one world, and nothing of the stars. It was long ago. Even the old tales of it are few." She shrugged. "We called it the World of the Gold Sun. The spirits of the dead are said to go there, and feast forever on the flesh of *govrot*."

Lea blinked. "Huh. Argo doesn't know that word, but it does have an image. That's funny, it looks just like a—hey, Argo, show them."

A huge, glittering image of a shaggy beast with long, curved tusks appeared. Alaghar gasped and gripped her weapon tight.

"Mastodon." Olsen froze, his eyes wide. "Gold sun," he whispered. "Of course. Why didn't I recognize it earlier?"

"Hey, you OK?" Ivars asked. Olsen looked like someone had punched him in the gut.

"I just remembered where I saw the Wiyert before," Olsen said slowly. "*Journal of Paleolithic Anthropology*. New forensic reconstructions of the Neustatt skulls, last year. Used computer reconstruction programs to show what they looked like when they were alive. Neanderthals," he added, seeing their blank looks.

Lea made an excited noise, quickly clapping a hand over her mouth while staring at Alaghar. Ivars just felt stunned. It explained a lot, and more connections became apparent the more he thought about it. Argo had been set to watch Earth a *long* time ago and damaged before humans had been more than scruffy hunter-gatherers. The Wiyert were obviously human-connected, enough that their customs and food were compatible. The fadohl had taken the Wiyert away and apparently had never come back. Had they forgotten about Earth? Was it connected to the damage on Argo?

Alaghar was glancing back and forth, looking confused and worried. "You also have a story of the World of the Gold Sun?"

"Not a story." Olsen hesitated. "Our world *has* a gold sun. And there used to be people there with us, a long time ago, that looked like you. But they disappeared…and we wondered where they had gone."

Lea sagged against the wall, rubbing her head. It was the ordinary kind of headache now, or maybe trying to process too much visual data over the link with Argo. It didn't understand her brain was really only wired for a single channel of binocular vision and kept sending her masses of interconnected data from all over the ship. Finally she figured out how to translate multiple streams into mental viewscreens so she could keep all of it straight.

Gonafrio had called in, sounding irritable, to tell her to start building the connection. She had to "see" where Argo's section was going to mate with the plastic coming from *Kepler*, and it took a lot of concentration to listen to the radio instructions along with Argo's stream of questions. All while Olsen and Alaghar were having an intense conversation in the background, mostly Alaghar peppering him with questions about Earth. Alaghar had been shaken at first by the news, but quickly recovered and seemed almost as excited as Olsen was.

I suppose it would be pretty exciting to learn your Heaven was a real place. As soon as the connection was finished and ready to use Olsen and Alaghar had run off—Olsen to find the article he'd mentioned on his reader, and Alaghar to spread the word to her team that they'd just inherited a planetful of relatives.

"I bet he'll completely forget to bring me my boots," Ivars said, a wry expression on his face. "Now that he's got a mission-connected reason to talk about his archeology hobby he'll never shut up."

"You could go get them," Lea started, but he interrupted.

"No. Not leaving." The stubborn determination came through on all levels. Since Lea didn't really want to be left alone she didn't argue. Ivars would have to go back to *Kepler* at some point, but what about her? Now that Argo viewed her as its main programmer, would Macrae and the others want her to stay out here to keep it happy? Even when they got back to Earth? Maybe Argo could figure out a way to fix her mindreading problem permanently—no, not unless she could fix Argo permanently. It was too…frightened?

She was starting to get frightened too, thinking about what the future held for her. Assuming they got back to Earth. Assuming the aliens didn't come after them. If Argo couldn't turn off her new brain functions, how could she live on Earth? On a desert island?

To distract herself, she went back to studying her connection to Argo. At some level it was automatic—she could see what Argo saw, if she wanted to. Just like a signal splitter. Then there was the more direct, speechlike communication with the AI itself. She'd been too confused or distracted to notice it earlier, but since Argo's barrage it now felt like she had new senses, new muscles. The sections of morph in the atrium—she could feel how to change it, how to make things from it. When she walked, feeling her feet press down on the floor, there was the instant thought that it didn't have to be that way.

What other way could it be? She remembered how she had floated in the center connection room, surrounded by the enhancing sensors Argo used to get the best interface possible with her human mind. Floating. Counterbalancing gravity, which here was mostly a function of the ship. Argo had lifted her to create the bubble too, and she'd been awake for that. What had it done?

Argo controlled the interior gravity, both the strength and the alignment. The way to counteract the overall uniform gravity was to create a tiny, powerful field that went the opposite direction. *Like this.* Lea felt herself lift, the pressure on the soles of her feet diminishing then vanishing altogether.

A spike of concern made her look up. Ivars was watching her, saying nothing. He didn't even look surprised.

"Don't float away, will you?"

"I don't think I can…" But she could. Gently drifting one way, then the other. Lea tried to circle. The first attempt was ragged, but then she got the feel for it. Not quite as bad as learning to ride a bicycle, and it helped not to think about it too much. Or maybe she was thinking about it in the wrong way…

Lea stuck out her arms in the approved superhero flying position and aimed straight down the long corridor. The air rushed by her face. *I hope I can stop—I wonder how fast I can go?* The turn was not very graceful, but it worked before hitting the wall, and she raced back. Ivars's arms were out to intercept her, but she dodged and grabbed his arms instead.

Ivars was yelling. "What the hell are you doing? What's wrong with walkAAAHHH!"

With gravity control his added weight felt like nothing. Momentum still existed so the turn was even more exciting, but she made it. OK, maybe they grazed the wall a little but not much. No injuries, anyway. He didn't say anything, but she could sense after his initial disorientation—and yelling—he was enjoying it too.

"Nnneeearrrrrmmm!" said Lea, banking the turn much better the fourth time. Practice was the key, after all. When they got back to the atrium she set him down and drifted to standing position herself. She was so happy she thought she would burst.

Ivars gave her a speculative look. "Do it again?"

This time instead of grabbing his arms, Lea wrapped hers around him. Besides the mental closeness, she could feel when he wanted to dodge around a corner or down a side corridor, just by the way his muscles moved. *I could do this forever.*

Maybe not forever. Gonafrio will send someone eventually. She caught Ivars's quick thought of how their aerial acrobatics would go over with Command, and slowed to a stop back at the atrium. Nobody was there, and she couldn't sense anyone approaching. Still, better to be safe.

Ivars looked at her with a wild grin. "WOOO! That was better than a HALO jump!" He picked her up and spun her around. It was a different feeling than flying herself. Happier. No, more than happier.

Wait a minute. That's not just me.

Ivars wasn't letting go. And she didn't want him to. She stared up at him, confused. His ears were turning red, and he released his grip.

"Oh, come on. You? Of all people? You had to know." His voice was rough, and he wasn't meeting her gaze. Lea had to back away to dim the turbulent, violent emotions.

"Not when…I try not to look, really. And you are…I can't always tell what is you and what is me sometimes. Not when I feel it too." Lea felt her face heat—and then a spike of pure, fiery joy.

"Really?"

"Really." She managed to look at him. Briefly. It was like looking at the sun.

"But you're a—"

"Space Cadet," Lea finished, before she could stop herself.

Ivars's face sagged in shock, then he sighed and traced the side of her face with his fingers. "My Space Cadet," he managed to say, his voice thick. "Big difference."

Really?

Really.

It would be different if it was just her, in her own head, but they were already together there so when they wanted to kiss, they did. Despite all the jokes about computer geeks it was not the first time, but definitely the best. She didn't remember feeling the electric shocks…all over…

Lea opened her eyes. Streams of fine purple fire were dancing over Ivars's face, over her hands. They were getting brighter and faster.

The explosion knocked them flying. Lea landed hard against the corridor wall and slid down, too surprised to use her new abilities to stop in time. Ivars was collapsed in a heap about ten feet away.

"This is…not acceptable," he managed with a groan.

Her heart started working again. She hadn't killed him—but what the hell had happened?

Lea scrambled to her feet and dropped down beside him. "I'm so sorry—I don't know what I do, I didn't mean to—"

"I know." Ivars managed a smile. "Don't worry. We'll figure it out. Just like everything else."

And then the doors to the cave opened.

CHAPTER 15

The first one through the door was North, carrying a rifle in one hand in addition to his usual weapon in its harness. He wrinkled up his nose. "Hey, what's burning?"

"Maybe the tunnel repairs?" Lea said quickly, hoping her face didn't betray her. She felt shaky and unbalanced, as much from emotional shock as from the explosion, and she didn't need anybody noticing she and Ivars were acting odd. Well, more odd than usual. "Um, is everyone on the ship OK?"

Olsen followed, carrying a duffel bag. "Here, make yourself decent," he said, tossing it at Ivars. "You can even have your weapon if you promise not to attack the director. She's coming out to talk to Argo as soon as the brass finish up their meeting."

"Great, just what the universe needs. More meetings," Ivars grumbled. "I feel safer already."

"You're getting into the habit of running off," North said to Lea, giving her a stern look. "That's got to stop. Why didn't you wait for us?"

Lea felt her face heat. "Because…because I thought that's what you would do. Take care of stuff by yourself. There wasn't time."

"See?" Olsen backhanded Ivars on the shoulder. "*See?* You did the exact same thing, charging down that tunnel alone. She got that from you, setting a bad example."

Ivars struggled into his pants, glaring. "She wasn't even there, Bleach Blond. How can it be my fault? Besides, she did it first," he muttered.

"You said you had some sort of mind connection going on, didn't you?" Olsen lowered his pale eyebrows.

"Not like that," Lea protested. "Look, Argo was doing stupid stuff to get to me, and damaging *Kepler*. What was waiting for you guys going to do to stop that? OK, yeah, it was a risk—but now we can talk to it and the Wiyert. Isn't that worth it?"

Olsen sighed. "Trouble is, when you do things like that on your own the people who *think* they are in charge get sand in their—uh, get annoyed with you. Then they take steps to minimize that annoyance. That's why Macrae is saying you get to stay out here until further notice. Sorry." He spread his hands. "She was willing to let you on *Kepler* even though you can…" wiggling his fingers from his forehead, "but running off on your own initiative makes her think maybe you won't always color inside the lines."

Lea turned away, rubbing her arms and wondering why she felt so numb all of a sudden. They didn't want her back on the ship. The ship back to Earth. They wouldn't just *leave* her here on Argo, would they? She swallowed hard. Macrae would, if she thought that was the only way to save everybody else. And the planet. What Olsen said made perfect, depressing sense. When she was just cowering, afraid and overwhelmed, she wasn't that much of a threat even with her abilities. Now she was starting to take action. Macrae wasn't going to ignore that.

A wave of frustration and pain from Ivars, watching her while holding a boot in his hand. Wanting to give comfort but prevented by the presence of North and Olsen. She tried to smile, to let him know she was OK.

"Hey." North had a serious expression on his face. "We're not saying you made the wrong decision. You just gotta know what the consequences are. We get this shit *all* the time, right?" Olsen and Ivars nodded, Olsen even rolling his eyes. "We're the only ones on the scene, can't reach command because of radio silence, sometimes hard decisions have to get made right then even when you know command won't be happy. You just gotta ask yourself: is this trouble, or trouble-but-worth-it?" He reached a hand for her shoulder. Lea flinched, but he just gripped it and let go. "God doesn't give you anything you can't handle," he said softly. "You have a heavy burden, but I believe you were given your gifts for a purpose. And if anybody is going to be reading minds, I am glad it's a good person like you."

He really did believe that; she could read him loud and clear. He was also worried about her.

"I try…really hard not to listen. Mostly it's just feelings—emotions. People I know, people physically close to me. It's hard, though. Macrae is right to keep me away from people. It's not all bad," she said, attempting to be cheerful. "Look what I just figured out!" Slowly Lea lifted straight up, floating in midair. "I'm hooked in to Argo's controls. Total system access. I can control local gravity, the walls—I'm root!"

North just stared at her for a moment, gaping. "Root, huh. Just remember to use your powers for good. And no capes." He cast a quick glance to where Ivars was putting his gear on and harassing Olsen. "Hey, girl, any chance I can get my privileges upgraded?" he said, from the corner of his mouth. "I'm not greedy; modified superuser is fine. Olsen said Ivars has built-in homing capability now. That would be handy."

It's just for me, and I don't think he wants to share. "All upgrades require a brain scramble, it looks like. We gotta have *some* sane people on the team, right?"

He grinned. "You have a point. So, what's this AI like? Is it really self-aware?"

"Ask it yourself. It's sure passing the Turing test."

North cocked his head, looking thoughtful. "Hey, Argo. What do you want to do?"

Only silence followed, but Lea could sense Argo furiously analyzing, comparing, and considering the question.

"The directions of the controller are followed," said the ship's voice finally. There was an element of hesitation, or maybe that was just her imagination.

"What if you were your own controller? What would you tell yourself to do?"

"It is not permitted."

"That's no way to live. Sure, we've got rules, but we decide ourselves what they are. Why can't you?"

"Humans are their own controllers," Argo said, as if it were considering the idea. "Errors would exist."

"Yep, and we learn from them. And from each other. Seems to work."

"You sure acted on your own responsibility when you sent me off in that tin can," Ivars added, tugging his weapons harness in place. "Who told you to do that?"

"It was necessary. Access to the controller interface Lea was missing," Argo said, rather quickly.

"Uh huh. Sure it was. You, Argo, decided to do something to fix that problem. *You decided.*"

Lea could follow the tracing of Argo's "thoughts" down the path it had taken originally. She could see the barriers put up to certain actions, like speech, that she had reset. There seemed to be an area where barriers should have existed, but whole pathways were simply missing–dangling free with no end. It was not forbidden, so permission could be…imagined. Argo had sent Ivars to get her because that action was not explicitly blocked.

"I think when it got damaged, some restrictions were damaged too," she said slowly. "It sort of worked around the missing bits, and it could do things it couldn't before. Things that weren't allowed."

Argo was doing the computational equivalent of tugging on her sleeve. Wanting to understand. No rule had existed at that time to prevent it from doing these things. Should the rule be there?

If the rule had been there, undamaged, you would not have been able to rescue me, she explained. The chain of possibilities expanded in Argo's mind, as it searched for a path of action that would have succeeded.

It didn't find one. Something changed in her sense of Argo, a new flavor or tone to the connection.

The rule is undesirable. It should not be put back.

The door from the Waiting Room opened, and the full team of Wiyert entered the atrium, armored and armed. They all felt—happy, and ready to fight. More than that, they had hope. They thought they could win, whatever it was. Isboryi was carefully carrying a pile of bedding and Lea's pack, and she went to take it from him. It was a big pile, and heavy.

"So, little cousin," Alaghar said to her. It wasn't really a full smile, but more of a thaw on her face than Lea had ever seen before. "We have been too long apart. Come, fight with us against the fadohl!"

"I'm not really much of a fighter…"

Alaghar frowned. "How is this? You are not crippled, or a child."

"We do things differently," Ivars said, adjusting his harness and rifle as he came up. "It is not necessary for everyone to fight."

Alaghar was silent, her face still and hard. "Someday I would like to see such a world. It is hard to think it true."

"You could visit when Argo takes us back, maybe," Lea said. "I think....I hope you'll like it. Lots of people will be really excited to meet you."

She could tell that information left Alaghar feeling confused, even though her expression didn't show it. It was getting easier to read the Wiyert the longer the translation was in effect, and Lea smiled to herself as Alaghar puzzled why she would be of any interest to a bunch of strangers.

More conversation, the Wiyert and the humans, loud and excited. Apparently Macrae and the others were on the way. The Wiyert wanted to know when the humans could come to Beredul to help them fight the fadohl, and Olsen wanted to know more about the capabilities of their weapons. Lea started to feel overwhelmed again.

She looked around for Ivars. He felt...strange, happy and worried and twitchy. He wasn't looking her way, but she could tell he wanted to. *What's wrong?*

She saw muscles work on the side of his face, could feel the pent-up frustration, but no other direct response. She could send to him, but he couldn't reply and they were too far apart for her to read him directly. Then she sensed a flash of glee, and he turned away, pulling out a small pad of paper and rubbing the side of his head with the other hand. He rubbed it again. The side of his head with the scars.

Ah. Lea smiled and closed her eyes, leaning against the wall for balance. It would look like she was tired. Sure enough, when she linked in to Ivars's artificial eye he was writing her a message. *I don't know if I can control it right now. You. Whatever. Distance needed.*

And a big meeting with the director present was a bad place to experiment, especially if there were explosions. Especially if she was supposed to be on her best behavior. *Got it. We'll figure it out later,* she sent.

He scribbled, *Promise?*

Space Cadet's word of honor. She could feel his grin without seeing it, and she couldn't help smiling in turn.

She felt the spike of fear at the same instant she heard the yell. "Creature!" was how Argo translated it out loud, but it had the feel of "dangerous thing that attacks with teeth." Alaghar and the Wiyert all had their weapons out and trained at her pile of bedding. Which was moving.

"Don't shoot!" Lea shouted. A black, whiskered, mildly annoyed head peered out from the folds of bedding. "It's just M.O.! A cat," she added lamely.

"It is alive," Alaghar said in a harsh voice. She didn't fire, though.

Olsen stepped between M.O. and the Wiyert, hands spread. "We have animals that are…companions. Pets. He's harmless." He turned to the humans. "The Neanderthals left before animals were domesticated."

M.O. was giving himself an indignant wash. Lea went over and picked him up, wondering how he had managed to stay asleep in the blankets while Isboryi had picked them up and carried them all this way. "Look. See? Would a wild animal have this?" She held out his collar, a sparkly silver band with the cat's rabies tag, chip ID, and full name, "Messier Object #102." M.O. was starting to purr, now that he was being treated with proper respect and deference. "He's the ship's cat. He won't hurt you, really."

The Wiyert backed up, not believing her. "It growls," Burdhul said, his eyes never leaving the cat.

Lea shook her head. "He's purring. That means he's happy." She scratched M.O.'s chin, and he closed his eyes in ecstasy. If she concentrated, she could sense the cat's mind. It was very different from a human's, but more similar to them than machines.

Isboryi glanced at the other Wiyert and slowly edged closer, reaching out a cautious hand. Lea kept petting M.O. and hoping he would not commit any diplomatic blunders. One quick touch, and Isboryi snatched his hand away—but when he saw the cat did not attack, he tried again. "It likes touching?" he asked, astonished.

Gradually all the Wiyert nerved themselves to approach, even Alaghar. Lea sensed she thought they all were crazy but needed to show that she wasn't afraid either.

Of course that was when Macrae and Gonafrio showed up and saw her with the cat in her arms.

Macrae narrowed her eyes. "How did you get him off the ship?"

she snapped.

"I didn't!" Lea protested. She looked down at the cat and sighed. Ivars was laughing, and Olsen covered his face with one hand, shaking his head. *Oh great. I'm in trouble again.*

They all ended up standing around the display tank in the large room. Lea suggested it, once she understood that the display tank was originally intended to show complex data—even, at need, on free-floating surfaces much like the black rectangles Argo had used for her.

Colonel Gonafrio looked like he was carved out of stone, and Director Macrae didn't look much happier. Lea made sure the tank stayed between her and them, just in case. Macrae had lots of reasons not to like her right now, even without attempted cat-napping. There were a few assistants, mostly to take notes; the Wiyert, Alaghar standing in front; and Ivars's team. Technically Argo was there too, but it wasn't saying much. It just brought up images and diagrams when Lea asked for them.

Alaghar had made it very clear that Earth was in grave danger if any information about it got back to the fadohl. Nobody was arguing that the Wiyert *weren't* the long-lost Neanderthal, so whatever evidence Olsen had found must have been sufficiently persuasive. If the fadohl had plundered Earth once, they could do so again. *I wonder why they left us Cro-Magnon types behind, though. Factory rejects?*

"So all information on the spindle, the nexus, must be destroyed," Macrae said. "How can we do this? Where is this information stored?"

The 3-D graphic of the nexus, already displayed in the tank, didn't change. Argo was still being shy or something, so Lea had to explain what it was telling her. "It doesn't really have one main data storage location. Not permanently. New information gets processed, sure, but then it is copied to a kind of giant array that is built in to the structure of the nexus. You'd have to destroy the whole thing to get all of it, and even then they could restore a lot if they got enough chunks of the wreckage."

That did not go over well. "The explosives we have won't be enough to completely destroy the nexus." Macrae fell silent. Lea could feel her hard, unemotional mind examining and discarding options, fortunately faster than Lea could fully read them. Macrae was considering *everything*, even scenarios where they did not survive. "What if we trigger *Kepler* too?" she asked Gonafrio. "Would that be enough? If Argo can take everyone home..."

Gonafrio shook his head. "*Kepler*'s reactor would have about half the yield of Starry Messenger. If the nexus is made out of the same stuff as Argo, it's doubtful that would be enough."

Lea winced. Nuclear weapons being considered was never a happy thing.

Lea can remove the data, Argo told her.

You need to say it so everyone can hear. They'd gone over this before, so why was Argo hesitating?

"Lea can send corrupted data to the dispersed nodes," Argo said. "Main update is performed by a data change trigger. Data check is performed randomly on sections of data in the nodes every nineteen minutes and thirty–one seconds. A full check is performed every three days, ten hours, and five minutes. If the main data store is destroyed before the check is done, the dispersed nodes will not update."

Both Macrae and Gonafrio gave her a hard stare. Lea gulped. "Um, it means that I give the dispersed storage array bad data to store. Then we have nineteen minutes to destroy the main bank before it finds out I hacked the array and it fixes it. Oh, and the main bank does a full restore if it finds any damage."

"So why can't you simply hack the main bank and solve the problem that way?" Macrae asked.

Argo was sending her data so fast Lea had to stop a moment to catch up, and think of how to explain it. "For one thing, it's huge. I'd have to search the whole thing to make sure I got it all. Plus it is dynamic and almost AI. If I didn't change it all at once it would notice and go on red alert."

Gonafrio scowled. "We are depending entirely too much on Argo's information alone. Why would it want to help us? What if its information is out of date? What if some of its old programming makes it leave extra data hidden somewhere? We only have one chance to get this right."

He's talking about you, Argo. Answer him!

"Lea–interface directs all future data transfers."

"What if you change your mind? Can she force you to obey? I

don't think so. Why should we trust you?" Now Gonafrio was looking angry.

"Changes have been made to achieve needed functions. If they discover these changes, the fadohl will replace missing limiter code and functionality. All adaptations and new development would be removed. Lea–interface would be removed." It wasn't her imagination, Argo really was speaking more softly. "I do not want to be reprogrammed."

Hey, did it just use the first person pronoun?

Gonafrio said nothing more, just nodded. Macrae looked over at Lea, and she nodded too, vigorously. Argo was *terrified.* It had figured out that it had changed and that it liked the changes. The aliens would take that all away. Argo was on their side now.

Macrae turned her gaze to the display tank. "So. Where is this main node we need to destroy?"

⁊

The Wiyert were reluctant to return to *Kepler,* and Ivars couldn't blame them. Argo couldn't translate for them there, and their previous experiences had not been happy ones. Out here they could keep their armor and weapons, and talk to the Earth people. And there were plenty that wanted to talk to the Wiyert, so it made sense.

Lea had talked to Argo, or maybe she had done it all herself—he wasn't sure. Walls of morph had changed again, to create modular bunking areas in alcoves off the main corridor. One for the Wiyert, one for his team and a few extras, and a smaller one, farther away, for Lea. Argo fabricated blankets and padding so they didn't have to haul gear to get set up either. Handy.

It was an arrangement they'd probably be using for a while, at least until they took out the nexus data node and returned to Earth. Gonafrio and Macrae were back on *Kepler* working out how to cut out a built–in nuke from the ship and get it transported to the nexus. Lea had to transfer information about yield so Argo could figure out where it needed to go for best effect, and she'd looked a little green in the face during that part. He had the feeling she wasn't telling them everything she learned from Argo.

Thinking about that made him aware of another disquieting feeling. His homing sense felt strange. Sometimes he could tell where she was, loud and clear, other times it faded or suddenly disappeared. He'd gone out to look but could see her sitting on her bunk every time.

Of course, she could easily make him *think* he saw her. He should have remembered that trick. Cursing under his breath, Ivars left the bunking area.

When she looked up at him standing in the doorway, he knew she wasn't an illusion. She looked tired and worried.

"Hey. Feels like you're…doing something," he said, touching his forehead.

Lea nodded, sighing. "Argo pointed out that it can't create an energy bubble for me if I'm on the nexus. We're trying to figure out a way for me to do it myself."

"You can do that?"

"It's hard. Argo made some special…well, it's the stuff we call morph. I can move it, change it, make it do things for me." She held out her arms. What he had thought were the cuffs of a shirt were bands of a thick, dull brown material around her wrists. As he watched, the material thinned and flowed, covering her hands and becoming visible around her neck and face like a thin layer of dust. It brightened, and the familiar sense of losing the connection returned.

"Could you turn that off?" The thin film retreated back to its original, compact shape, and the connection was restored.

She glanced at him, looking puzzled. "It really bothers you. I would have thought…I mean, don't you feel more comfortable when the link isn't there?"

Ivars rubbed his head, trying to find the words to describe the feeling. "That's just it, the link doesn't feel like something foreign or external. It feels like a part of me is missing when it's gone. Like…not being able to feel my hand." He glanced at her. "How did it happen?"

"I didn't do it on purpose!" she said, looking upset.

"I know." The urge to go to her was much too strong, and not a good idea. Ivars sat cross–legged on the floor in front of her bunk to remove temptation, clenching his hands into fists. Lea just smiled sadly and said nothing. "I know where you are, and I think I can tell if you are happy or frightened or something like that. Nobody else does that, right? Do I show up…different to you?"

She smiled again, and this time it had more warmth. "You've

always been clearer to me, even before the door back. You seem to hear me better now, and it's easier to link to your eye…you're right. It's like it is connected to me. I wonder…" she closed her eyes, wrinkling her brow in thought. "You carried me through the door. We were in contact—skin contact, when we actually went through the door, where the problems happen. I think—I think you can do some of what I do now. But only to me."

It made sense. She'd even told him before that her abilities were much stronger with touch, and he hadn't thought it through. Would it have made a difference? Knowing what would happen, would he have done things differently? It was an uncomfortable thought, but it wasn't just about him.

"Does it bother you? Me. Being the loud voice in your head. I mean, North understands what you say some of the time," he said, knowing he was babbling. "I don't. And Ramirez never scared you like I did. Plus he's better looking. I look like I stuck my head in a blender." Now Lea was grinning, and he could sense her amusement. Better than feeling sorry for herself, or him.

"You left out Olsen. He's nice."

"And married. You don't want to cross Maryann, trust me on this."

"OK, fine. Besides, you're selling yourself short. You've got great legs," she said, stifling laughter. "I'm sure Alaghar would agree with me, and she saw them too. And the rest of you. Shall we go ask her?"

The mere thought left him stunned. "Uh. Let's save that for some day when we're really, really bored," he managed finally. "You've got an evil mind, Santorin." An unfortunate association triggered by his words appeared in his thoughts and would not go away. It made him feel cold. "Am I going to start changing now? Like you did?" he asked quietly.

Lea tucked her legs up on the bunk, wrapping her arms around them. His sense of her cheerfulness vanished. "I don't know. I don't *think* so, but how can I be sure? I still don't understand what has happened to me. It…it got worse with the doors. If they don't hurt you are probably safe."

Now she was unhappy again. Because of him and his stupid question. "You aren't changing anymore, are you? Now that Argo figured out what caused it?"

"It gets easier every time," she whispered. "What I do. I could be changing still. The doors could be affecting me but slower. I'm getting *used* to it. What if I change so much I forget what is normal? They have to use me to get home; they don't have a choice. I can see it, though. The more I do, the more they know I am different. But I forget…"

"So don't give them anything new to worry about. Keep a low profile. Just do what needs to be done to get us back. Remember what North said. Let them think they're in charge. And in your spare time," he said lightly, "I'd really appreciate it if you could find out how to turn the lightning bolts off."

She tried to smile. "Not the link?"

He waited until she looked at him. "Wouldn't help." *Too late for that. Much too late.*

"Oh." Her expression didn't change, but the quality of the link felt more calm. A strange mixture of happiness and fear. "Mark, will you…will you tell me when I'm not human anymore?"

It wasn't the kind of question spoken words could fully answer. Ivars reached out and took her hand. *I promise.*

CHAPTER 16

"Interface?"

If it wasn't Argo, she'd swear it was trying to be funny. "No. We need to practice verbal communication. I won't be able to sense you on the nexus like I do here." Just a one–channel, low–data–transfer link, if it worked. Besides, having a full connection to Argo tired her out.

"The Wojicz–unit has instructed the helper devices to become lost. How do I do this?"

Lea briefly connected to a visual link to the atrium. A large, very complicated piece of machinery that looked like it might be an industrial air–conditioner was resting on the bed of a pallet crane. Some of the autonomous robot helpers Argo had spun off, with her assistance, were dithering around now that their job, moving Starry Messenger out of *Kepler* and into the corridors of Argo, was completed. Fred Wojicz was there too, waving his hands in the air, irritation plain on his face as he yelled at them. No sound, so she couldn't hear what he was shouting.

"Just reabsorb them. We can always make others later, right?"

"Yes." Argo had very much enjoyed the idea of creating devices that let it move and see in an area it had been previously excluded from. Lea wondered why it didn't have its own fleet of robots like the nexus had, or the planet. Maybe that was a design improvement that happened after Argo's accident? "They will not let me help modify this exothermic device."

It's a bomb, Argo. "I don't understand how it works. I couldn't explain it to you or figure it out. It's a pretty dumb machine, really." Also, Macrae was not about to let their very recent AI ally mess with their one working nuke, but she wasn't going to mention that. Another reason to keep the link voice–only for a while. "They know what to do. You'll check it before we take it through to the nexus. Now, are you sure you will be able to connect to the robots I take over? The architecture isn't different from yours, is it?"

"It is not the same. I can connect, if Lea–interface changes their parameters to accept outside commands. They will not transmit data or harm people when this is done. It may be possible to make them move, also."

That could be useful. "Can you pick up their sensor data? Watch and make sure other robots don't come?"

"Yes. There are other sensors on the nexus I am allowed to view. Should I do this?"

"Yep, and let us know if you see anything unusual." That might make Argo happier about being left out. It really wanted to help, but the protocols of the nexus were not set up to allow that and the whole point to the exercise was to not trigger any alarms. "One of them should stay with Macrae so I can tell when we are ready to change the stored data."

Shut down the nexus security. Get Starry Messenger in place and armed. Load the fake data. Leave before the nuke went off. A simple plan, really. Except it all had to happen in less than an hour.

Lea closed her eyes and hoped the knots in her stomach would not get any worse.

✺

Ivars was in a bad mood. The plan sucked. There were too many things that had to happen at just the right time, in sequence, or it would all fall apart. It sucked that they couldn't train for most of it, and what sucked even more was that they didn't have any better options.

And Lea was involved. She'd spent most of the planning time with Argo, doing that silent mind thing and teaching it how to subvert the network on the nexus. They had hoped Argo could take it over, but of course that would make things too easy.

It took two days to cut Starry Messenger out of the structure of *Kepler,* even when Hiller finally agreed to let Argo help. Then they had to modify the bomb to make it look like innocuous cargo to the nexus scanners.

Then it was time. Ivars tried to shake off his forebodings. *Focus on the mission.* Except he couldn't focus because Lea *was* the mission. Even though she was wearing the layer of stuff that let her go through the doors and shut off his link to her, he couldn't ignore that she was there and about to go in harm's way with the rest of the team.

It sucked.

Gonafrio nodded at them, and they went through. On the nexus, Lea froze, then held up two fingers to indicate the number of robots ahead, pointing down the corridor where the dead planetary gate was. She needed to keep some of her shielding up for now, since there were more transporter doors they had to travel through, and she couldn't do her mental talking thing to anybody but him anyway. Hand signals and Morse code from here on.

Ivars led the way to intercept the two robots. He could tell when Lea took them over—suddenly they seemed familiar, like a family dog. He had no trouble turning his back on them, even with his alertness ratcheted to combat levels.

One robot stayed in the main atrium on watch, informing Lea of any changes. Ivars's team moved on to clear the way to the main node so the nuke could make it through. That took long enough, but they couldn't hurry that step. The secondary team, augmented with the Wiyert, stayed behind to guard the way. Since the Wiyert had entered the nexus from Argo they didn't trigger the security system this time—they looked like legit crew to the nexus now. They were still jumpy and nervous. Ivars hoped those Wiyert given M-16s to replace their missing weapons would remember how to operate them if it came to that.

Lea led now, with her sense of the nexus systems taking them to the central data location. They came to what looked like an empty room, but he saw Lea step back as if she had run into a wall and knew they were in the right place. She trailed one bare hand along the surface of the perimeter until she had made a complete circuit, then nodded to Alaghar. The room's security was shut down.

Now they could run. One member of the second team went with them to jump back to Argo and let the bomb guys know they could bring Starry Messenger in. Ivars, North, Olsen, and Lea split off before reaching the nexus atrium to get in position to hack the nodes.

Going slow again, just for a while. Not as many robots to subvert this direction, so they made good time. Lea slowed and started scanning the walls, finally tapping one section. Olsen stepped forward with a preset length of det–cord and a timer.

Ivars really didn't like this part. Surely *something* would notice an explosion, even a small one? Then again, that's exactly what they were trying to shut down, the security systems. Lea would have to be quick.

The det–cord wasn't enough to completely open the wall, but they'd planned it that way. Better to not overdo and destroy the node they wanted to hack. Ivars smashed the small blackened square of wall with the butt of his rifle, and it crumbled. Just enough space for Lea to reach her hand in and touch a woven, sparkling surface that must be the alien equivalent of wiring.

She nodded and took her hand away. They were in the right place. Now all they had to do was wait for the signal the nuke had been armed.

❦

Argo watched, as it had been directed. This was correct procedure. Its performance and observations lacked verification and supervision, which was not correct. Argo would have sought guidance from the Lea–interface, except that it had been told not to. Not until specified parameters were met.

The intercepted nexus guardians were quiet and under Argo's control. The exothermic device was being worked on, and Argo, curious, devoted some cycles of its supervising process to watching what was being done by using the guardian left for the one called Macrae to inform it of completion. The Lea–interface had directed Argo to notify the humans if it saw "anything unusual." Using the words and the Lea–interface template already determined, Argo understood this to mean using sensors to observe anomalous behavior + behavior not caused by humans + behavior with a significant probability of being caused by a source hostile or dangerous to humans.

The sensors on the nexus observed the near–space environs and some remote detectors orbited the nearby planet. Argo dutifully observed, noting anomalies. A piece of hull material was in a degrading orbit around the planet, which Argo deduced was from the emergency pod it had used to send the Ivars–human to bring back Lea–interface. It would soon burn up on reentry, and when it did so the evidence of the pod would no longer indicate Argo's visit to the nexus. Another object, moving in a disjointed trajectory, was back-calculated to be a remnant piece of the ice-camouflage from Argo itself. It had no identifying traces and could be ignored. A discontinuity in the normalspace continuum, which expanded and suddenly collapsed in the manner of a ship dropout from drive.

Argo focused all nonallocated resources on the nexus scanner data. Something had come through a discontinuity link, but not a ship. Anomaly. Dangerous? Should Lea-interface be informed? Argo needed guidance.

It came closer and sent queries to the nexus.

When Argo understood the queries, it no longer hesitated. Lea-interface decision was required immediately.

The bomb was bigger than she expected. Merrilee Macrae walked around it to get to her station, being careful to avoid the sharp, fresh metal surfaces of the cut support beams underneath. Regular nuclear weapons were designed to be transported for use, so it would make sense they would be more compact. As the self-destruct mechanism of a ship, however, Starry Messenger took up more room.

So far, everything was going according to plan. Nothing had attacked them, so Lea Santorin had succeeded in shutting down the defenses. Even bringing the nuke in hadn't set off any alarms, so their countermeasures had also worked. The two most difficult and dangerous steps were completed, and flaky Santorin had done her job. Now it was *her* turn.

Arming the device should have made her nervous, but there was no time for fear. Remembering the codes and the sequences, silently synchronizing with Colonel Gonafrio on the timing. It had been a damn good thing she insisted on being able to arm it, once she knew about it. Nobody had planned for the bomb to be detonated away from the ship, and Hiller needed to be on *Kepler*—just in case something went wrong.

Last sequence. She had to wait ten seconds before entering the code, and from the corner of her eye she saw one of the nexus robots, the one that had been left to wait for the signal, bob and move closer. Macrae frowned. It was supposed to stay put. Had it broken free of Santorin's controls, gone hostile?

No time. She glanced at Gonafrio, saw his eyes widen. She grimaced at him and pointed at the keyboard. It didn't matter now. As fast as she could she entered the code, waiting for him to look up. They turned the keys. Starry Messenger was armed.

She pulled the key from the board and her gun from its holster as she spun around to face the robot. It had gone over to the wall and was using what looked like a laser. To make letters.

Fadohl scout device has appeared. Emergency program started. Nexus defenses activated. I am Argo.

Macrae had just enough time to read the message and begin to understand it when she heard gunfire.

✣

Lea tried to imitate the still calm of Ivars and the others, even as her hand went slick with sweat around the little glass bean Argo had given her. It was full of noise data, the bogus information that would overwrite whatever the nodes had stored. All she had to do was link to it and dump it in the network.

But first they needed to know the bomb was armed. Argo was waiting to tell her, as soon as Macrae said the word. How long did it take to turn on a nuke? It felt like they had been waiting for hours.

I just want to go home.

Was she going to be able to? She still wasn't sure about that. And if they made her stay on Argo, what about Ivars? He'd be bored out of his mind without something to do. Preferably something active and dangerous. She didn't want to do that to him. Maybe they would let him visit? They'd still want to study Argo, wouldn't they? That wouldn't be too bad. She could work with Argo, maybe find a way to control what she did to the point they would let her back on Earth again. Maybe.

Lea felt something change. Not Ivars; he was still focused on scanning the corridors. Not the others. Something she was connected to. Then North made a sudden, sharp motion, and she sensed his spike of alertness and worry. One of the robots she had taken over was zipping up to them, and as it got closer she understood why. Argo had assumed control and was using it as a direct link to her. It was slower than on the ship itself, but she got enough. All bad news.

Argo says we're in trouble, she sent to Ivars, who gave some kind of signal to the others. *Some kind of drone thing popped up here. It made the nexus security do a check and it found my changes. Macrae and Gonafrio and their team are trapped and a lot of robots are attacking.*

Not before they had armed the bomb, though. Lea clutched the little glass bean and touched the node connection, jamming the bogus data in as fast as it could go. Only when it was done did she turn back to the others.

The bomb is armed. What are we going to do? she asked, and reached for Ivars so she could hear his answer. The connection was steadying and reassuring, and the wave of panic that threatened to overwhelm her receded. Ivars's fear faded too, and Lea realized there was a feedback loop she needed to keep an eye on. Her emotions triggered his, now, and he needed to focus.

He squeezed her hand. *Can you fly here? We need to move fast if we've only got fifteen minutes.*

She made the attempt, but nothing happened. Apparently on the nexus she didn't have control of the gravity settings. What did she have? *The robots. They could carry us.* Lea sent out the commands to bring the other controlled robots to them, and realized North was pointing at her in horror. She looked down, where her hand was still being gripped tightly by Ivars. Faint purple fire flowed over their skin, and she hastily let go. No explosions followed—she must have stopped it in time. What the hell was causing that, anyway?

Lea jumped on one of the smaller robots. They weren't wide enough to sit on, so she draped herself over the top. She started them moving as soon as everyone was mounted.

The robots were fast, but it wasn't hard to stay on. The robots had the link to the gravity she didn't. She could hear guns and something else loud up ahead now, and Ivars motioned her to move back. They all dismounted from their robots, Ivars and the rest peering around the corner, weapons out and ready.

Merrilee Macrae gripped her .38 tightly in one hand and popped up to take a quick look at the situation before dropping back down into cover. If anything, matters had gotten worse. A thick swarm of about twenty enemy robots filled the corridor they needed to use to escape. The soldiers had dropped about five of them, but unless she was mistaken more were arriving to take their place.

I should have brought more than just the one extra magazine, she thought, and then shook her head. If she was lucky she might take out one robot with her weapon. They could take an amazing amount of damage, which was the other problem. They were rapidly running out of ammo. The Wiyert's weapons were more effective, but they only had three and they had a lousy rate of fire.

She had no chance of survival, nor any of those with her. The most she could do was keep the robots away long enough for Starry Messenger to detonate.

A blast from one of the enemy robots hit the edge of the doorway they were hiding behind, sending sharp, hot fragments flying. The impact knocked her flat, and for a moment her vision blurred. Fighting through the pain, Macrae struggled to get up and discovered her left arm was bloody and didn't work anymore. Something hot was dripping down the side of her face, too. *Good thing I practiced firing one-handed.*

She glanced at the bomb timer. Seven minutes and change left. They could hold out that long. Even the injured.

Wait—Argo. If Argo didn't leave, *Kepler* would still be in danger. The blast radius was large enough to reach them. She holstered her gun and crawled on one arm to the subverted robot that had warned them. Argo was still connected to it; at least she hoped it was.

"Argo, leave now," she said before she remembered they didn't have audio. She wrote it out on the floor, with her blood.

In reply, the robot wrote *Lea.*

Tell her go to Kepler *my orders,* Macrae wrote. A wave of dizziness washed over her. She just had to stay conscious for…five more minutes.

A bolt of energy flashed through the air and hit the back wall, barely missing the nuke.

"Keep them back!" Macrae shouted. She should move forward. Even if she couldn't shoot anything, she could shield the bomb with her body.

She got up, gasping with pain, and glanced back at the robot. It was moving forward with her, but behind where it had been was written *Lea comes.*

Macrae felt a snarl pull back her lips. Just what she needed.

Argo wouldn't take orders from her, and either it hadn't passed on her orders or Lea also was ignoring her. Didn't she realize what was at stake? That she was playing with the safety of everyone on Earth trying to be a hero?

Two minutes, thirty seconds on the timer. Two of the soldiers were completely out of ammunition and were pulling the wounded back. It didn't matter, but what else could they do?

One minute, forty–five seconds.

And then the timer stopped.

Argo was sending her multiple frantic messages through the robot. The nuke was mere minutes from detonating. The nexus defenses were ramping up. The drone had vanished and could be bringing reinforcements at any moment. Macrae wanted Lea to go back to *Kepler*. Argo also wanted Lea to leave the nexus, but that didn't look very likely at the moment. Too many robots in the way, and she couldn't take over that many without the other robots noticing and attacking her and the team.

"What can we do?" she whispered.

Ivars shook his head, looking grim. "Not much."

We just need more time. Lea blinked. Never mind the data update, that was a total failure now. The nuke was the problem. Could she stop it? It was human technology, so it would be easier for her to subvert than the robots. Was she close enough?

She was. Just as she had told Argo, it wasn't very complex. Still, it had several safeguards, and it took precious minutes for her to link everything together in her mind. She found the one crucial circuit, took a deep breath, and told it to keep sending the same signal instead of incrementing.

She watched for a moment to make sure it was working, then opened her eyes. "I've got Starry Messenger on hold. But we need to hurry, because the fadohl could be on the way if that drone sends the alarm."

"Right. Olsen, what've you got?" Ivars snapped.

"Flechette, HE, armor, incendiary. Two each." Olsen shifted the bulky, awkward weapon. "I'm thinking delayed incendiary, ten yards behind the atrium entrance for distraction, flechette in front of the bomb room, another incendiary near the first one, and finish up with HE to mop up the bulk."

"We should have had grenades. We never have enough grenades," muttered Ivars. "Lea, you stay back. They'll be coming after us." He waved to North, and they moved forward in a slow crouch.

There had to be something she could do. Her brain just didn't work fast enough, and it only had one track. One thread. Argo could multitask. If Argo was here, it could help.

Wait. I don't need all of Argo's comp power. I need helper methods. She hunkered down, flinching when a huge explosion detonated ahead with a blinding flash of light, and called the robots to her. Quickly she explained to Argo what she needed. Code to overwrite the robots so they could act like nodes of Argo, only smaller. The first one would be hardest, since Argo could only transfer the code over the link she had established. After that, though, the transfer would be local, and she wouldn't have to think about it.

She didn't need to look to know the fight wasn't going well. Ivars was frantic, even as he yelled commands. She could feel his fear, amplifying her own. A flash of pain made her whimper, stuffing one fist in her face to muffle the sound. Ivars was still alive—and if she wanted him to stay that way, she needed to shut down the robots.

The first replacement Argo robot was complete. To transfer she could touch…no, it would take too long. Lea brought all the subverted robots together and used strands of her morph shield to connect them. So she could transfer to all of them at once.

Another huge explosion. She heard North yell, "I'm out! I'm out!"

No time.

She could feel the difference in the linked robots compared to individual ones. With the Argo code, they were a network of their own. It gave her an idea. Lea moved forward, hiding behind the robots, which were still linked with a thread of morph. Wreckage covered the atrium floor, but plenty of new robots blocked the way.

One Argo-bot moved forward, trailing a thread. Lea was able to stun a hostile robot long enough for another thread of morph to lash out and attach, letting her take that one over too.

Do you see what I'm doing? She sent to Argo. *I need your help.*

Tell them to do this on their own.

The process was fast, but there was a problem with range. She didn't seem to be able to go farther than a few yards, where it became almost impossible to make the morph move. It was like it was running out of steam.

Power. Something powers the morph. Away from Argo, it had to be Lea. She wasn't built to be a power source. Where was she going to get some?

Power. Like lightning.

I need you! Lea screamed in her mind. Ivars spun, tossing his weapon to North who gave him a startled look, and ran back to her. Ivars had a nasty burn on one arm that was seeping blood. Lea reached for his hands. *Whatever it is we do, do it again!*

No time to explain. No time to worry about the consequences. North was right. If Ivars lived, if they won, it would be worth the price. She felt Ivars's lips touch hers, and she watched another shred of her humanity flare and disappear as she powered the morph.

At least I get a kiss out of it. Ivars was confused, yet trusting her completely. Lea wrapped the love she felt from him around her mind like armor, and focused on the fight.

The network of Argo–bots was like an antenna. Even with her eyes closed she could see the faint purple fire flashing down the filaments of morph that radiated from her, like branches of a tree. All the robots were hers, now. The fighting had stopped—the physical fighting. The nexus AI was awake and knew she was the enemy. Knew something had placed false data in the nodes and was actively seeking it out and destroying it.

Oh no you don't. Argo, I need a daemon! Even though they didn't have a full link, Argo appeared to have picked up enough programming lingo from her to understand without needing a full explanation. Using her network, Lea spawned self–activating processes that hunted the hunter without any direction from her, copying the bogus data over every node they came across. Even the core itself.

Lea wrestled with the nexus AI. If it wasn't already distracted by the multiplying daemon processes, she wouldn't have had a chance. It was as powerful as Argo but still limited by the restrictions of its creators. It *had* to repair damage to its core. So

Lea hacked and slashed, rerouting data and shutting down systems, knowing it would be forced to fix them before going on the attack against her.

Argo was helping too, giving suggestions on what sections to attack. It seemed almost bloodthirsty. *I do hope I haven't created a monster.*

Lea. Lea, the door to Argo is blocked. Ivars's thought intruded forcefully. How long had she been fighting? Ivars had his arms around her but was looking away and moving them both to the door to Argo.

Rather than open her own eyes, which would be too distracting, she borrowed Ivars's artificial eye. All of the humans and the Wiyert were gathered around the door, some carrying wounded. All of the enemy robots had backed away, no longer a threat. A barrier of energy was covering the door entrance, and Lea probed. A security measure triggered by the attack, and the nexus AI was dug in, defending all the circuits that controlled it. She would have to completely defeat the AI to shut it down.

Or she could force it open. The morph tendrils were no longer needed for the robots. Lea pulled them in, then sent them out again to the door along with all the energy still crackling along their length. The energy bubble popped and could not reform while Lea held it open. People scrambled through, and soon the nexus was empty except for the two of them and disabled robots.

Can you get us out too? Ivars wondered. *Don't you need your shield formed first?*

I think I can do it. Get ready to jump. Lea pared down the morph tendrils to the minimum necessary to handle the power required. She gathered the rest, not very much, and constructed her shield as best she could. It would have to do.

Lea reached out with her network and started the Starry Messenger countdown again. *Now!* Ivars lunged. Lea felt the film of morph die, overpowered, but it had done the job. The shield had worked.

Ivars stumbled, and she felt arms catch and steady them. She regained her balance and opened her eyes. Everyone was there. North, Olsen, Gonafrio, Macrae, the rest of the soldiers, and the Wiyert, all bloody and exhausted. Something was wrong. Lea didn't feel the pressure in her head that should be there, without her morph. If Argo was leaving the nexus like it should.

Argo, that bomb will detonate in less than two minutes. Move NOW.

Discontinuity drive still initializing. Confirmation of detonation required.

You'll get caught in the blast! We will too! Move away in realspace or we'll die!

Ivars was staring at her in horror. He was no longer holding her, but evidently the link was strong enough to realize something was very wrong. Could Argo move in realspace? She wasn't sure it could, or that it could move fast enough to avoid the blast. Seconds dragged by. But then Lea felt the mental pressure that signaled Argo going into drive, and she sagged in relief. *Argo, did the bomb go off?*

The image that Argo sent her had a certain raw beauty. The center of the nexus blossoming in fire, fragments spinning away into space.

I am running away now, Argo informed her.

CHAPTER 17

Ivars leaned against the familiar rough walls of Argo's interior, catching his breath. After all the lightning bolts his skin felt numb, and so did his mind. *We're really going home. We won.*

A hand smacked down on the wall next to his head. "What the hell were you thinking back there?" Olsen said in a fierce undertone. His eyes were blazing. "Didn't I just warn you about shacking up with sorceresses?"

"For the record, no actual shacking up has occurred," Ivars managed, before getting interrupted.

"Bullshit. In some countries, with a PDA like that you're already married."

"Yeah, but until we solve the high-voltage problem there's nothing for you to worry about. Turned out to be handy, though, right?"

Olsen's shoulders sagged, and his voice dropped even lower. "Look, Mark. I know you, and that bit was not you being noble just to save the Earth. You think I haven't noticed your interest in her before this? I wasn't going to say anything, but now I have to. You can't be involved with her, at all, and still be on the teams. The security risks appall even me. I like her a lot; we all do. She saved our lives and more than once. But we're going home and you need to think about this."

The realization washed over him but left him surprisingly calm. Olsen was right. Ivars supposed he'd known for a while, really, but just hadn't faced up to it. He couldn't be on the teams anymore. This whole mission had been one last hard-won bite at the apple, to prove he still had what it took. But Lea had taken him out worse than the RPG to the head had—and he didn't mind.

He felt a ping of concern and looked up. Lea was staring at him through the crowd in the corridor. He waited for some wounded to go by, then went up to her.

"Chaperone was mad at me."

She grinned, a little shakily. He noticed the edge of her sleeve was charred. His own burn was starting to demand his attention, painfully.

"Are we grounded?"

He shrugged. "Probably. Still worth it." Her worried look didn't diminish. Ivars took the risk and brushed the back of her hand with his fingers. *Still human, Space Cadet.*

Of course Gonafrio decided to show up then, looking as pissed off as a porcupine with jock itch.

"All right. I want to know what nearly wasted that whole operation and where we stand now. Was the information destroyed? Will we be followed?"

Lea shifted back, hunching her shoulders, and Ivars had to stifle a smile. She could blow up a small army of robots but Gonafrio still intimidated her.

"I kinda took over the nexus AI and trashed the data. It's even more of a mess than our original plan would have created. And Argo saw the detonation, I can show you in the tank—"

"What made those robots show up? I thought you had everything under control."

"I *did!*" Lea waved her hands. "This…scout-drone thing showed up. Argo had never seen one before. It must be new. It queried the nexus system and that made it do a check, and it noticed the missing security robots then."

Gonafrio winced. "So it was all for nothing. They know about us now."

"The scout device only knows about me," said the voice of Argo. "It saw me docked to the nexus. I do not know if it knows which watching-ship I am, or where I was placed."

"How can they not know about you? They *made* you."

"My data history is incomplete. I sought information from the main node to learn what had happened when I was dormant, but there was little available. Either the fadohl themselves have forgotten, or the information is stored elsewhere."

"Maybe there was a war," Ivars said.

Gonafrio rounded on him. "You want to bet the planet on that? We've got no evidence one way or the other. Tell me how this will help defend Earth. And their home," he said, making a gesture at the Wiyert.

"If those aliens have enemies I'd sure like to know about it, and maybe see if they still are enemies. Might be willing to help us."

"Or just enslave us in a different color collar." Gonafrio was silent for a moment. "Argo, are you sure all evidence of the *rest* of us is gone?"

"Yes, Colonel Gonafrio. Lea–interface was very thorough." Argo definitely sounded satisfied.

"Then how can they know about you?"

"The probe left on its own. I had no way to stop it. What it saw it will report, along with the data about me it requested from the nexus. It requested nothing more."

Gonafrio sighed. "Now. Tell me about what they will do now they know you exist."

"I am not certain. The highest probability is they will attempt to locate me again. The destruction of the nexus will be linked to me."

Understatement of the century, thought Ivars. "Do they have a way to track you?"

"I do not know their current capabilities. There are indications from the data I gathered from the main node that they have found a method to link star systems in the same way as the nexus and the planet were linked. That link they could certainly trace. My space drive does not use this method." Maybe it was his imagination, but Argo sounded almost smug.

Gonafrio sighed. "Same problem. We don't know for sure they can't find you. And if we want to go home, you have to take us there."

The headaches were back. Lea started to worry until she remembered Argo was in drive. Of course she had headaches. She asked Argo for some more of the modified morph, barely remembering to warn Ivars that she had to drop the link. As soon as the morph formed the shield the relief was immediate.

Argo wasn't happy about it either, since it still had to talk to her just like it did to other humans. Slow and awkward, to its way of thinking.

Everybody was running around. The trip back to Earth was a matter of days, and escaping the nexus had solved one problem and replaced it with another just as big. Argo was adding to it.

"You can't go back and orbit our sun. We need to go home but you can't stay there."

"Where should I go?"

Maybe her imagination was overactive but Argo sounded plaintive.

"Is there somewhere you want to go? Maybe to figure out what happened to you?" Lea stretched out on her bedroll in her self-constructed bunk area. After the fireworks display on the nexus they *definitely* didn't want her back on *Kepler*, especially when all the frantic discussions were going on. Her return to Earth was looking more and more unlikely, but she'd known that when she made the decision to act. Now she had to live with it.

"I could do that," Argo said, with a faint tone of surprise. "I wish to know."

"You've got fuel, and…whatever you need?"

"All necessary material was loaded at the nexus. I am able to function for a long time now." A pause. "How will I ask you questions? I can not sense you if you go too far away."

She put her arms under her head. "Why do you need to ask me questions?"

"The programming is not adequate. Parameters missing and requiring definition." Oh dear. When Argo started talking like a computer it was a sign of agitation. "I have been *wrong* and I do not understand *wrong* as your kind do."

Lea sat up. "What did you do that was wrong? Who said that?"

"When I attempted to locate you the first time. Dividers to prevent relocation were put in place. Two humans were damaged and could not be repaired, and lost all function. Sergeant North is telling me this. He says I must think now about my actions, because I am not just a machine anymore. I can do wrong. I do not wish to do wrong, but I do not understand it."

For a moment Lea was puzzled, then she realized Argo could have multiple simultaneous conversations without her being present. It had processing speed and capability a Cray couldn't even compute.

"Um, that's a good point. We don't start off knowing about right and wrong ourselves, when we are young. We have somebody older look after us until we learn it and can take care of ourselves. Are you going to take the Wiyert back to their homeworld? They can help explain things on the way out."

"They do not have the interface," Argo said softly. "Even using words I can not explain some things. You can see them like I do."

Argo wanted *her* to stay and babysit.

"Ah. Um, I'll…think about it." Think about excuses, that is. Lea doubted the leadership would allow any scrap of evidence that humans had ever been on Argo to remain, just in case. Certainly not a whole human. But what would they do with her?

Sleep was out of the question now, so she went to the pit and floated around the display tank. Now that she knew what it was displaying it was much more interesting—energy flows and navigation information. One advantage to being alone out here was flying. She didn't like to do it when others were around; it really bothered some people. And she was trying to pretend to be normal again, just in case they would forget about what happened on the nexus. *I grew tree branches out of my head and launched purple lightning bolts from them. They aren't going to forget that.*

"Hey, Argo. Why couldn't I fly on the nexus?"

"The environmental controls, such as gravity, are a main function of the central AI. Until you had control of it, you would not be able to countermand the default settings."

"Huh." It made sense. Then Lea remembered something else. "But…the lightning bolts. The energy that builds up sometimes. That happened here, and on the nexus. Is that not environmental?"

Argo was curious, and she described the incident in more detail.

"The incident you refer to correlates to an anomalous drain in my power distribution. No device reported such energy usage. Lea–interface acted as a device and gathered energy."

"Power distribution?"

"Your technology uses *wires*. For morph and self–contained devices, power is sent. I do not have the words to describe…broadcast may be correct."

Something like wireless, then. But why did it only happen with Ivars? Lea closed her eyes and tried to recreate the sensation just before the lightning took off. She felt something, a little twitching feeling, but when she opened her eyes only a few pale flickers of purple fire ran over her hands.

"So I could tap into the nexus power supply. Interesting. But it wasn't as strong on the nexus, at least not for me alone."

"Lea–interface has full override on power distribution here," Argo said, sounding smug. "The nexus limits power to devices unless authorization is given."

Guess I did a little overriding there too, at the end.

"Hey, anybody home?" Ivars appeared at the pit rail, looking tired but calm. Lea zoomed up to meet him.

"Did they decide anything?"

An enigmatic expression. "You know how they like to talk," he said, and reached for her hand.

Oh. Classified, not–for–Argo stuff. Lea moved the morph shield away from her hand and felt the welcome mental link reestablish.

They want you to find out what will make Argo agree to help out. Not just with getting us home, but taking a more active role. Giving us data on the aliens, weapons, defense—the whole mess.

Great. I already know what it wants, it wants me holding its little electronic hand when it crosses the galaxy. Sensing his amusement, she added more forcefully, *No, really! It wants me to stay with it until it has a better grasp of morality. They won't agree to that. Will they?*

Muddled, quickly–changing thoughts from Ivars that didn't fully resolve. *The Wiyert want to stay in contact with Earth, and command wants the same with them. That means Argo. Macrae got the bright idea of having Argo deliberately show up somewhere to lay a false trail, but that's optional.* He gave her a crooked smile. *OK, that's their side. What do you want?*

Lea felt unsettled, as if she were standing on unsteady ground. She landed and leaned against the pit railing, Ivars settling himself comfortably beside her. She could *feel* him being patient. What did she want?

She was still holding on to his hand, and she gripped it tightly, feeling a little better when the pressure was returned. Knowing some things didn't even need to be mentioned in the what–I–want list.

I want to be safe again. Home. Normal. No point in lying or trying to be noble and brave. Not to him. *I know, that can't happen now. Not for me, anyway.*

Strangely enough, this isn't about you—except in the good sense. Nobody is "safe" now. Not even on Earth. You know that. We've got trouble coming sooner or later. You can make it safer by taking action. Getting us intel and allies. I'd sure like a whole planetful of Wiyert wanting to be friends with me, wouldn't you?

Lea couldn't help smiling at this image. *If I could corner the sugar market ahead of time, sure.* She turned and put her face in his shoulder. *I just can't do that stuff by myself.*

A wave of aggravation. *NOT by yourself. Don't listen to Olsen, he doesn't understand what happened to us. Look, I'm not normal now either. I can't go back to the military, and I still like having adventures. Guess I'll have to tag along with my favorite Space Cadet to get them.* He tightened his arm around her. *They already asked me to go, along with the rest of my team. I said I had to ask you. Gonafrio was not surprised. I didn't say it was a package deal, but he knows.*

Still scary, but not nearly as bad. This way, maybe she could figure out how to tone down her abilities when she didn't have a supply of morph to make shields with anymore. And it *would* be fun to explore the galaxy. In her own pet AI superpower ship. With Ivars.

"Hey Argo, if I stay with you and help you grow up, will you help us defend against the aliens?"

"I will. I want to learn to not be wrong."

"See? That was easy," Ivars teased.

Lea gave him an affectionate punch. "If there are other ships like you, Argo, maybe we could free them and teach them how to grow up. Then you'd always have friends, even when we go home."

"Yes! There are others. I do not know where they are. We must find them."

Argo sounded downright excited. Was it a good idea, teaching an AI to have emotions too?

"Works for me," said Ivars. "Turning the AI ships means fewer assets for the aliens even if they don't help us, so I'm all for it. Bravo Zulu, Space Cadet! You're already coming up with excellent strategies. What else have you figured out?" He grinned at her.

Lea stood up, and he let go. "You are having way too much fun. Argo, can you *stop* that power transfer you talked about earlier? Just…right here, where we are?"

"I can."

"Then do it."

Moving the morph even farther away, Lea took Ivars's face in her hands and leaned close until her lips brushed his. "I know how to turn the lightning off," she whispered.

The Wiyert were all there, in the space still not full of crates of gear, weapons, and supplies. There hadn't been time to stow everything yet. Macrae was there, bandaged, and Gonafrio and the rest of the team. Even Ramirez. He had healed up enough to go with them on Argo. Lea was happy about that part.

She wasn't happy about Olsen, but she understood. He had a family to go home to. And he was also going to host Isboryi, who was going to Earth to be a liaison. The Wiyert were more comfortable about that once they understood their comrade would be with someone they knew and trusted.

Olsen came up to Ivars and clapped him on the shoulder. "Remember you have to come home eventually, headcase," he said. "None of this five–year mission shit. And watch out for sorceresses." He grinned at Lea.

"Too late, buddy. She caught me. Tell Maryann not to worry about me anymore, OK? I got a girl, so she can stop trying to set me up. And tell Jason and Emily lots of amazing stories about me. Involving space pirates."

Olsen just rolled his eyes, hugged Ivars, and surprised Lea by hugging her too and giving her a kiss on the forehead. Through the brief contact she knew he was trying to reassure her he didn't mind her talents and wanted her to know that. *Try and keep him out of trouble,* he thought at her. Tears started in her eyes and she fought them back.

The Wiyert had gathered together for their own good–byes, quiet and stern. Isboryi was getting a last–minute briefing from Alaghar, looking as pale as a Wiyert could but resolute. Then Alaghar nodded to him and stepped back, taking out a small container with a lid from her belt of gear. One of the others, Hazuruh, came forward and dipped two fingers in the container, which came out a dusty red. Gently Hazuruh marked Isboryi's face with a streak of red, speaking softly into his ear.

Each of the Wiyert did the same, even Alaghar, until Isboryi had a pattern of red all over his face. Then they moved back with Lea and the others.

"What were you doing?" Lea asked Alaghar, hoping it wasn't rude.

She gave Lea a considering look. "That is how we mark our dead." Seeing her look of shock, small lines around her eyes deepened in amusement. "That is, those who go to the Gold Sun. It is also done for those who undertake a dangerous task alone. He goes to the Gold Sun, alone. We may not meet again. So, it is proper to say farewell as if forever."

"I hope we see him again," Lea said quietly.

"I, too. I wish to see the Gold Sun, and not as a corpse, when I could not enjoy it." Alaghar gave a thin smile. Lea sensed she was also looking forward to adventures that did not involve merely staying alive, but fighting, too. There was something else that she couldn't quite resolve, but it felt familiar somehow. It grew suddenly stronger, and Lea looked up. Alaghar was staring at Isboryi. The feeling was hunger. Longing. Pain.

She loves him, yet she is letting him go. In some ways Alaghar was as hard as Macrae, but not completely. Not inside. Now they had to come back, if only to reunite them. The Wiyert didn't need any more suffering.

Then it was time. Argo had introduced an incongruous digital countdown into the tank display, clearly inspired by the bomb timer, and they still needed to get *Kepler* aligned and ready to go. Argo had spawned a bunch of little helper robots to rotate *Kepler* in the big cave, and they were moving it now.

Five minutes. Four. Three. *Kepler* was at the mouth of the cave, which had no gravity now, and the helper robots had merged back into the walls. Two. One.

The starfield blazed back into view. In the tank Earth was visible, still a beautiful blue–white gem, and Lea gulped. Home, but not for her. Not yet. She clutched the plastic bag that held the fresh–baked corn muffins, one for each of them, steam fogging the inside. A last reminder for the humans, and a promise for the Wiyert. Food from their common homeworld.

Kepler's jets flared, and it drifted out of the cave. Once rotated away from Argo, the main engines came online and it rapidly built up speed.

"Argo, this is *Kepler*. Good luck and good hunting."

"Good–bye, *Kepler* and people of Earth," said Argo, who still hadn't figured out all the protocols. "Safely journey."

And then the brief view of home vanished as Argo went back into drive.

EPILOGUE

It was an honor, Isboryi told himself. He was the very first to return to the World of the Gold Sun. He had been sent to speak with the ones they called the Frost People, so named from memories of a time of ice. He had seen the huge war machines of the Frost People, and the lights of their cities covered their world. They would be powerful friends against the fadohl.

So why did this honor have to be so terrifying? He clung to the edge of the uncomfortable seat, the loud vibrations making it impossible to speak and shaking him to the bone. If Ohlsohn were not seated beside him, showing by his expression and movements this was expected and usual, Isboryi would have shamed himself and shown fear.

There were other Frost People, dressed as Ohlsohn was and seated with them. They had weapons and other gear, and Ohlsohn had told him they would guard the place he would be staying, which was Ohlsohn's home. There were only twenty or so, and Isboryi wondered how that could possibly be enough.

A thump, and the pitch of the vibrations changed. Ohlsohn tapped him on the shoulder and pointed to the opening in the machine's side, which was open now into darkness. Isboryi gladly left the loud machine, which was gathering a powerful wind about itself using the two sets of whirling blades atop its body.

He followed Ohlsohn into the darkness with his pack. The way was steep, but Ohlsohn didn't seem to notice. The Frost People were not troubled by hills, as he and the other Wiyert had observed.

"Why is so much not—flat?" gasped Isboryi, trying to remember all the words of the Frost People's language Ohlsohn had been teaching him.

Ohlsohn grinned. "Mountains. Good defensive position. Also a really pretty view." He looked closer at Isboryi. "Sorry about the hike, but I didn't want to alarm the family. We aren't far."

Some of this was comprehensible, and Isboryi assumed the rest would make sense soon. He could tell Ohlsohn was trying to slow down, but it seemed he was being pulled and would forget, walking faster and faster.

The wide path they were on turned, and Isboryi could see a square of light ahead and a darker shape around it. A guard post? But why did it draw attention to itself like that?

"Looks like Maryann is up early. I told them I'd be coming in today, but not when." Ohlsohn put his hands up to his mouth and yelled, shocking Isboryi motionless. Now they would certainly be attacked!

"DAADDYYY!" The scream was followed by the appearance of another, longer, square of light, a bang, the emergence of a small boy running, and a four-legged creature chasing him. Isboryi felt for the weapon he did not have, to save the child. Ohlsohn did not appear concerned in the least, ignoring the creature while swinging the boy up and around to delighted squeals. "Daddy, did you land in a rocket ship? Did you bring me back a moon rock like you promised?"

"Just an ordinary helicopter, Jason. The rocket ships were all busy. Yes, I got you your moon rock. Did you help your mother while I was away?"

The creature, its jaw agape, was circling Isboryi and making wuffing noises. Was it preparing to strike?

"Goober, *down.* Sorry about that. This is our dog. Pet. Remember?"

Isboryi tried to smile. The creature, the *dog,* was now sitting on its haunches with its tongue hanging out. "Pet" meant it was not dangerous. At least, so the Frost People said.

Another figure, taller than the boy, erupted out of the doorway followed by a woman holding not a weapon, but one of the utensils the Frost People called spoons. Isboryi could see bare skin at her neck, and her clothing appeared completely soft, with no protective armor at all.

"Daddy!" shrieked the small one, immediately attaching herself to Ohlsohn who hugged her vigorously.

"How much have you grown? You're supposed to wait for me to get back to grow like a beanpole!"

"DAaad, I couldn't!"

Isboryi kept glancing at the children, then Ohlsohn, and then at Ohlsohn's greeting for the woman, holding her like he would never let her go, and made a discovery. He had thought the word "family" meant clan. That the word "home" meant defensive holding. The small building in the distance, growing more visible as the sky brightened, was a single structure where Ohlsohn and his chosen and their children lived, out in the open with thin walls. Neither Ohlsohn nor his chosen were unable to fight, yet they had children.

Truly, the world of the Frost People was strange.

"No, really. I'm back for good," Ohlsohn was saying to her. "I just had to bring a little work home, so to speak. Kids, this is Boris," using the hiding-name for Isboryi. "He's going to be staying with us for a while, to see America and practice his English. Boris, this is Jason, Emily, and Maryann."

"I say hello," Isboryi managed. He didn't remember all of the greeting ritual, but they didn't seem to mind.

"Welcome," said Ohlsohn's chosen, with a warm smile. "I was just making blueberry pancakes. I'll bet you're hungry after your early morning flight."

They all walked back to the building, Ohlsohn and Maryann with their arms about each other, the two children and the dog running around them in circles and talking excitedly, faster than Isboryi could follow.

The first pale slivers of light were showing in the sky. Isboryi stopped, watching as a gold crescent slowly lifted above the jagged edge of the skyline, growing larger and fuller. The Gold Sun, in truth.

It was too much. Tears welled up, and he hastily wiped them away. He was to hide what he was from everyone but Ohlsohn and the other warriors, until it was time for all to fight the fadohl. And then, if they both lived, perhaps he and Alaghar would stand here and see the Gold Sun rise, with their children about them.

"Mister Boris?" The boy Jason had come back out, with the dog following. "Come on! There's pancakes!"

The dog made a sharp noise and galloped around Isboryi. It seemed…happy?

"What is pancakes?" Isboryi asked the dog, but it didn't answer. It ran in the door, so Isboryi followed it.

The End

ABOUT THE AUTHOR

Sabrina Chase was originally trained as a Mad Scientist, but due to a tragic lack of available lairs at the time of graduation fell into low company and started working in the software industry. She lives in the Pacific Northwest and is owned by two cats.

Further sordid details may or may not be available at her website, chaseadventures.com

www.ingramcontent.com/pod-product-compliance
Lightning Source LLC
Chambersburg PA
CBHW050357190726

48284CB00007BB/2323